’cla

Chris

CA

‘For romance ce

married life, readers n.’

—*RT Book Reviews*

‘Her novels go beyond romance
to the depths of the ultimate healing power of love.’
—*RT Book Reviews*

CAROL ARENS

‘Fans of rollicking romps and rip-roaring adventures
in the Wild West are in for one exhilarating read
as Arens pits a ditzy Easterner against a rough and rugged
bounty hunter. The pace is faster than a lightning bolt,
but Arens manages to paint a vivid portrait of the era
and bring her characters to life in a short, fast format.
Take a deep breath and enjoy!’
—*RT Book Reviews* on REBEL WITH A CAUSE

‘Arens sweeps readers to another time and place with grit,
sweetness, and tender sensuality.’
—*RT Book Reviews* on RENEGADE MOST WANTED

LAURI ROBINSON

‘By capturing the atmosphere of Colorado’s mining
towns, and the unique characters who populated the area,
Robinson adds appeal and depth to a delightful Western.
There’s enough humour, realism and sweet emotion for
fans of light, quick Westerns to make everyone happy.’
—*RT Book Reviews* on INHERITING A BRIDE

‘Robinson’s heartwarming Western style
is perfect for this story of a mail order bride
and a proud rancher. The small-town backdrop,
an adorable matchmaking teenager and the engaging
and often humorous plot are simple and ideal.’
—*RT Book Reviews* on UNCLAIMED BRIDE

Reading, writing and research—**Carolyn Davidson**'s life in three simple words. At least that area of her life having to do with her career as a historical romance author. The rest of her time is divided among husband, family and travel—her husband, of course, holding top priority in her busy schedule. Then there is their church, and the church choir in which they participate. Their sons and daughters, along with assorted spouses, are spread across the eastern half of America, together with numerous grandchildren. Carolyn welcomes mail at her post office box, PO Box 2757, Goose Creek, SC 29445, USA.

While in the third grade **Carol Arens** had a teacher who noted that she ought to spend less time daydreaming and looking out of the window and more time on her sums. Today Carol spends as little time on sums as possible. Daydreaming about plots and characters is still far more interesting to her. Carol lives with her real-life hero husband, Rick, in Southern California, where she was born and raised. She feels blessed to be doing what she loves, with all her children and a growing number of perfect and delightful grandchildren living only a few miles from her front door.

With a degree in early childhood education, **Lauri Robinson** has spent decades working in the non-profit field, and claims once-upon-a-time and happily-ever-after romance novels have always been a form of stress relief. When her husband suggested she write one she took the challenge, and has loved every minute of the journey. Lauri lives in rural Minnesota, where she and her husband spend every spare moment with their three grown sons and four grandchildren.

CHRISTMAS COWBOY KISSES

Carolyn Davidson,
Carol Arens,
Lauri Robinson

First published in Great Britain 2013
by Mills & Boon, an imprint of Harlequin (UK) Limited.
Harlequin (UK) Limited, Eton House, 18-24 Paradise Road,
Richmond, Surrey TW9 1SR

ISBN: 978 0 263 89858 3

Harlequin (UK) policy is to use papers that are natural, renewable and recyclable products and made from wood grown in sustainable forests. The logging and manufacturing process conform to the legal environmental regulations of the country of origin.

Printed and bound in Spain
by Blackprint CPI, Barcelona

CONTENTS

A FAMILY FOR CHRISTMAS

Carolyn Davidson

Dear Reader

One of my most beloved memories of childhood was the sight of our Christmas tree on Christmas morning. We never saw the tree before the 25th December, nor did we help to decorate it, but come the morning of the big day there it was. Always touching the ceiling, strung with big lights of a sort now out of use, and hung with hundreds of strands of tinsel—put in place by some elf, we decided.

The ornaments were a mixture of heavy German balls in solid colours and glittering spun glass pieces with gold dust scattered hither and yon. I still have one of my grandmother's German balls—not the prettiest decoration on the tree these days, but one holding fond memories of a woman much loved and revered in the thoughts of her grandchildren.

There was nothing to equal the scent of our Christmas tree, for it was redolent with the aroma of a pine forest, and we spent long hours lying on the floor long after the gifts were opened, simply enjoying the sight and scent of our tree, which was always 'the best ever.' Somehow the trees of today cannot compete with such beauty and majesty. Ah, the joys of childhood that shall forever dwell in our hearts.

Carolyn Davidson

DEDICATION

This story is dedicated to my sister, Nancy,
who shares my thoughts of Christmases past.

And, as always, to Mr Ed,
who fills my life with the rare beauty of his love.

Chapter One

Connor's Falls, Missouri
December 18, 1887

It was snowing again. Joy stood at the window and looked out, her hopes of having a Christmas tree fading as she considered the white landscape that seemed unending. October had brought the first snowfall of the year and it had continued, inch by inch, and now lay several feet deep in the drifts by the porch. The tree she'd had her eye on for almost three months was at the edge of the woods, but it might as well be in St. Louis for all the good it did her today. She was tough by her own estimation, but hauling the sled through three feet of snow was an impossibility, even to her hopeful eyes. In all her twenty years, she'd never gone without a Christmas tree. But even though she told herself it wasn't necessary for celebrating the sacred holiday, she'd still hauled out the decorations from the attic, just in case the snow stopped falling and she could shovel a path to the barn and then make her way from there across the meadow. She turned back to the stove and stirred the sausage gravy she was making for Grandpa's breakfast. From the sounds of it, Grandpa was moving about in his bedroom directly overhead, where the register caught the early-morning heat from the wood-burning stove she cooked on. He called to her from the top of the staircase and she walked down the short hallway to answer his summons.

"Joy, I can smell sausage cooking up here. Did you make biscuits to go with it?" he asked hopefully as he made his way down the stairs. It was slow going, for he'd passed his eightieth birthday just months ago and he was becoming more frail by the day. In this weather, he had to stay inside, off the porch; in fact, for the most part, he was limited to walking back and forth between his bedroom, the kitchen and the parlor. She reached for his hand just as he touched the floor in the hallway and bent to press a kiss against her cheek.

"You're a pretty sight to behold this morning," he said with a chuckle, leaning on her a bit as they made their way back to the kitchen.

She settled him in his chair at the table and poured a cup of coffee, placing it before him as she waved at the nearby window.

"Just look out there, Grandpa. More snow falling this morning. I don't think I'm going to be able to drag my tree home for Christmas, do you?"

He shook his head. "Not a chance, child. Neither of us is fit to go stomping through the snowbanks out there. Thought sure we'd had our share of the white stuff, but you can't argue with Mother Nature. The good Lord must have thought we needed an extra helping for Christmas. You can't argue with the depth of that drift out there. Must be four feet already, and the cow will be anxious for you to make your way to the barn."

"I know," Joy said with a sigh. "I'm going to bundle up good and try to shovel off the porch as soon as I get you settled with your biscuits and gravy. I'll eat mine later, for poor old Daisy will be miserable if I wait much longer."

"You'll need my high-top boots, girl," Grandpa said with a laugh. "Stuff 'em with some socks so they'll stay on you. And don't forget to put your shawl over your head. I don't want you getting another case of the quinsy."

Joy took two biscuits from the warming oven atop the stove and split them with a fork, then ladled a good helping of sausage gravy over them before she placed them before her grandfather. She brought him a knife and fork and dropped a quick kiss on his head as she headed for the rack by the backdoor. She took down her winter coat and shawl, then tied the shawl over her head as Grandpa had instructed. Her mittens were in her coat pocket, and she slid them on her hands and picked up Grandpa's boots.

She laughed as she looked up from her task of stuffing his boots with a pair of socks she'd brought out for the purpose, for she'd surely not make it through the snow in her own shoes. The boots slid onto her feet with ease and she was ready. She reached for her broom and the broad shovel she used on the snow and opened the door just far enough to ease through to the porch.

The wind caught her unaware, taking her breath, and she ducked her head, covering her mouth with a fold of the shawl. Propping her broom against the house, she bent with a will to the chore of shoveling the snow that lay over a foot deep on the porch. She'd need only a narrow path to the steps and then, between her broom and the shovel, she'd be able to clear a path to the ground.

The sound of a man's voice coming from nearby startled her. She brushed snow from her face as she turned in the direction of the sound and saw a stranger approaching through the deep snow.

"Hello, there," he called, and lifted a hand to wave at her. "I don't mean any harm, ma'am, but I need some help, I fear."

He was huge, tall and broad shouldered, and in his arms he carried a child, from the looks of things. "Come on up on the porch," Joy answered him, immediately worrying that no child should be out in this cold weather. "I was just going out to milk the cow, but I'll take you inside first. My grandfather is eating breakfast and there's more than enough for us to share with you."

Hunched over the child in his arms, the man made his way to the steps and lifted his head to meet Joy's gaze. "My son is about frozen, I fear," he said quietly. "I don't know how long

I've been walking through the snow. More than an hour, I think. My wagon slewed off the road back a ways and the horse fell and broke his leg. I had to shoot him and that left us without transport. I'm much obliged for your help, ma'am."

Joy held out her arms for the child he carried and took him quickly to her bosom, turning back to the door to carry him inside. The stranger was behind her as she went back into the kitchen, and her grandfather looked up from his breakfast, a forkful of biscuit halfway to his mouth.

"We have company for breakfast, Grandpa," Joy said, sitting down on the chair near the door with the child on her lap. "This young'un could do with some warm food in his stomach, I'll warrant, and so could his father."

"I can't thank you enough, ma'am," the stranger said as he quickly removed his coat and hung it on a spare hook by the door. He took the boy from her and sat on a chair, working at the buttons of his coat, and then shook his head in frustration.

Having taken off her coat and shawl and hung them up, Joy now recognized that her help was needed once more. "I fear my fingers won't work well enough to undo him," the boy's father said, standing once more to deliver the child to Joy's arms so she could work at his coat herself. He couldn't be more than three or four, judging from his height. She pulled the scarf from his face and looked down into eyes so blue they were almost purple. His mouth was tight shut and as he looked up at Joy, he opened it. Before he could cry aloud, as she was certain he was about to do, she bent close and whispered words of comfort.

"Hush, sweetheart. I'm only trying to undo you so I can get you warm and feed you some breakfast. Are you hungry?"

He brightened at her words and nodded slowly, as if he was unsure of himself here in this strange place. And well he might be, she thought. The best thing was to slide him from his coat and drop it to the floor, then scoop him from his bundling and settle him near the warm stove.

"There you go," she said brightly, rising to lift him in her arms. "Look what I have for you here." She carried him closer to the warmth, his shivers telling her his cold body welcomed the heat. She bent her head to the skillet of sausage gravy still simmering on the stove. "See, there's your breakfast. Shall I put you on the chair so you can have a plate full of biscuits with gravy on top?"

The boy nodded against her chest, and she felt warmth spread throughout her body from the movement. It seemed that his trust in her would extend as far as breakfast. She backed to the table and placed him on a chair, then found a bowl in the dresser and placed half a biscuit from the warming oven on his dish, cutting it into small pieces before she covered it with sausage gravy and put it before him. He bent his head to inhale the fragrance. It must have been a long time since his father had been able to feed the child, Joy mused, and the tall stranger's words confirmed her silent thoughts.

"We haven't eaten since yesterday noon-time," the man said in a hushed tone. "I fear I set off from the farm where we stayed last night without knowledge of the nearest town. I wanted to get an early start, but by the time the snow had covered all the tracks on the road, I was thoroughly lost and had no way of cooking something for us to eat. Then we landed in a ditch and spent the hours till dawn huddled together beneath the overturned wagon."

"Well, I'll guarantee you could use something to eat, too, sir," Joy said, waving at the chair across from the boy's seat. She handed the boy a spoon from the spoon jar in the center of the table. "Eat up, sweetheart," she said cheerfully. "It'll warm your tummy."

"Let me shovel off your porch first," the stranger said. "Then I'll come in and eat while you tell me what else I can do to help you."

"I'd be much obliged, sir, but I'd feel better about things if you'd eat first. I'd set out to shovel when I heard you calling. I have to milk the cow before much longer, but I'll feed you first and then you can help me make a path to the barn."

The man stood hesitantly and walked to the sink. "Then I'll just wash up a bit first, ma'am, if that's all right with you."

Grandpa pushed his chair back a bit, then bent to the lad who sat a foot or so from him and whispered to him in his husky voice, "You're a fine-looking boy, sure enough. I'll bet you can eat another biscuit when that one's gone. Joy made lots this morning. Musta known we'd have company."

The child looked up at the old man and lifted his small hand to touch Grandpa's beard. "Is that what it looks like when you haven't shaved for a long time?" he asked.

Grandpa chuckled. "Sure enough, boy."

The stranger bent over the sink basin and splashed his hands and face with water from the pump. Joy handed him the jar of soap from beneath the sink and he nodded his thanks as he poured a bit into his hands and scrubbed them together to form a mountain of suds that soon turned dark from the dirt he washed off. She poured a bit more soap on him, and he again rubbed it into suds, which he used to wash his face. She pumped the water again and he rinsed off with the clean flow.

"Come sit down, sir," she said, taking two biscuits from the warming oven and placing them on the plate that had been before her own chair. "Split these and I'll dish up some gravy for you."

He did as she'd told him and watched as she poured a good helping for him. "I'm sure enough thankful for this, ma'am. I fear I've not even introduced myself to you and your father."

"He's my grandpa, for my parents are both dead and buried," Joy said quietly.

"Well, I'm Gideon Burnley, and this is my son, Joseph. We're without my wife, for I lost her when Joseph was born and she's buried this side of St. Louis, where we had a home."

"Pleased to make your acquaintance. My name is Joy Watson."

"How do you happen to be in this neck of the woods?" Grandpa asked, settling back into his chair.

"I decided to head west and look for a bit of land, for we lived in the city and I'd been raised on a farm. I'd been thinking that a new start might work well for us, so I set out with my boy and all the cash I got for our furniture and such to find a place for us to settle. The weather was fine when we started out and I wasn't expecting the snow to start falling right away, figured we would have a month or so of decent weather to travel first."

"It's been a hard winter thus far," Joy said. "We haven't had any relief from the snow and ice since October."

Gideon Burnley took the knife and fork Joy had given him and cut up the food before him. His son, Joseph, spoke up quietly. "Daddy, we forgot to bless our food."

"So we did, boy. Why don't you do that now. The good Lord will excuse you from eating first."

Joseph bent his head and spoke simple words of thanksgiving for the food and then looked up at his father, as if seeking his approval. Gideon nodded his head and smiled. "Go ahead and eat, Joseph."

Joy found a bowl and fixed herself a biscuit, deciding the cow could wait for another ten minutes, for she was beyond hungry herself. Pouring a cup of coffee, she set it before Gideon and received his thanks. She then filled a glass from the pitcher of milk and offered it to Joseph. He reached for it and drank eagerly, as if it had been a long time since he'd had a glass of milk in his hands.

Joy settled across from her grandfather and quickly ate her own breakfast, then rose to place her empty bowl in the dishpan. She poured a bit of soap into it and added a pan of hot water. The rest of the dirty dishes were added quickly and she fortified herself for the walk to the barn with a last sip of coffee.

"I'm going out to milk now, Grandpa," she said, touching his shoulder as she passed his chair. "You just sit still and enjoy your coffee, won't you? I won't be long."

"If you'll hold up a moment, ma'am, I'd like to go ahead of you and make a path for you," Gideon said, rising from his place to scoop his coat from the hook behind him. He slid into it quickly, then took Joy's from her and held it for her, easing it onto her arms carefully. She snatched up her shawl and wrapped it around her head, tucking the ends into the front of her coat to provide extra warmth on her chest. She buttoned her coat, stamped her boots into place on her feet and opened the backdoor.

Joy's heartbeat thudded in her chest as Gideon led the way, for he'd reached for her hand to tug her close behind him. "Hold tight," he said. "I'll break the path for you, Joy. Just stay close."

The man threw off heat like the potbellied stove at the general store and she felt his warmth radiate as she followed him from the kitchen. *Stay close.* The man had no idea how tempting those words were, Joy thought, and she obeyed him, stepping in his footprints as they made their way across the yard.

In but a few short minutes, Gideon had made a fair-size path halfway to the barn and she took a short detour to the milk house to reach in and snatch up the pail she'd left there last night, ready for this morning's milking. Gideon looked back at her and grinned.

"We're almost there, ma'am. Another couple of minutes should do it."

Joy nodded her agreement, then ducked her head against his back and followed closely behind him. Tall, strong and blessed with a smile that warmed her heart, he tempted her. And though it might be folly to think of him in such a way, she allowed her thoughts to dwell on him and the moments they would share as they worked together, tending her animals. She'd never known such a man, never felt such happiness as she did this very minute, catching his eye as he turned toward her as if to make sure of her well-being.

His mouth curved in a smile. "All right?" he asked. And Joy thought she'd never been so *all right* in her life.

Chapter Two

The barn loomed before them and Gideon applied his strength to the task of pushing the wide barn door aside, reaching for Joy to draw her close to his side as they entered. She found herself inside the warmth of the barn, which in reality was more of a shed, holding but three stalls and storage space above for hay for the animals. There was a straw stack outside the backdoor, already half gone with months of winter yet to pass before the hay would once more be ready to cut and the wheat ready for harvest. Luckily, their neighbor was good enough to cut the wheat for them and bring a stack of straw to the barnyard for their use, all for allowing him half the harvest.

Gideon spoke to her, his voice booming now

that the barn door was closed and the wind was held in abeyance. "I'll clean out the stalls for you, ma'am, and put hay in the mangers for the animals. It looks like you have a good supply up above."

"Yes, hopefully it will last until the first cutting of hay in June or July. We cut the last in September and had a good crop to pile up top. It keeps the barn warm and the animals fed. Can't ask for more than that, can we?" Joy smiled up at Gideon from her perch on the milking stool next to Daisy. She'd tossed an armful of hay into the cow's manger before sitting down to milk her, and Daisy lowed contentedly as she bent her head to munch on the hay set before her. Joy propped the milk bucket between her knees in preparation for the chore of milking, an event Daisy was more than ready for, according to her low murmurings that Joy understood after long association with the cow. She found herself talking to the animal as she milked, much as she might speak with a friend, knowing that the sound of her voice kept Daisy contented and placid.

Joy looked up as a pair of big feet paused to stand beside her. "I can't thank you enough for your help," she said to the man who had worked his way to Daisy's stall, having already hefted last night's leavings from the animals out the backdoor. "It would have taken me almost an hour to plow through the snow and get out here, and then I'd have to carry the bucket of milk back and hope I didn't spill it on the way. I've fallen more than once traveling back and forth, and it was much easier to follow in your footsteps and get here so quickly today."

"I'm more than grateful to you, ma'am, for feeding me and my son and giving us a warm place to roost this morning. I don't think I'd have lasted much longer if I hadn't seen your lit window from the road out front. I was about winded from plowing through the drifts and carrying Joseph. I fear we'd have frozen to death had I not caught sight of your place."

"Well, you're welcome to stay with Grandpa and me for as long as you need to. We have a loft with plenty of room for you. Grandpa sleeps up there in one room my pa walled off over the kitchen range. It keeps him warm in the winter, and when he opens his window in the good weather, he's right next to the big maple tree out front and can see and hear the birds in its branches. We use the rest of the space up there for storage and have a bed set up in one corner. It used to be my room before my mother and father died. It seemed like a waste to have their bedroom empty, so I moved downstairs and put my things in their old room a couple of years ago."

"How long have your folks been gone?" Gideon asked quietly from behind her. She felt the warmth of his big body and wondered if he hadn't moved to keep the draft from the door off her while she milked Daisy.

"It's been four years, since I was sixteen. They apparently got hit by a log while they were crossing the stream on their way home from town. It must have tipped the wagon and they were caught beneath the lumber Pa had bought there. The weight of it was too much for them and they drowned before they could get free. Our neighbor found them and managed to pull them from the water, but it was too late to do more than bring them home."

"We never know why things happen as they do," Gideon said quietly. "I often wondered why my wife died in childbirth as she did. I had to find a wet nurse for Joseph. She lived with us until he was six months old, when I began to feed him from the table and taught him how to drink from a cup. My housekeeper took over his care when the wet nurse had a chance to go to a family that needed her more. She was a lifesaver for me and for Joseph, of course. But it was good for me to take over his care as much as I could after I came home from work. Mrs. Bates had her hands full with cooking and cleaning and such, so Joseph and I spent a lot of time together. We've become much closer than most father and sons, I think. He means the world to me."

"Well, I'm pleased to have you with us for Christmas, Mr. Burnley. Perhaps you can even help me chop down the tree I've had my eye on."

"First off, why don't you call me Gideon, ma'am?" he asked nicely.

"I will if you can bring yourself to stop calling me ma'am and call me Joy instead."

He grinned at her and she was warmed by his smile. She stood and lifted the milk pail, not surprised when he reached to take it from her hand. He placed it by the barn door and then turned back to her.

"Where will I find the straw to put in the stalls?" he asked.

"I'll show you, Gideon. Follow me."

She went to the backdoor and slid it open, revealing the small corral and the straw stack that was covered in piles of snow. Gideon set her aside and stepped outdoors, pitchfork in hand. "I'll toss it in if you can push it to one side until there's enough for the stalls," he said. He stuck the pitchfork into the hollowed-out space from which she'd dug straw for the past months and turned back around with the fork piled high. In a quick movement he sent it sailing into the barn and Joy nudged the straw to one side, then awaited the next load.

In just a few minutes Gideon had tossed enough straw inside for the stalls and he came back into the barn, pushing the door closed behind himself. "It's not so bad out back. The wind is broken by the barn and it makes it easier to work when you're not being blown hither and yon." He laughed as he turned to fork up the straw and spread it in the stalls. "This won't take at all long now. Why don't you let the cow out of her stall and into the aisleway while I clean her space and then give her a share of this stuff."

Joy undid Daisy's lead rope from the manger and backed her up, giving Gideon room to toss the soiled debris from her stall and then replace it with the clean bedding. When he'd completed his chore, she led the cow back to her breakfast and Daisy immediately tucked into the fresh hay, lowing contentedly as she did.

"I'm about done out here," Joy said. "And it

looks to me like you've finished all my chores for me, Gideon. I surely do appreciate it. Now to carry this milk into the house. I usually leave it in the milk house until the next milking, but I think I'll just take it on in with me and let you pick up last night's bucket from the milk house, if you will. It's just to the left of the door, with a towel draped over the top. We'll put them both in the pantry and by tomorrow I'll have enough cream for churning."

"I'll be glad to carry both pails, Joy. I think I can manage if you'll hold this one while I get the other from the milk house."

Joy tucked her shawl around her head and inside her coat collar, readying herself for the blast of wind that would surely be waiting on the other side of the door. Gideon led the horse into his stall and closed the door behind him, and then they stood by the wide barn door, both of them obviously dreading the trek back to the house.

"Might as well set out. It's going to be hard going, no matter how long we wait to begin," Joy said, inhaling deeply of the warmer air inside the barn. She watched Gideon open the door and pick up the milk pail as he waited for Joy to pass in front of him. She set out, ducking to keep her face inside her warm shawl, away from the blowing snow. Gideon followed closely behind her, his hand grasping her elbow as they made their way to the milk house, where Gideon picked up last night's milking. As they set off back down the path, which was fast filling with new snow, she looked up, hoping for a break in the heavy clouds that had dumped so much of the white stuff on them in the past weeks. But as it stood, they would have to shovel again tonight to get to the barn.

"I was hoping for some of it to clear, at least enough to allow me to get across the meadow to the trees before Christmas," she told Gideon, hoping he could hear her voice speaking to him.

Apparently he got the gist of her muttering, for as they stomped their way up onto the porch, he leaned forward enough to answer her. "What do you want to go out across the meadow for, Joy? Is that where you spotted the tree you spoke of earlier?"

She nodded, then opened the door and stood aside, allowing Gideon to carry the milk into the kitchen. She shivered as the heat from inside warmed her suddenly.

After shaking the snow off their coats and hanging them up, they stood in the kitchen grinning foolishly at each other, as if they had surmounted some great task set before them and were celebrating their victory over it. And so they had, Joy decided. They carried the two buckets of milk into the pantry and placed them beneath the shelf, covering the most recent milking with a clean dish towel to keep dust and critters out of it while the cream rose to the top. Then she uncovered last night's milking and stirred it with a wooden spoon before pouring a good bit of it into the pitcher she kept there for that purpose. It was enough to keep her in milk for baking and drinking for the day. Joy left the rest beneath the shelf and carried the pitcher to the kitchen.

"Would you like some more milk, Joseph?" she asked. "It's nice and cold from being outdoors, but if you'd rather have it warmed, I can do that for you. In fact, I can put some chocolate in it, and with a spoonful of sugar, you'd have hot cocoa to drink. Would you like that?"

"I've never had hot cocoa," Joseph said eagerly. "Can you show me how you do it?"

"I surely can. Let me put your chair a bit closer to the stove and you can stand up on it and watch me fix it." It only took her a few seconds to move the chair and prop him up next to her. While she prepared the cocoa, she kept her left arm around his waist lest he fall forward.

"Would you like to share Joseph's drink, Gideon? I can add another cupful of milk easily enough."

Joseph turned in her grasp to look over his shoulder at his father and added his plea. "Why don't you, Daddy. We never had this before, did we? I don't remember it anyway."

"No, I suspect we haven't, son. I'll be glad to share some with you if Joy doesn't mind."

She added the extra milk to the saucepan, along with another scoop of cocoa and some sugar. Joy lifted the saltshaker from the back of the stove and shook it over the pan, as her mother had taught her, the salt enhancing the flavor of the chocolate.

"Would you find some mugs in the dresser, Gideon? The door on the left."

With a grunt of assent, her guest rose and brought back four thick china cups, which he placed on the table. "I assume you'll both be joining us," he said, taking his seat once more.

Grandpa got up from his chair and made his way to the kitchen door. "No, you young folks enjoy your treat while I find my whittling knife and a likely piece of wood to work on," he said, then walked from the room with the aid of a cane he kept nearby at all times.

Joy lifted Joseph from his perch and set him away from the hot stove before she poured the mugs full, the milk foaming almost to overflowing as she drained the pan. "That ought to do it, gentlemen," she said with laughter lacing her words. It seemed there was much to be thankful for this morning. Two guests to share the coming days until Christmas and the hope of having a tree this year after all.

"How about a piece of bread and butter to go with your cocoa? I can slice some right quick if you like."

"Have you the heel handy?" Gideon asked. "Joseph likes the middle of the loaf, but I've always been partial to the first slice. My mother used to spread it with butter, right to the edges she always said." He looked up at Joy with a smile that was strangely tender, as if his thoughts of home and hearth were warming him. "It's odd how little things stick in your mind, isn't it, ma'am? I can still see my mother at the stove, standing as you are right now, ready to serve her family."

She felt the sting of tears as she turned away, her thoughts bittersweet as she recalled her own mother. "Memories are to be cherished, especially the ones that warm us from within," she said quietly.

"I wish I had a mama to remember," Joseph said, and Joy sat, reaching across the table to take up his small hand within her own.

"Perhaps one day your father will find a woman fit to be your mother, Joseph. We never know what life has in store for us, and surely a mother isn't too much for a little boy to hope for."

Gideon lifted his cup and sipped carefully. "I fear he'll have to make do with one poor excuse of a father, ma'am," he said. "I wouldn't ask any woman to take me on, unless she was looking for a repair-and-restoration project."

She smiled at him, almost chuckling at the woebegone expression on his face. "Do you think you are such a poor specimen as all that? I see you as a shining example of fatherhood, Gideon. Your son would not be as he is without your influence."

"My daddy says I'm a good boy," Joseph said with a speck of pride showing in his shining eyes.

"I'm sure you are. You certainly know how to behave well and that's about all that can be expected of a child your age," Joy told him, leaning close to speak to the lad as if he were an equal and would understand her words. She marveled at how she'd misjudged the small boy at first, thinking him to be three or four years old. Gideon had since told her that Joseph was small for his age; he was actually six. That explained his ability to communicate so well, Joy thought.

"Thank you, ma'am," Joseph said politely, his wide grin showing his delight at her attention.

"Well, I'd better get busy and start something cooking for dinner. These dishes aren't going to wash themselves and I have dish towels to wash and hang to dry," Joy said, listing her agenda for the morning.

"I'm a pretty good hand at dishes," Gideon said, offering his help.

"I'll take you up on that." Joy rose and took her cup to the sink, adding it to the pile already awaiting warm water in the dishpan.

As the two adults did the dishes, Joseph watched from his place at the table, not seeming surprised at the sight of his father with his hands in dishwater.

But he totally missed the warm look Gideon bestowed upon the woman who stood beside him, nor would he have understood the message his father sent silently with but a wink of his eye and a subtle twist of his mouth that signified his delight in her.

Chapter Three

The pantry shelves held a multitude of Mason jars, chicken filling some of them, beef and gravy in others, but nothing there seemed to appeal to Joy this morning. She thought of the ham hanging in the smokehouse, the venison hanging on the porch from the latest buck that had stood in her meadow and dared her to take aim in his direction. She'd performed the task ruefully, not looking forward to the chore of dressing out the animal and then dragging it to the yard to wash the meat at the horse trough.

The best part had been the fine hide she'd hung and cleaned, thinking of the slippers and, perhaps, a vest she might make from its soft leather. She'd cooked stew from a hindquarter, sliced slabs from the roasts and spread them out in a flat pan to freeze and even ground up scraps to make venison sausage they had for breakfast when the pork supply ran low. Perhaps a chunk of stew meat would be good for dinner. There were potatoes and carrots left in the cellar, along with several squashes and the pumpkin she planned to cut up and cook for pies for Christmas dinner.

And somehow the thought of Christmas held new visions of cheer as she contemplated cooking for more than just herself and Grandpa. There were several leftover bits of yarn in her knitting basket, surely enough to make a pair of mittens and a cap to match for Joseph. It would be a hodgepodge of colors, but she doubted the boy would mind, so long as the end results kept him warm.

"I think I'll go out to the porch and cut off a piece of venison for stew," she said, turning to watch as Gideon wiped the table clean.

"Can I do that for you? It'll save you getting cold again, and if you'll tell me how large a piece you need, I'm sure I can handle the job." His words halted her as she reached for her coat and shawl and she turned to face him, a smile wreathing her face.

"I can see that you'll come in right handy, sir. I need a piece about the size of that kettle there," she told him, pointing at her medium saucepan.

"Sounds good to me," Gideon answered, then reached for his coat and pulled on his hat. Joy found her large butcher knife and handed it to him, then watched as he went out to the porch. It was overcast, with snow still falling, but the light from the kitchen was sufficient to see from the window where he reached for the hanging venison and sliced deftly at it, cutting loose a large piece that would fit readily into her stew pot.

She went to the door to take the meat from him, then sent him back out to the cellar to fetch vegetables for tonight's dinner. He turned away and held the porch post as he went down the steps and headed for the cellar door next to the porch, careful not to slip and fall on the snow that had already coated the slick wood.

In less than five minutes he reappeared, holding the kettle she'd given him to fill. It almost overflowed with the vegetables she'd asked for, and she opened the door to allow him entrance as he stomped his feet to leave the snow behind on the porch. Again he shook his coat outdoors before he hung it on the hook, and she decided he'd been trained well by some female.

"How far west did you plan to travel, Gideon?" she asked, wondering if his memories were happy ones or if he'd decided to start a new life with his son because of overwhelming sadness in his past. "I know the weather came on quicker than you'd thought it would, with an early winter setting in and putting a stop to your trek."

"I'd hoped to get closer to the Rockies before winter," he said. "There's a lot of land west of here waiting for a man to homestead it."

"Perhaps you could find a place left behind by folks who have headed back East. There are places like that for sale hereabouts at good prices. Some of them only want the taxes paid."

"I fear I'm going to have to stay in the area until the snow clears and it's safe to travel with Joseph. I'd hoped to get farther west in my travels, but if you wouldn't mind a couple strangers to tend to, we'd surely appreciate staying in the room you mentioned upstairs for the time being. We can pay our own way, for I've got a bit of money saved up, plus what I made from the sale of our house."

His words were welcome ones, though she hadn't planned on having houseguests. A pair of strong arms to handle the snow shoveling and a willing man to do the chores sounded like manna from heaven this morning.

"I don't expect you to take me at my word," Gideon said. "I had my pastor back home write me a letter of introduction and the banker there vouched for me in his note. I didn't know if I might need some sort of credentials when I found a place to stop. I'll be glad to show them both to you, Joy, and to whomever you think might be able to verify my word."

And those papers he spoke of might be faked, she thought cynically, but a long look into the blue eyes that met her own gave her a feeling that they weren't. He looked like a man of his word. A fellow in search of somewhere to stay until he could find a more permanent place to set down his roots and raise his son.

Bedtime came at dusk, for Joy had learned to be stingy with the kerosene that fueled the lamps. She curled in the middle of her bed, her thoughts of the man and boy sleeping in the loft enough to warm her. If Gideon took over the chores, she'd have time to spend with his son. Joseph looked to be needing the touch of a woman in his life, and Joy felt a tenderness toward the boy she couldn't explain.

She awoke at dawn, sliding from the warmth of her quilts to don her dress and wrap a shawl around her shoulders before she made her way to the kitchen. There she found Gideon, busy adding small logs to the fire he'd banked in the stove last evening.

"Good morning," he said in his low, almost husky voice. "Thought I'd beat you to the punch and have your stove ready to cook on when you got up."

"I surely appreciate it, Gideon. I'm used to doing everything myself, and though I don't mean to sound like I'm complaining, I'll have to admit it will be a pleasure to have some help."

"I'll head out to the barn while you fix some breakfast. I heard your grandfather moving around upstairs, so he should be down right shortly. Joseph slept like a log last night and I may have to shake the sheets to get him up when I come in." As he spoke, he donned his heavy coat, pulled down the knitted hat he wore to cover his ears and the shawl Joy wore outdoors, tucking it around his throat and across his chest beneath his coat.

From the pantry, Joy called out softly, "I'll have this ready in half an hour or so, and if you're not in by then, I'll hold it in the warming oven."

As Joy prepared breakfast, she looked through the window and caught a glimpse of Gideon shoveling his way to the barn. He moved more quickly this time, tossing fresh snow to either side as he went. The path from last night was still visible, but at least another six inches of snow had fallen.

From upstairs she heard Grandpa's voice mingling with the youthful tones of Joseph. After a few minutes they made their way down the stairs, the boy holding Grandpa's arm as if he would keep him erect with his childish strength. Grandpa made a big fuss of him when they arrived in the kitchen, sitting down at the table, Joseph taking the chair next to his.

"This young'un will sure enough come in handy, Joy. He gave me a hand with putting my slippers on and helped me down the stairs."

Joy smiled, pleased at Grandpa's welcoming words. Joseph beamed his pleasure as he listened to every syllable passing the old man's lips. "I like to help when I can," he said. "My pa says the good Lord expects us to do our best and always lend a helping hand."

"Your father is a smart man, I'd say," Joy

told him, turning from the stove to smile at him. "He'll be in shortly for breakfast, probably by the time the biscuits are done."

"Are we gonna stay here with you?" Joseph asked the old man next to him.

"As long as this weather lasts, I'd say. Your pa will be a big help to Joy. Gettin' back and forth in the snow is too much for a woman. Joy's been doing it all along, but if your pa wants to help and ease her load, I'd surely appreciate it."

The backdoor rattled open and Gideon stepped inside, carrying Joy's blue-speckled bowl in one hand. He hung his coat and Joy's shawl on the hook by the door, and then sat to slide from his boots. "Things are looking good out there, Joy," he said. "I found your pan on top of the chicken coop and gathered the eggs. Fed the chickens first, though, to lure them off their nests. The cow gave me almost a full bucket of milk and I put it in the milk house. Every bit of stock is fed and the barn is warm enough with the heat they put out to keep them all safe and sound."

"I can't thank you enough, Gideon," Joy said sincerely. "Now, get washed up and sit down at the table. I'll fry up the eggs and we'll eat."

* * *

By breakfast time a few days later, the snow was piled up higher than the windows. Finished with his meal, Gideon leaned back in his chair and shot a look at Joy. He was amazed at how quickly they'd settled into a routine, almost like a real family. And now his suggestion would make it feel even more so.

"If you've a mind to, we could head out across the meadow after a bit and see to cutting you that tree you've got your eye on, ma'am. The wind's died down some and I think we could make it without any trouble."

Joy's heart skipped a beat as she thought of the thrill of decorating the pine she'd marked as her own. "That would be such fun, Gideon. I'd about given up hope of a Christmas tree this year. If you could make that particular dream come true, I'd be most grateful."

"Can I go, too, Pa?" Joseph wanted to know. His face glowed as he considered the joy of having a real Christmas, tree and all.

"I fear not, Joseph. It'll be all we can do to make our own way out there, and besides, Grandpa here needs you inside to keep an eye on things while Joy and I are gone."

"That's right, sonny." Grandpa's words were firm as he backed up Gideon's stance. "I need somebody to look after me a bit and tote things hither and yon. Maybe you'd like to watch me whittle something to hang on the Christmas tree once your pa drags it into the house."

"I'd like that, sir," Joseph said, rising to stand by Grandpa's chair. "Can I go get your whittling stuff for you?"

He'd apparently watched when Grandpa had wrapped up his knife and the wood he was working with and laid it behind the stove yesterday. Now he waited impatiently for the chance to retrieve it and put Grandpa to work at his task.

Gideon spoke up. "Let's you and me get going, Joy. I think your grandfather is in good hands, don't you?"

Joy chuckled as she prepared for the trek across the meadow, bundling up warmly and waiting at the door for Gideon to lead the way.

They made it to the barn quickly, and then Gideon found the bucksaw hanging on the wall. "You ready, ma'am?" he asked with a grin.

"Whenever you are," Joy said, her heart lifting as she considered the man standing before her. She tilted her face upward and smiled at him. "I'm so glad you're here, Gideon."

In a swift movement, he held her shoulders

in his hands and bent to her, dropping a quick kiss on her forehead. "So am I," he said, his voice husky, as if some emotion held him in its grip.

Joy smiled at him again, feeling the residue of warmth he'd left behind on her skin. She felt a blush rise to her cheeks and ducked her head, fussing with her coat buttons as if they needed attention. "Let's go then," she said finally, savoring the memory of her first kiss.

Chapter Four

The expedition was a rousing success, for within an hour Gideon had formed a crude tree stand and nailed the small evergreen onto it before carrying it into the house. Joseph clapped his hands with glee as his father carried the tree to the parlor and gave it pride of place before the front window.

Joy and Gideon toted the boxes of decorations from the corner of the parlor where Joy had left them after her foray into the attic in hopes of her dream tree becoming reality. Dishes were forgotten as they gathered in the parlor to place the homemade wooden stars, the gingerbread men and even an angel on the fragrant tree. Joy brought out tinsel left from years gone by and hung it strand by strand on the branches. Gideon found the candleholders and clipped them on the ends of the branches while Joy located the box of candles, most of them with hours of burning left in their slender white lengths.

She found some colored paper left over from another year and showed Joseph how to make chains, cutting the paper and then sealing the loops with paste made of flour and a dab of water. They were soon joined by Gideon, and by the time they'd used up all the heavy paper Joy had saved, the chain was almost twelve feet long and Joseph pronounced it "beautiful." They wound it around the tree several times and the little boy beamed at the sight.

"After it gets closer to dark, we'll light the candles," Joy decided. "It's only the twenty-third of December, but we'll enjoy it awhile. Tomorrow, we'll make cookies and bake a pumpkin pie."

"I can't thank you enough for letting us join in your Christmas celebrations," Gideon said in a low tone as they stood before the tree, Joy reaching to make sure the candleholders were firmly in place.

"We wouldn't have had it without you here," she said softly. "I'm so thankful you came to our door, Gideon. Even though I didn't like the circumstances behind it, what with you losing your horse and wagon."

He slid one arm around her waist and bent to whisper in her ear, "I'm thinking it was meant to be, Joy. That we were meant to find each other this way."

She blushed and cut a quick look at him. "Maybe so. I only know that you and Joseph are welcome here, and Grandpa and I are thankful for you.

"I have some knitting to catch up on, Gideon. I think I'll ask you to light the fireplace and warm up the parlor a bit. Then I'm going to sit on the sofa and work on my project. I have to have it done by Christmas."

He grinned at her. "I watched you a bit last evening before we went to bed, just knittin' away on what looked suspiciously like a hat for my young'un."

"I got out all my odds and ends of yarn, so it'll be a hat of many colors. I won't be able to knit his mittens to go with it until after Christmas, but I might be able to work on a scarf. The hat's almost done and straight knitting on a scarf takes no time at all."

"You're a kind woman, Joy. My boy's already taken a shine to you. You're the first female he's latched onto since he was born."

He cleared his throat and glanced to where his son sat next to Grandpa, watching as the old man whittled away, paper spread on the floor to catch the whittling scraps.

The low murmur of voices reached them as Joseph and the old man next to him considered the small manger Grandpa had formed from the wood. "How'd you do that, sir?" the boy asked softly.

"Just as easy as pie once you get the hang of it, sonny. I thought I'd do a couple of figures to hang on either side of it, maybe Mary kneeling by the manger and Joseph standing by." Grandpa grinned at the boy. "Did you know you had such a famous name, sonny? Joseph has been revered since the days when he taught the boy, Jesus, about being a carpenter."

"I never knew my name was special. I just thought it was what Pa wanted to call me."

"Well, your name is almost as special as you are, my boy. You're a fine young man, and you'll be a terrific man when you've grown, if you take after your pa."

"Thank you, sir," the child said, as if he was flustered by the attention bestowed upon him.

"Can we light the candles, Pa?" he asked Gideon as his father and Joy crossed the room to where he sat.

"That's up to Joy, I'd think," Gideon said, bending to her wishes.

"I don't know why not. The fireplace is making it warm enough to sit in here till bedtime. Let's enjoy the tree for an hour or so."

"I'll light a candle in the stove and bring it back in here," Gideon offered. He made short work of his task and in minutes he was back, his hands efficient as he lit the two dozen candles they'd anchored on the tree.

"Oh, Pa. That's the most beautiful thing I've ever seen," Joseph said, his eyes widening, his mouth stretching into a grin and his excitement knowing no bounds.

"Why don't we sing some carols," Joy asked them. "I'll play some chords on the organ and we can all join in. I have a book somewhere in the organ bench with Christmas carols in it."

"I wondered if you could play that thing," Gideon said with a chuckle. "I noticed it over in the corner there and I didn't know if it was in working order."

Joy nodded. "Oh, it works, all right. I'm not very good at it, but my mother taught me some music and how to read notes before she died. I don't play often, but I think this celebration calls for it, don't you?"

"I'd love to hear you play, and I think I know

the carols by heart. We used to sing them when I was a youngster. My mother and father took us to church regularly and Christmas Eve was always a big night, with caroling and reading the scripture from the book of Luke about the birth of the Savior. Then we'd go home and have hot cider and cookies and usually we'd have a houseful of folks follow us home and join in more singing."

"What a wonderful memory to have," Joy said. "We used to go to church on Christmas Eve, but after my folks died it was too much for Grandpa to harness up and then hope we could get through the snow. I sure hadn't planned on it this year. I've never seen so much snow in my life."

"Well, we'll have our own celebration right here," Gideon said stoutly. "I can squeeze some of those apples in the cellar and make some cider for us to drink and you can make cookies tomorrow, enough for us to have a real party."

"Can I help, too?" Joseph asked, excitement riding high as he hurled himself into his father's arms.

"Sure you can, son. We'll figure out how to press those apples in the morning, as soon as I finish with the chores."

"And in the meantime, if Joy starts cookies maybe I can help her," Joseph said, casting a yearning glance at the woman he'd obviously come to think of very fondly.

"You sure can," Joy said quickly. "I'll mix the dough and roll it out, and you can use my cookie cutters to cut out stars and angels and bells and all sorts of good things."

Joseph leaned from his father's arms to hug Joy's neck. "I'm so glad we're here with you and Grandpa," he sang out.

"Well, I'm glad you're here, too," Joy told him, returning his hug and then turning to the sofa to sit beside her grandfather. "Come sit on my lap, Joseph," she invited, and the boy lost no time in accepting her summons. Joy leaned back a bit and Joseph cuddled close as they both turned their attention to the tree, glowing brightly as the candles flickered and flamed.

"Time for you to show us how talented you are," Gideon said, approaching Joy a bit later. He reached for his son and then helped Joy up from her seat with his other hand. She went to the organ and lifted the cover from the keyboard, settling herself on the bench and pumping the pedals for a moment.

"Now watch, Joseph," his father said. "Watch how Joy pumps the pedals that feed air to the organ and make it sound out the notes she presses with her fingers. I think we're in for a treat."

"I hope so," Joy said with a laugh. "I haven't played for a while, but some things you never forget." She stood quickly and pulled the proper songbook from the bench beneath her, opening it and placing it on the music rack. Within moments the sound of "Silent Night" filled the room as Joy played with more proficiency than Gideon had expected.

"All right, you lead off, Gideon, and we'll all join in," she said, completing the short introduction.

Without hesitation Gideon's baritone voice rose in the opening words, and Grandpa rose from the sofa to join them around the organ. Joy sang a low alto part, harmonizing as her mother had taught her, and even Joseph was caught up in the words, singing along as best he could.

"I remember that song," the boy said after they'd sung the first verse. "We sang it at Aunt Rosie's house back home."

"So we did, son," Gideon replied. "I wasn't sure you'd remember the words, but you did really well."

"How about 'Joy to the World' now," Joy

asked, turning the pages to find the carol she'd mentioned.

"I know that one a little bit, too," Joseph said with glee. Following his father's lead, he sang out, not always getting the words correct but following as best he could. Grandpa cut in with his rusty bass and their harmony rose in the small parlor as they sang. The words were a paean of joy and Gideon found himself focusing on the woman who sat before him, her music rising in accompaniment as they sang. She was flushed and excited, her voice melodic and sounding much to him as the angels must have on that first Christmas Eve.

They sang on, turning pages in the songbook, until finally Joseph's head began to loll against Gideon's shoulder. "I think this boy needs to be in bed," he said quietly as Joy finished the last song.

"He'll have a big day tomorrow and he's about tuckered out right now," Joy said agreeably. "We'll be up early. I'll hold breakfast until the chores are done, Gideon."

He nodded and offered her a smile that carried a wealth of feeling. "I'll sort out some apples in the cellar after I do the chores. Joseph and I will do our apple squeezing in the kitchen, I suspect. It's too cold for him in the cellar."

"We'll have lots of space. The kitchen is the largest room in the house. We spend most of our time there," Joy answered.

Grandpa yawned widely and grinned. "I'm on my way up to bed right now," he said. "This old body needs a lot of sleep these days."

"I'll come back down and bank the fire as soon as I put this boy of mine into bed," Gideon offered.

He left the parlor on Grandpa's heels and they climbed the stairs to the loft. Joy snuffed the candles on the tree, then went to the kitchen and checked in the pantry to be sure she had enough of everything she needed for the cookie baking. It was there that Gideon found her just a few minutes later. She turned and almost walked into him, stepping back as he took her hands in his.

"What are you working at now?" he asked, grinning as he saw the look on her face, one of surprise and pleasure, if his guess was right.

"Just making sure I have everything we need for the big day tomorrow. I'll mix the cookies in my bread-dough pan. It'll hold enough to make ten or twelve dozen."

Gideon drew her closer, his hands tightening on hers in a firm grip. She stood before him looking like the angel on the Christmas tree, he decided, lifting a hand to brush a lock of hair from her cheek. "Joy, would you think poorly of me if I stole a kiss from you? I wouldn't do anything to cause you distress, but since the first brush of my lips against your smooth skin, I've yearned for another chance to touch you. Perhaps a kiss more suited to a man who has come to care for a woman more quickly than he'd planned."

"And what is the difference between the two?" she asked, her eyes sparkling in the dim light within the pantry.

"I believe I'll just show you," Gideon said quietly. He bent a bit, his mouth touching hers gently. And then with a murmur in his throat, he released her lips and scooped her closer to him, his arms wrapping her in a firm embrace. His mouth sought hers once more and this time he began a foray of kisses across her cheeks and forehead, ending up once more at her lips. His tongue touched her upper lip in a caress she had apparently never felt before, for she moved back quickly and opened her eyes to meet his.

"I haven't had a lot of experience at kissing, as you've probably guessed," she said quietly, "for aside from a few hasty kisses on my cheek, I've never allowed a man to come any closer to me, Gideon. I fear my experience is far overshadowed by yours."

He smiled down at her, holding her closely against his big body. She was small and delicate, and though gently rounded, she was all woman and filled his arms. "You're a woman to be cherished, Joy. I hope you know that I mean only what is right and honest between us. I feel deeply for you, but perhaps that sounds foolish after such a short time."

She blushed and touched her forehead against his shirt, there where his heart beat, a bit rapidly, she thought. "I don't know what to say to you, Gideon. I've been sheltered here with Grandpa, and men are beyond my experience for the most part. But I have to admit that I feel something…" She looked up at him. "I don't even know what I feel, to be honest with you. I just know I'm glad you and your son came to us. I feel like you were put here for a reason, and if that's nothing more than to be a help to us through this storm, so be it. I'm just happy to tend to Joseph and keep him safe and warm and well fed. And the same goes for you. If you'll lend a hand with the work here, like you already have, then I'll be thankful for it."

"I'm here for you, Joy. For as long as you need me I'll be here. You may be right. Perhaps I was sent here for a reason, whether for Joseph's well-being or my own. I'm happy here with you and your grandfather, and Joseph is tickled pink by everything that's happened since our arrival."

"Well, I think we both need to turn in," Joy said firmly. "Tomorrow will be a big day for everyone, and I plan on getting up early. And I still have some knitting to do tonight. I'll sit up in bed and finish Joseph's cap. Shouldn't take more than a half hour or so, and I want to begin his scarf early on tomorrow, after the cookie baking is finished."

Gideon stepped back from the pantry, then made haste to bank the cookstove after ushering her into the kitchen. She watched him finish his task, then walked into the hallway and toward her bedroom. Gideon made his way to the stairs. "Good night, Joy," he sang out cheerfully, for he felt he had much to be pleased with, given the events in the pantry and Joy's response to him.

"Good night," she called back, bending to light a lamp on the hallway table to carry with her into her bedroom. She disappeared from his view and he quickly went up the stairs to the loft, where Joseph slept soundly. He undressed, slid beneath the sheet and quilts next to his son and curled his arm around the boy, the better to keep him warm throughout the night. The heat from the stove in the kitchen made its way upstairs and he found himself ready to sleep, even as visions of the woman downstairs drifted through his head. His lips curved in a tender smile as he closed his eyes.

Chapter Five

The scent of apples filled the kitchen as Gideon used Joy's grinder to fill a large pan with juice and pulp from the fruit he'd gathered from the cellar. He'd washed the apples, sorting through them and discarding the ones with bad spots. Although this was a new endeavor for him, he felt confident he would be able to make a decent batch of cider in his own makeshift way.

The grinder worked well for the job, and he set about straining the apples into another container with Joy's large strainer. By the time he was finished, he had over a gallon of the fragrant juice, along with a goodly amount of pulp, and had set aside the rest of the pulp and skins for the pigs who lived in a pen with a sheltered lean-to attached to the barn. There were three pigs, all of them ready for butchering, a job Gideon meant to inquire about in town or perhaps with the nearby neighbor once the snow cleared up. Surely there would be someone in the area who specialized in such things.

Joy worked at the table, mixing the dough for the cookies, finally dumping a part of the dough onto the flour-covered table. She patted it into a circle, then used her rolling pin to flatten it and ready it for Joseph's task of cutting out cookies. He knelt on a chair, one of her aprons tied around him to protect his clothing from all the flour that would be flying about as he worked.

He cut out first one star, then another, until he had almost two dozen, not all of them perfect, but all of them suitable for the cookie sheets Joy had readied. Using her spatula, she transferred one after another of the stars until she had filled the sheet.

"This one goes into the oven, Joseph. We'll give them ten minutes and then check them out. They should be pretty near baked by then." After sliding the pan into the hot oven, Joy brought her other cookie sheet to the table.

"Now let's fill this one," she said with a smile for the eager boy who watched her.

In no time, she found room for the rest of his stars on the cookie sheet and placed it on the warming shelf to await its turn in the oven below. She piled up the remnants of the dough and added more from her bread pan, then went through the same process as she had the first time. This time, Joseph was given a cookie cutter that resembled an angel. His tongue was caught in one corner of his mouth as he worked, and Joy and Gideon exchanged smiles as they watched him, Joy lending a hand when needed, for Joseph wasn't yet adept at fitting the angels closely together on the cookie sheet.

The morning passed quickly as one pan then another left the oven. The cookies were just a touch brown, marking their readiness for the next step. After the table was piled high across one end with ten dozen cookies, according to Joy's count, they got ready to frost them. Joy filled a bowl with white icing and found some small bottles of colored sugar in the pantry, which she transferred to empty salt and pepper shakers. "I never did this before," Joseph announced as Joy began frosting the cookies.

"Well, it'll take you and your father both to

keep up with me, I fear," Joy said with a laugh as she moved her frosted cookies closer to the boy. Gideon joined him, and they all sprinkled the colored sugar on the stars and angels before them, Joseph more than generous with his shakers, colored sugar flying about with gusto. Gideon announced that one of them was damaged by too many sugar crystals and must be eaten immediately, calling forth laughter from Joy and his son.

He made a big production out of eating the angel he'd considered to be damaged, sharing it with Joseph bite for bite. "That's the best cookie I ever ate, ma'am," the boy declared fervently. "It surely was good. I'll bet I could eat another one, if you wouldn't mind."

"I'd be happy to get you a glass of milk to go with it, if you'd like, Joseph. And perhaps even one for your father," Joy said happily. She hadn't had this much fun in a month of Sundays, she decided, watching the wide grin spread across the boy's face.

"Would you, ma'am? I'd sure like that and I know my daddy would, too," Joseph said, smiling through the icing that adorned his lips and cheeks.

Within a few minutes, Grandpa had joined them, and all four sat at the table, drinking milk and sampling the cookies before them. Joy moved as many cookies to the cooled cookie sheets as she could and then found two more in the cupboard to hold the excess. The kitchen dresser held all four sheets and still the table was almost half full.

"We'll have enough cookies to last us for a month," Joy said happily. "We'll hang some on the tree later on, when the icing is completely dry. Probably by tonight. And in the meantime, I have some other tasks to finish up before the day is over. If you'll all excuse me, I'm going to sit on the rocker in the corner and get out my knitting."

"Can I go in the parlor and look at the Christmas tree?" Joseph asked. "I just want to sit on the sofa and enjoy it."

"You sure can, son," Gideon said, ushering the boy away from the knitting scene lest he figure out that the work keeping Joy so busy was intended for him. She'd finished the hat last night and had begun working on the scarf before her eyes closed midway through a row, almost causing a calamity when the stitches came close to sliding from her needles. Now she knit the final ball of yarn into the length she'd determined would fit around the boy's neck and crisscross on his chest to keep him warm beneath his coat. The mittens would have to wait till after Christmas, for she had another task she wanted to complete before dark.

She'd found a large ball of brown yarn in her basket of supplies and determined to do a scarf for Gideon, even if it took all evening. She was quick at the task, for she'd been knitting since she was but a youngster. She'd made Grandpa a new hat and scarf over the past weeks, working at it in her bedroom to keep it a secret from him, and had fashioned a vest for him out of the deerhide she'd cleaned and stretched. Now if Gideon's scarf was ready in time, she'd wrap them in the tissue she'd bought in town a while ago. It was red and would look festive under the tree come morning. She needed only to make out small name tags for the packages and then scoot into the parlor after everyone else was in bed to put them beneath the tree.

Christmas morning began before the sun came up. Joy was busily making cinnamon rolls, having put them to rise atop the warming oven the night before. She fried up a panful of bacon and a dozen eggs, sliding them onto her big platter to sit in the center of the table when everyone had assembled for breakfast. She toasted six slices of bread in the oven, then buttered them and presented them on another small plate.

"This is a feast fit for a king," Gideon pronounced. His cheeks were ruddy from the cold and he sat closest to the stove to soak up the warmth. The chores were done, he'd said as he came in the backdoor, and after he'd washed up at the sink, he helped Joseph wash, then sat him on a store catalog atop his chair. Grandpa came in, a smug look on his face as he joined the group around the table.

They held hands while Gideon said a blessing over their food, and then they all tucked in with a will, the bacon and eggs disappearing quickly. The cinnamon rolls were hot from the oven and Joy cut them up in big squares and passed the butter. They drank coffee and ate the rolls almost in silence, so tasty were the sweet offerings. Joseph drank two glasses of milk, declaring the rolls to be the best thing he'd eaten in forever, causing his father and Joy to laugh heartily.

They lit the candles on the tree, and then all sat down on the sofa but for Gideon, who announced he would distribute the gifts. Joseph was delighted with the hat and scarf Joy had made and thanked her profusely. Grandpa was surprised at his own knitted gift and muttered his thanks with a low growl. His misty eyes needed wiping with his big kerchief as he unwrapped the vest Joy had stitched so carefully from the deerhide.

"I sure didn't expect such a wonderful surprise, girl," he said in a gruff tone, his smile belying the sound. With Gideon's help, he donned his gift and beamed as he smoothed his hands over the front, examining the buttonholes Joy had worked into the suede fabric. Gideon was more than happy with the scarf he received, declaring it a lifesaver, for he needed something to keep his ears warm.

Grandpa pointed at a brown-wrapped package and Gideon lifted it from beneath the tree and cast a questioning look at him. "Give it to Joy," he said, and Gideon did so with a flourish. Joy took it on her lap with a cry of glee.

"How did you…? What did you…?" she asked, her cheeks pink with confusion and pleasure as her fingers untied the string that encircled the package. She folded back the paper, and within the wrapping lay a navy blue cloak, three frog fastenings at its throat. Joy stood up and held it before her, admiring the red binding that accented it, encircling the neck and then running down the front of each lapel and down to the hem.

"Oh, my! Oh, my!" she crooned, unfastening the loops and swirling the cloak about her, holding it closely against her throat and turning in a slow circle before her audience. Grandpa smiled, Joseph clapped his hands with glee and Gideon could only watch in admiration as the woman before him cast warm glances at all the males in her family.

"You surely do look like a Christmas angel, Joy," Grandpa said with a hint of tears in his voice. "I knew you'd look beautiful in that thing. Had it ordered from the catalog for you and picked it up a while ago when we went to town."

"I didn't know," Joy said. "You sure are good at keeping a secret, Grandpa. And I thank you so much. It's just beautiful and will keep me warm. I'll even put it over my quilt on the bed when I go to sleep." She bent over her grandfather and kissed him across his forehead and down one cheek, murmuring soft words of love to him as she did so.

"You look pretty enough to put on the top of the tree, Joy," Gideon said. "You sure enough look like an angel in that beautiful cloak. Your grandfather knew just what would look lovely on you."

"I have something else for Joseph," Joy said hesitantly. "I didn't wrap them, but I thought he might like something I've enjoyed for many years. In fact," she said, bringing a pile of books from beneath the tree, "if Joseph would like me to, I'd enjoy reading one of the stories to him tonight before he goes to bed."

"Would you really, Joy?" the boy asked, his eyes pleading as he stood before her, his hands reaching for the books she held. "Oh, look, Daddy. Just look at the books Joy gave me." Joseph sat down on the floor and looked over the assortment Joy had gathered together from her own library for him.

"Here's a whole book about horses and another about dogs. There's lots of stories in this one, and look at the pictures of all kinds of horses in this one. And here's *Black Beauty*, too." He hugged the book to his chest. "I've always wanted to have someone read this story to me. And now Joy says she will. Will we be here long enough for her to read the whole thing, Daddy? Will we?" the boy asked pleadingly.

"Of course you will," Joy said quickly. "I'm sure you and your father aren't going anywhere in a hurry, Joseph. You'll be here for a good while, I'm certain."

"As long as Joy and her grandfather will let us stay," Gideon added with a quick smile at Joy. "There's lots of work I can do here to make life easier for Joy and Grandpa this winter. We'll stay for a while."

"You betcha," Grandpa added. "We've been needing someone to lend a hand around here. It's too much for Joy, and I can't do much to help her. At least not in the snow."

"That's settled, then," Joy said with a wide grin. "You can stay as long as you like, Gideon."

"Well, this has been the merriest Christmas we've had for several years," Gideon said, bending to pick Joseph up in his arms. "I just know my son hasn't been so happy in a long time." And then Grandpa called out for Joseph to draw near to him.

The boy scooted over to stand by Grandpa while the old man dug in his pocket, finally drawing forth a wooden figure. It was a small horse, and the boy watched wide-eyed as the old man held it in the palm of his hand. "Maybe this could be Black Beauty, sonny," Grandpa said with a wide smile. "Not the right color horse, but you can pretend he's black till your pa can paint him for you one day."

"Oh, I can pretend without black paint, Grandpa," the lad cried, holding out his palm for the small figure.

Grandpa placed the figure in Joseph's hand and then had to stop and wipe his eyes and nose, so caught up in the lad's pleasure he almost shed a few tears. "I'm happy you like it, Joseph," he said, reaching to hug the boy in a quick embrace.

Joseph ran to his father. "Lookee what Grandpa made for me, Daddy. Ain't it the prettiest thing you ever saw?"

"Sure enough it is," Gideon said, casting a thankful look at the old man who watched the boy so closely.

Joy rose from the sofa, bent on making it to the kitchen before tears escaped her control. "I'm going to clean up and get ready to fix our Christmas dinner," she said, hurrying from the room.

"I reckon I'll give her a hand." Gideon put his son on the floor and headed after the young woman he'd barely been able to keep his gaze from all morning. Joseph ran to the sofa.

"Can you and me just sit here and watch the Christmas tree?" he asked Grandpa, who held out an arm to enclose the lad's shoulders as he sat beside him.

Gideon went to the kitchen where Joy was wiping the last of her tears and had set about with the breakfast dishes. His arms encircled her and she rested against him for a few moments. "It's been a wonderful morning, but now the dishes await me, Gideon," she said with a sigh.

"Tell you what, ma'am. I'll dry if you'll wash," he said, picking up the dish towel and waving it with a flourish, as if intent on drying her tears with his foolishness.

And so the day passed, all enjoying the dinner Joy fixed for them, Gideon doing the chores closer to nightfall and Grandpa whittling another figure for Joseph to match the horse he'd given him. "This way you'll have a team of 'em," Grandpa said, busily carving the long legs on the figure in his hands.

It was truly the best Christmas Joy could recall as she sat on the sofa after replacing the candles on the tree and lighting them anew. Gideon came in from the barn and stomped his feet as he hung his coat and then joined them in the parlor.

"I'm going to see about putting this boy to bed. He's had a big day and he's about ready to shut his eyes and doze off," Gideon said quietly, picking Joseph up and holding him close.

"Well, get him ready for bed and send him down to me if he's still wide-awake. I'll read to him for a while from *Black Beauty* and see how he likes it. It's a good story, for sure," Joy said.

So it was that she curled up on the sofa with a lamp on the table next to her on one side and a small boy gathered to her on the other. The book lay open on her lap and she found herself with an audience as Gideon joined them, sitting on the floor by her feet as she read. Joseph snuggled close as if he hadn't been cuddled in a long while and his head drooped against her, finally dropping to her lap as he snoozed while she read.

Joy closed the book after inserting a bookmark she'd knitted, a miniature scarf, only an inch or so wide.

Gideon smiled as he saw it. "You're just full of talents, Joy," he said. "You not only cook and clean, but you know how to tend to a family in every way possible. I'm in awe at your abilities."

Joy flushed, nodding her thanks for the compliment, placing the book she'd been reading on the table beside her. "This boy is about

out for the night," she whispered to Gideon as he approached.

"I'll take him up now. And I think I'll crawl in beside him. We're both nearly tuckered out. Will you being going up, too, Grandpa?" he asked the older man.

Grandpa nodded and headed for the stairs, dropping a quick kiss on Joy's cheek as he passed her chair. "Good night, Grandpa. And you, too, Gideon. I'll lock the doors and be on my way, too," Joy said, stifling a yawn as she spoke.

"It was the most beautiful Christmas I've ever had," Gideon said as he paused by her chair. "And you made it possible, Joy. You and your grandfather. I can't thank you enough, both from me and my son. I'll bank the fire in the kitchen and be right back to tote my boy upstairs."

Joy looked up into his eyes and felt warmed from within. Gideon's smile was one she'd never seen before, filled with more than affection, for he bestowed upon her a smile that spoke to her heart.

"I'll be turning in, too, once I make sure all the candles are out," she said.

"I'll see you in the morning, Joy. God bless you, for you've been a real blessing to me.

And to Joseph." He bent, leaving the touch of his lips against her cheek, then went into the kitchen where she heard him lifting a burner on the stove, preparatory to banking the fire for the night. By the time she'd gone to her own room he was back in the parlor, picking up his son and carrying him to the stairs, where she heard his footsteps touch each step. She watched from her bedroom doorway as he climbed, looking down at the lad he carried, lifting him close to his heart as he reached the top of the stairs and headed to the first room on the right.

The house was quiet as Joy found her bed. Before she snuggled beneath her quilts, she lifted herself up a bit to blow out the candle she'd brought to light her way. Her fingers touched the spot on her cheek where Gideon had left his warmth. The man seemed to have crept into her life and her heart in a way she'd never have dreamed possible. He was the very image of what she had long harbored in her heart as the perfect man for her future. Not only tall and strong and handsome but a wonderful father to his son. Perhaps it would be her Christmas gift from the powers that be, that Gideon would find her pleasing. For though he'd told her she was to be admired, she could only wish for more.

Her head swam with images from the whole day as she sank into slumber. And all of them included the tall man who had swept into her life and somehow…into her heart.

Chapter Six

The days following Christmas passed swiftly, Joy caught up in the pleasure of watching from the window as Gideon went about the chores inherent in running the farm. For he had told her she must not leave the house, but rather stay inside and keep Grandpa and Joseph company while he braved the cold and snow outdoors.

She could not find it in her heart to dispute his edict and so cooked and cleaned the house, then washed the ever-present laundry, hanging it on the rack behind the stove to dry. Gideon brought in bacon and sausage from the smokehouse and even half a ham for their supper one night.

"There's still a lot of meat out there," he

told Joy as he presented the ham to her that afternoon. He ducked back to the porch and brought a pail of eggs into the house, carrying them to the pantry for her. "I'd say we're in pretty good shape," he said as he hung his coat and cap on the hook. "If we seem to be running low, I can always take the gun and find a deer for us. I'd think we could eat for a good long time on a nice buck. And we could always have one of the hogs butchered if need be."

"I'm so glad you're here, Gideon," Joy said with spontaneous happiness. "I've never felt so well cared for before. It seemed I had to be the one to do chores and look after my grandfather and keep everything up to snuff. It's a real pleasure to have you here, and especially with the way you've taken over the chores for me."

"I've been blessed by you and your grandpa, Joy," he said in a low tone as he sat at the kitchen table to watch her as she put together their supper. "Joseph and I would have been goners if you hadn't welcomed us into your home."

"I think there is a power that watches over us," Joy said, turning to face him. "Things work together for good, the good book says, and I believe it." She lifted the coffeepot and filled a cup for Gideon, placing it before him.

"I made a fresh pot while you were out taking care of things. I thought you'd be cold and ready for some hot coffee to warm your innards," she said with a chuckle.

"I can't imagine why a woman such as you hasn't been snatched up by some young fellow," Gideon said softly, his words carrying only to her ears. "You are the epitome of womanhood, Joy. A real treasure for the right man." And then she watched as a flush rose to cover his cheeks.

"I can't believe you're blushing," Joy said, seating herself next to him at the table, her own coffee steaming before her.

"I'm trying to smooth the way for a question I want to ask you, Joy. I've wanted to go to town and speak with your minister there, but the weather hasn't allowed for travel yet. And I need to deposit my cash into the bank, too. I'd thought the minister or even your sheriff might check up on me for you, kinda relieve your mind about me if you've any questions He could write or wire to the folks who wrote my letters of referral and see for himself that I'm exactly what I've said I am."

"I don't have any questions about you, Gideon. I read the letters you showed me the first day you were here and I have no doubt that they are genuine. If you want to speak with my pastor or the man at the bank or even the lawman in town, I'd say go right ahead. But I trust you thus far. And unless you give me reason not to do so, I'll let things ride."

He bowed his head in a courtly gesture. "Thank you, Joy. As to what I began saying earlier, I really hesitate to be too bold, for we've only known each other for a short while. And yet I feel that I've known you forever. Does that make sense?"

She lifted her cup to sip at the hot brew within, then smiled at him as she lowered it to the table once more. "I know what you're saying and I understand what you mean, Gideon. I didn't know I could come to love a child in such a short while, but I feel that Joseph is almost my own. That sounds a bit… presumptuous, I suppose, but it's how I feel."

"Joseph asked me last night when we went to bed and after he'd said his prayers if he could call you his mama. He'd already prayed for a mother of his own, as he has several other times, but for some reason, he has latched onto the idea of calling you mama and I didn't know how to answer him. I told him I'd ask you today if you wouldn't mind."

Joy folded her hands on the table before her

and bit her lower lip, trying her best not to shed the tears that had formed at his words. "I'd be honored, Gideon. I love your boy."

He reached out and took her hands in his own, sending his warmth to her very depths. "Joseph will be pleased to hear that, Joy. I'll be sure to tell him when he wakes up in the morning that you're agreeable to his plotting."

"Let me loose, Gideon," she said as a sound of bubbling from the stove caught her attention.

The potatoes had begun to boil and she slid the kettle to the rear of the stove to simmer for a bit. The pork roast she was baking would soon be ready to take up and she'd make gravy by the time the potatoes were finished cooking.

"I think I'd better check on Grandpa while I have a few minutes free," she told Gideon, wiping her hands on her apron and heading for the parlor. "He wasn't feeling just right this morning and he's been resting on the sofa, enjoying Joseph from a distance. Said he didn't want to spread around any germs if he had something going on."

She went into the parlor, hearing Joseph's clear tones as he "read" from the picture book he held. It was one from her own childhood and Joseph had felt he'd struck gold when she'd allowed him the use of her outgrown library. Grandpa sat on the sofa, an afghan tucked around him as he listened to the boy make up a story to go with the pictures in the book before him.

Joy touched the old man on the shoulder and bent to whisper in his ear. "Are you feeling any better, Grandpa?"

Grandpa shook his head. "I'm not sure what it is, Joy, but my chest is hurting some, and my breathing seems to be not quite right. I'm thinking it would be a good idea for Gideon to ride to town on your mare and see if the doctor would come out here."

Joy felt dread strike her soul at his words. She'd feared early this morning that there was something amiss with her grandfather, for he'd not eaten breakfast and had only had hot milk to drink, saying he felt a bit under the weather. Now to hear that his chest was paining him gave her real cause for alarm. She bent to his ear and whispered words of comfort, and then made a decision. "I'd feel better if you'd lie down on my bed, Grandpa. My room is warm, for the stove is just on the other side of the wall and the heat radiates into there. Maybe you'd do better to lie down."

"I don't think so, Joy, for I can breathe better when I'm sitting up. If you'll bring your quilt out here, I'll put my feet up on the sofa and lean into the corner and let Joseph read his picture book to me."

Joy squeezed his shoulder in reply and went to her bedroom to get the extra quilt from her bed. She lifted Grandpa's feet to the sofa and tucked the quilt around him, then put the afghan around his shoulders to keep his back warm. "I'll go and talk to Gideon now, Grandpa," she said. "I'll be back in a few minutes to check on you."

Her heart beat in a rapid cadence as she walked to the kitchen, unwilling that Joseph be frightened by anything going on, then caught sight of Gideon. He stood when she came into the kitchen and grasped her shoulders.

"What's wrong, sweetheart? Is Joseph all right?"

"It's Grandpa, Gideon." She felt the tears sliding down her cheeks and Gideon's warm arms enclosed her tightly, muffling the tears she couldn't help but shed against his chest.

He whispered soft words into her ear. "Whatever it is, we'll take care of it, Joy. Is he not feeling any better? Shall I go for the doctor in town?"

She could only nod her head at his words, grateful for his quick understanding of the problems they faced. "Probably there's been enough folks driving by in wagons and sleighs to make the snow packed down enough if you ride my mare. She's a good size and well able to handle your weight. Take the town road back about two miles, and in the center of town you'll find the bank. Next to it is a white house where Doc Stevens lives. Stop there and ask if he can come out to see Grandpa. Tell him his chest is hurting him and he's having a problem breathing." She choked on the words, but Gideon nodded his understanding and patted her back as if he would lend his strength to her own.

"I'll go right away, Joy. I'll let you tell Joseph for me, for I don't want to alarm him in front of your grandfather. Let me just get my warm sweater on under my coat and I'll saddle the mare and be off. If I'm lucky, I should be back in time for night chores, so don't you try to do them, you hear me?" He bent to look directly into her eyes as he spoke and she nodded, assuring him of her cooperation. "Joy, I'm going to take my references with me and drop them off at your sheriff's office. Won't take but a few minutes while I'm waiting for the doctor to ready himself for the trip back here. I'm anxious to have my word verified somehow."

"All right, Gideon. Your papers are right here on the kitchen dresser where I put them after I read them." And if the sheriff checked him out, she would feel better about things, she decided silently.

He picked up the papers and approached the stove where she was tending the kettle of beans. "If you would, Joy, fix me some of that pork if it's done enough. Just cut a slice and put it on one of those biscuits left from breakfast. I'll eat it as I ride." As he spoke he pulled his sweater on and buttoned it closely at his throat, then donned his jacket and cap, bending finally to pull on his boots.

"Let me wrap your scarf around your neck," Joy said, snatching up the scarf she'd made him for Christmas from the hook where he'd hung it earlier and wrapping it closely so that he could pull it up over his mouth if he wanted to as he rode.

"Thank you, sweetheart," he said, dropping a quick kiss against her forehead. He reached for the doorknob and turned to face her, his eyes warm as they swept over her from her feet to the top of her head. "You're a real beauty,

Joy. I'm happy that you're in my life. Just be patient, and I'll be back as soon as I can. The roads are treacherous, but at least it doesn't look like we've got any snow coming tonight. Don't go outside, you hear?"

"I won't. I'll stay in here and feed Joseph and see if I can coax Grandpa to eat a bit. We'll be fine. I want to stay close to Grandpa and be sure he's all right. Please tell the doctor to hurry."

"I will." With a last, long look at her, he opened the door, quickly pulling it shut behind him. She watched through the window as he went to the barn, the path he'd shoveled the day before free of fresh snow. The barn door stayed open as he saddled her mare quickly, put on her bridle and then led the animal from the barn, closing the door tightly behind him.

He looked toward the house and then mounted the mare in a swift motion, waving at Joy as she waved back from the window. And as he passed by the porch, he lifted a hand to his mouth and blew a kiss in her direction, a wide smile following it. Then he was gone and she felt the warmth of his kiss as though he had delivered it to her from close at hand. *"Sweetheart", he'd said. He'd called her sweetheart.*

She pulled the curtain over the window, keeping as much heat in the house as possible, then checked the potatoes, drained them in the sink and covered them again. She opened the oven and lifted the cover on the roast, then added a bit of water to have plenty of gravy. She could mash the potatoes later, she decided. The green beans she'd cooked half the day were more than done and she set them aside to keep them warm while she checked on Grandpa and Joseph again.

Joseph had moved to sit on a small stool next to Grandpa and was still telling him a fanciful tale he made up as he went along. Grandpa was snoozing a bit, his head tilted to one side, leaning against a pillow; she felt relieved that he seemed to be resting well.

"We'll eat in just a bit, Joseph," she whispered. "Your father has gone to town, so you keep an eye on Grandpa for me while I make the gravy and fix our plates. We'll have a picnic here in the parlor. Will that be all right with you?" she asked, and the boy grinned widely at her.

"Oh, yes, Joy. That will be fun and Grandpa can stay where he is and not have to get up."

"I'll bring our food in very shortly," Joy said,

leaving the boy in charge, a job he seemed to relish.

After putting the finishing touches on the meal, she filled their plates well and carried them all into the parlor on a cookie sheet. Joseph grinned widely and whispered that Grandpa was sleeping.

"I'll put your food on the quilt on the floor, Joseph," she told him, snatching up an extra quilt from the rocking chair and arranging the boy's plate before him on the floor. Then she sat next to him, hugging him close as she closed her eyes and prayed a fervent blessing not only on the food but for the elderly man she loved so dearly.

Joseph picked up his fork and tasted the potatoes and gravy. "You sure are a good cook, Joy. I like the way you fix the food for me and Daddy every day. I'll bet he'll like some of this when he gets back from town."

"We'll save a good bit for him, Joseph," she assured the boy.

She tucked into her own dinner, urging Joseph to eat as she did. The meat was tender and tasty and the green beans were nicely flavored with the onion. When they had finished their meal, she took Grandpa's plate from the cookie sheet and removed the cover she'd kept atop his food to keep it warm.

Kneeling by his side, she whispered quietly, deciding that if he didn't answer, she'd leave him dozing. But he surprised her by opening his eyes and speaking in a low voice, "I thought you'd never get to my dinner, Joy." His eyes twinkled, but the lack of color in his cheeks alarmed Joy more than she could say.

"I thought you might eat a bit of potato, Grandpa," she said, holding the plate before him and handing him his fork.

"I think maybe you'd better feed me, honey girl," he said, his voice seeming weak to her ears.

"I surely can," she said, holding his fork and then offering it to him with just a bit of potato on it and a mere scrap of pork on top.

Grandpa opened his mouth and took the food from his fork, chewing a bit and then swallowing. "Just a few bites, Joy. I'm not feeling up to snuff yet, and I don't want to risk eating more than my stomach can handle. Just enough to keep me going for a while."

Joy gave him another small morsel of meat with some potatoes on it and Grandpa ate it readily. "Sure is tasty, Joy," he managed to murmur, then closed his eyes as if he was too weary to keep them open.

"I think you've had enough for now, Grandpa. Just rest easy until Gideon gets back here. If things go well, he'll be bringing the doctor back and we'll get you taken care of."

Grandpa nodded his agreement, but his eyes remained closed and Joy tugged the quilt up to his throat, the better to keep him warm. She held his hand for a moment and bent low to his ear. "I'm praying for you, Grandpa," she said, and was pleased when he nodded his head a bit.

"Can I help you take the stuff back to the kitchen?" Joseph asked from behind her, and Joy was pleased at his offer.

"You're a good boy, Joseph," she told him, turning to hand him Grandpa's plate.

"He wasn't very hungry, was he?" the boy said sadly. "Can I give him a hug, Joy? I want him to know how bad I need him to get better. I don't have any grandpa at all, and I want to keep this one for a long time."

"Come over here, Joseph. Put the dishes on the cookie sheet first and then come tell Grandpa you want him to feel better real soon."

Joseph did as Joy had bid him and then

backed off. "I think he's sleeping. He's got his eyes closed and he's breathing real soft, isn't he?"

Joy nodded. "Let's clear this food away, Joseph. I wouldn't be surprised if your father arrived home pretty soon. Let's go out to the kitchen for a minute so I can tend to the food on the stove and you can put the dishes we used into the sink."

The boy seemed to be agreeable to anything she suggested and she was pleased. They went to the kitchen and Joseph put the dishes in the sink in short order. Then he went to the window, pulling the curtain aside.

"Come look, Joy. I think Daddy is in the barn." As if in response to Joseph's voice, a whinny came from the barn and the boy grinned. "He's back, for sure. Your mare must be glad to be home, too."

"Yes, and here comes a buggy down the lane. The doctor must have followed right on your father's heels." Joy watched with tear-filled eyes as the buggy halted before the back porch and two men climbed down, joined quickly by Gideon, who apparently had finished in the barn.

The three figures headed for the porch and Joy opened the backdoor, welcoming them into the house. Then she bent to Joseph. "Run and stay with Grandpa for a few minutes to keep an eye on him. The doctor will want to come in as soon as he hangs up his coat."

Joseph did as she asked, and within seconds the kitchen was filled with the sound of masculine voices as the three men took off their coats and hung them near the door. They took their boots off and stood them behind the stove, and then Gideon turned to hold out his arms for Joy.

She walked into his embrace and bent her head against his chest. "I'm so glad you're back, Gideon. I think Grandpa is dozing again, and I sent Joseph in to keep an eye on him. But I'll be happy to have Doc Stevens check him over."

"Well, I think your grandfather will be pleased to see our other visitor, Joy. We saw the pastor of the church walking home from the general store and the doctor asked him if he'd like to come along and talk to your grandpa. He just hustled home and dumped his packages with his wife and climbed into the buggy. I'm pleased he was so willing to take a ride in the cold weather. He seems to think well of Grandpa and wanted to see if he could help in any way."

While they spoke, the doctor went into the parlor, followed by Pastor Wright. When Joy and Gideon stepped into the front room, they saw the two men kneeling before the sofa, speaking to Joy's grandfather.

Doc Stevens opened his bag and brought out his stethoscope, warming it in his palm as he spoke to the old man on the sofa.

"Sounds like you're having a bad time of it, sir," he said, his keen eyes assessing the elderly man. Grandpa nodded and pulled aside his warm sweater, leaving space for the doctor to get beneath his clothing.

Joy went to the sofa and spoke to the doctor. "Can I help with anything? Grandpa is still wearing his nightshirt beneath his sweater. I wanted him to be warm."

"I'll just unbutton it a bit, Joy." He made a space for the instrument he held and placed the earpieces in his ears. "Let's take a listen, Grandpa. Just breathe like you usually do and I'll check out your old ticker here." He smiled at his patient and moved the instrument easily across Grandpa's chest, listening carefully to the sounds that carried to his ears.

"I think I need to listen to his back, too." Dr. Stevens withdrew his stethoscope and handed it to Joy. "We'll have to sit him up. I can hear all right through his nightshirt, I think."

Gideon stood behind the sofa and placed his big hand on Grandpa's back, supporting his weight easily. In a few minutes, the doctor had done his job, muttering a bit, then helping Grandpa to lie back against the pillow Joy had provided.

"I've got some medicine I think will help you feel better, sir. Your heart needs a bit of help to keep it beating as strongly as it should, but I think you're going to be right as rain before too long, Grandpa. But, the thing is, your heart is telling me that you've worked hard all your life, so now it's time to rest a bit and let the younger ones take over. I think Joy is capable of running things here, and this young man seems to have the chores in hand. The best thing for you is to stay in bed or on the sofa and get rested up. I'm going to leave the medication I think will help you. Once the snow clears up, I'll be back to check on you again. If things go well, a week or so will see you feeling a bit better. I'll tell Joy how to measure out the doses of your medication so you'll get the most help from this stuff."

Grandpa nodded his agreement and Joy bent to kiss his cheek. "We'll keep him down, Doc.

And I'll be sure to give him the medicine just like you tell me." Joy felt a huge relief at the doctor's diagnosis.

"I think we'll just leave you alone for a few minutes with your pastor now," Doc Stevens said. "He wanted to see you, said with the bad weather you hadn't been able to make it to town to attend services, so this would be a good chance to catch up with you."

Grandpa shook the doctor's hand and the medical man seemed pleased at the gesture, holding the elderly man's hand in his own for a few minutes while he explained all about the medicine he was leaving and the way Joy would fix it for his consumption. Then he withdrew, leaving Grandpa alone with Pastor Wright.

In the meantime, Gideon had scooped Joy up in a loose embrace, his arm around her waist and his other hand reaching for Joseph, who was more than pleased to follow his father from the parlor. Together the three of them went to the kitchen and Gideon sat at the table. "Did you save some for me?" he asked, sniffing the aromas that filled the room. "I can tell you cooked beans, Joy. The onions smell good, and I'll warrant the meat you fixed is tasty."

"Why don't I fix you a plate and you can see

for yourself how it tastes," Joy said. And then as the doctor came into the room, she offered him some of the same. "I'd be pleased to have you eat a bit, Doc Stevens. I hope we didn't take you away from your dinner."

"No, I was walking back from the store with Elda's groceries. Thought I'd better come out here and see how things were, once this fella here told me what was going on." He motioned at Gideon. "Seems like you've got yourself a fine man here, Joy. I'm sure he's been a godsend to you and your grandpa."

Joy turned from the stove where she was filling Gideon's plate. "You have no idea, Doc. He's only been here for a short while but he's saved me a lot of work, and Grandpa is quite taken with him and especially his boy, Joseph." She carried Gideon's plate to the table and placed it before him, offering a knife and fork along with a clean napkin.

"Can I fix you a plate, Doc?" she asked.

"It sure looks like good food to me, Joy. I'd be happy to join Gideon here and sample your cooking."

So it was that the two men were hungrily making their way through dinner when the pastor appeared in the doorway a bit later. "It sounds like you fellas are having a good meal out here without me," he said, peering over Joy's shoulder at the food on the stove. And as Joy offered him a plate from the cabinet, he nodded, heading for the sink to wash his hands. She heaped the plate with food and placed it across from Gideon, then filled coffee cups from her big pot that was always at the ready.

"I'm going in with Grandpa while you gentlemen eat," she said to the men at the table. "I'll be back in a bit." Her skirts swished as she turned to the doorway and made her way from the kitchen, followed closely by Joseph and the doctor, who had cleaned his plate in no time.

The pastor sat down and ate several bites, swallowed and then nodded at the man across from him. "That girl can sure cook up a storm, Gideon. She'll be a fine wife for the right man—and after talking to her grandpa, I think I need to speak with you. The old fella in the parlor is determined that you stay on here and relieve his granddaughter of the job of running this farm. I don't know her feelings on the subject, but I thought I'd better come out here and talk to you to see how the land lies, so to speak.

"Her grandpa and I talked for a bit and I prayed with him and heard his viewpoint on things, like I said, and then he kinda tucked himself in and went to sleep. I sat there for a few more minutes, but he's resting nicely. I think hearing his favorite psalm from the Bible gave him some comfort. Told me he was feeling better just seeing me walk in, and after the doctor checked him over, he was agreeable to do as he was told, so long as he didn't have to worry about Joy any longer."

Gideon spoke up, his voice firm, his intent clear. "I'll take care of Joy and keep Grandpa's farm running just the way he wants it, Pastor."

"Well, that isn't all Joy's grandpa wants you to do, Gideon," the young preacher said. "He thinks maybe you and Joy should be married, what with you living here and planning on staying on."

Chapter Seven

Gideon grinned as the preacher spoke. "He whispered that to me just now, too. And I'm most agreeable. But it's up to Joy. I don't know if she'd like the idea, but she's been right nice to me and she sure loves that boy of mine. Give me a few minutes and let me talk to her. Since you're here and it's what her grandfather wants, maybe she'll be amenable to the idea."

"You go on ahead and speak your piece, Gideon. I'll wait in the parlor with her grandpa until you get an answer from the girl." He took Gideon's hand and squeezed it tightly. "The very best to you, Gideon. I'm thinking this would be an answer to a prayer, for her grandfather tells me he's been praying for a good husband for Joy. He said he wants to see her settled before he dies. I'll go on into the parlor and send her out here to you. If she's agreeable, we'll have us a wedding today. I always have my book of sacraments with me and the doctor can serve as your witness."

So it was that in a few minutes' time Joy walked into the kitchen and approached Gideon, who stood at the window awaiting her arrival. "The pastor said you wanted to speak with me, Gideon," she said quietly. "Is there a problem?"

"Not with me, Joy," he replied. "I'm just hoping you'll be agreeable to what the preacher man and I were speaking about out here. He tells me that your grandpa and I are kinda on the same track with our ideas about you. I dropped off the paperwork we spoke of at the sheriff's office and he's checking up on my credentials, and I told the preacher what I'd done and he approved of it. Said it spoke well of me that I was willing to let my past be looked into by the authorities.

"Now for the important part of things. I've been wanting to persuade you into us joining forces here on the farm. If you'd see fit to spend your life with me, I'd be the happiest man on earth today. And now your grandpa has stated right out that he'd like for us to be married, and the pastor is ready to do the job. So now it's all up to you, Joy. Can you find it in your heart to wear my ring on your finger and share your life with me?"

Joy looked floored by his words. Her mouth opened, then closed, and she turned away, lifting her hands to her face.

Gideon held her firmly by her shoulders as he bent to whisper in her ear. "I didn't mean to alarm you, Joy, or cause you to be upset. I know we're almost strangers, but I feel such a link between us, as if our meeting was meant to be. I'm not trying to push you into anything. I just want what's best for you, and for me and my son. Joseph needs a mother and he's already looking at you as a candidate for the job. I told you already that he wants to call you his mother and I'm ready to call you my wife. The rest is up to you."

Joy was silent for a moment, then stepped back a few inches until her back was warm against Gideon, and he felt the full length of her pressed against his own sturdy frame. He bent to her again and his lips pressed a kiss against her cheek, then visited the softness beneath her ear. "I'm trying so hard not to press you for an answer, Joy," he said quietly, "but at the same time I want to kiss you and hold you close and know the sweetness of your mouth pressed to mine."

Joy moved from him, then turned and lifted her face to his. "I keep remembering how wonderful it was to hear you call me your sweetheart, Gideon. When you rode off to town to get the doctor for Grandpa, I kept hearing you in my mind and it gave me such comfort to know that you would call me by that name."

"You are my sweetheart, Joy," he answered, holding her hands in his and yearning to enclose her in his embrace. "I haven't looked at another woman since my wife died so long ago. It's been a long, dry spell for me without a woman in my life. I love my son dearly. I'm sure you know that, but I wouldn't marry just to give him a mother. It would have to be a woman I could love wholeheartedly, one who could return that love."

Joy smiled up at him, as if she was pleased with his words. "I've never known a man, Gideon. Grandpa and I have lived here alone. We go to town when the weather is good, to church in summertime when we can travel in our wagon. But Grandpa has kept me from the men who would have made themselves a part of our lives. He saw a few who wanted the property and were willing to marry me to get it, and some who just wanted a woman to tend their own homes. He knew he couldn't let me be snatched up by a man who was selfish in such a way, and so I've just lived here with Grandpa and done my best to tend things for him."

"You've done more than any woman should, Joy. But there is much about a farm that only a man can tend to. I'd like to be that man for you and for your grandfather, too. He's agreeable to my suit, and if you feel the same way, I'd like you to consider me as the man in your life. I'd like to be your husband and give you Joseph as your child."

"You said you wanted to hold me, Gideon. That you wanted to kiss me. Would you do that now?"

Gideon felt his heart swell within his chest. To have such an invitation from Joy was almost more than he could imagine. His arms went around her as he stepped closer. His head bent and his mouth touched hers softly, then more firmly as she responded to his kiss. He blessed the fullness of her lips with his own, then dropped countless kisses along the length of her cheek, beneath her ear where her pulse beat rapidly, making him smile at her response. Then he visited the smooth skin of her forehead until he reached her temple, where her soft tresses met his lips.

He buried his nose in the sweet scent of her hair, and then finally lifted his head, breathing deeply as if he could not hold all the clean, pure aroma of her within his lungs. "You overwhelm me, Joy," he murmured. "I can't believe you would allow me the privilege of holding you and loving you this way. I don't want you to fear me, sweetheart, but know that I ache to possess you as my own." He held his breath as he awaited her reply, knowing that she was as innocent as could be about what was involved in a man and woman coming together in marriage.

She lifted her head to meet his gaze, and her words were slow but confident as she answered his query. "I don't know the full meaning of which you speak, Gideon. I'm without much knowledge of men, but I feel that I can trust you and I'm willing to give my heart into your care. Your willingness to be investigated by our local lawman speaks well for you. I trust you, Gideon, and I want to be a mother to your child. I truly love him, and if we marry and one day I bear your children, Joseph will always be my first son. Can you believe that of me, that I will love him and care for him as my own?"

Gideon's heart lifted in his chest at her words and he reached for her again, his lips covering hers, his kiss a promise of what was to come in the future. "I love you, Joy," he said softly, the words a plea, as if he would ask her to repeat the phrase to him.

"I've never loved a man, Gideon. But what I feel for you is honest and my words are sincere. Know then that I feel for you as I have no other person. I love my grandfather, but that is different than what my heart feels for you. When you left here to get the doctor, I prayed you would be safe and return to me swiftly. When you came back, I felt such joy to see your smile. I knew such happiness when I realized that you cared for us enough to tend to our needs. But most of all, I felt a closeness to you."

"Can you accept that as enough, then, Joy? Do you feel enough for me to marry me? Will you agree to be mine? To live with me for the rest of our lives and to accept me as your husband?"

She nodded her head, holding his hands within her own. "If the preacher will speak the words over us and record the wedding in his books and make out a certificate for us to have, I'll be proud to stand beside you and speak the words of marriage with you."

"Glory be! I've never been so happy, Joy," he said, lifting her from the floor and holding her against himself, whirling her in a circle around the kitchen and kissing her as if he thirsted for her, as if his body yearned to draw her within himself.

And Joy appeared to be overcome with happiness at his words. "Will the preacher do as we ask, Gideon? Will he really marry us today? Will I be your wife that soon?"

"Oh, yes, sweetheart," he said, holding her close and walking with her out of the kitchen and into the parlor, where the doctor sat watching her grandfather and the preacher stood near the front window. Joseph looked up from his perch on the end of the sofa, his grin a happy greeting for them both.

"Well, from in here it sounded like someone was mighty happy out there in the kitchen," the preacher said with a smile as he held out his hand to Gideon. "I'd like to be the first to congratulate you, Gideon, on your forthcoming marriage."

Gideon placed his own palm against that of the parson and his own smile glowed with happiness. “Joy has agreed to be my wife, sir. I couldn’t be happier, and all that stands in the way of our marriage is for Grandpa to give us his blessing.”

“Well, we can tend to that right now, I’d say.” Pastor Wright nodded at Grandpa, who was watching the two men from his perch on the sofa.

He lifted his hand toward Gideon. “If you and Joy will come over here to the sofa and kneel by me, I’ll be happy to do just that very thing, young man.”

Gideon’s arm tightened around Joy’s waist. “I want this more than anything,” he told her. “I want your grandfather’s blessing on us, Joy.”

“I want it, too, Gideon. I want him to be pleased with our decision to marry.”

Gideon led her to the sofa, where they knelt and placed both their hands in her grandfather’s.

“I ask only that God will place His hand on Joy and Gideon and make their union one of peace and happiness, so they will live in harmony and know the full pleasures a good marriage can bring to two people. I give my blessing on their marriage, and ask that God will also bless it according to His words in the good book. That two people will come together and be joined as one and live as one, accepting each other's burdens and loving each other to the end of life." The old man leaned back against his pillow, his breathing slow, his words halting as he seemed to recover from the exercise he'd undertaken.

"I couldn't have said it better myself," the preacher said with a laugh of pleasure in hearing Grandpa's words of blessing.

"Well, if all is in order, I'd ask you to do the deed, Preacher," Gideon asked nicely, holding out one hand to Joseph, who rose quickly from the sofa to join his father.

"As I told you, I just happen to have my book of sacraments with me, Gideon," the pastor said, reaching in his pocket for the small black book he carried with him. "If the doctor wants to stand as a witness, then we'll ask Joseph to stand between the bride and groom and you can all join hands for a moment."

They did as he asked, Joseph fairly shivering with happiness as he joined his father and Joy, his smile a beacon of delight as he reached his hands out to them. The preacher read the beginning of the marriage ceremony to them, then reached to join Joy's and Gideon's hands together, allowing Joseph to stay in place between them. His words were spoken slowly, as if to emphasize their importance to the two who sought marriage. And then he asked them to repeat the vows. Gideon spoke first, his voice resounding with fervor as he gave his promises to love, honor and cherish the woman beside him.

Joy spoke then, repeating the words the pastor read aloud. Her vows were much the same, to love, honor and obey the man she'd chosen as her husband. She smiled up at Gideon as she said the words.

Within a few short minutes, the preacher spoke the final words of the ritual, the most important in the sight of those present. "And now I pronounce you man and wife, in the sight of God and these witnesses. Amen."

It was done. Gideon was awash with the happiness of knowing he and Joy were united in marriage and he had been given the responsibility and privilege of looking after her and keeping her safe and secure in his love. He bent to her at the preacher's words and touched her lips with his, brushing the soft surface with a kiss of promise.

Joy looked up at the man who had claimed the title of husband to her. He was tall and handsome and his smile held the promise of happiness she craved for her future. It was as if Christmas morning had arrived once more.

Gideon turned his attention on the boy who stood to one side now, observing the scene, not missing a word spoken or a gesture of any of the two who had become one.

"Joy is your new mother, Joseph," his father said quietly, placing his hand on the boy's head as he spoke. "Will you accept her as such and call her Mama from now on like we discussed?"

"Of course I will, Daddy," the boy said, as if there was no doubt in his mind as to the *real* meaning of this ceremony. "I told you I wanted Joy for my mama and now I can call her that for real, can't I?"

Gideon laughed aloud. "You bet you can, son. She's your new mama and you can use that name from now on when you speak to her."

Joseph reached to hug Joy, his arms tight around her waist, and she bent low, kissing his forehead and cheek.

"Well, I'd say this has been a day of joyous miracles," the preacher said. "First we have Grandpa feeling some better and willing to rest and recuperate as the doctor has ordered, and then we have a wedding to beat all," he announced with a joyous sound that almost brought to mind church bells and the sound of angels singing.

Doc Stevens was making ready to leave, putting his bag together and issuing last-minute instructions to Grandpa. The preacher came to Gideon and shook his hand again. "I can't tell you how pleased I am that I made this trip along with Doc Stevens. I felt like I should come out and see Grandpa, and lo and behold if I didn't get to perform a wedding. I'm hoping to see all you folks in church when the weather breaks and Grandpa is feeling a bit better. We'll introduce you and Joy and Joseph, too, as the newest family in our congregation."

After saying their farewells, the two gentlemen made their way out the backdoor to the horses and climbed into the buggy, then headed out together toward the road to town. Gideon stepped back from the window and sought Joy's attention.

"Did you have any idea you'd be a married lady by the time this day was over, sweetheart?" he asked, his smile announcing his own happiness in the matter.

"I'm stunned, Gideon," she said softly.

While Gideon did the evening chores, Joy, Grandpa and Joseph passed the time in quiet celebration. Joy sat in the rocking chair with Joseph on her lap, reading to him from his favorite book, his sigh signifying his pleasure at the arrangement.

"I've surely enjoyed hearing you read every evening, Joy," Grandpa said softly after listening for a while. "Reminds me of when I was but a small boy and my mother used to read to all of us every evening in this very parlor."

When they were done reading, Joy reached over and grabbed the hymnal from the organ-music rack and sat back again in the rocker, then cuddled Joseph close as she opened the book to a familiar hymn. Her voice rose as she began, and Grandpa kept time with his index finger, tapping the sofa cushion as she sang. Joseph joined in on the chorus, seeming to recognize the music, and Joy sang another verse before she turned to a second hymn.

"That's one of my favorites," Grandpa said from the sofa. "I remember my mother singing it when I was but a wee lad."

In no time at all, Gideon came in the back-door and within but a few minutes he joined them, sitting on the floor by the rocking chair and nodding at Joy to take up the reading.

She did, until she realized that Joseph was about to close his eyes in slumber. The boy sighed as his father lifted him in his arms and headed for the stairway with him.

"I'll put him to bed and be right back. I doubt he'll even stir, he's so tired," Gideon said quietly, leaving Joy and Grandpa with a smile as he carried Joseph to his room.

"Why don't you sleep in my bed tonight, Grandpa," Joy said to the older man. "I hate to see you climbing the stairs in your condition, and I can sleep in your bed."

"That sounds like a good idea," Grandpa said. "In fact, I'm going to take my leave right now."

Before long, Joy had tucked Grandpa into her bed, gathered her nightgown and robe and made her way up the stairs. Gideon was just leaving his bedroom, where Joseph was already asleep.

"Now, where are we sleeping, Mrs. Burnley?" he asked Joy.

"I forgot altogether, Gideon. My name is Joy Burnley now, isn't it?" she said.

"It sure is, sweetheart. And I can't tell you how happy that makes me," Gideon told her.

"We'll sleep in Grandpa's bed up here while Grandpa uses my room downstairs. I thought he'd better not use the stairs for tonight, at least, and this way we'll be close to Joseph in case he wakes."

"That's all right with me," Gideon told her. "I'll just go down and lock up and bank the fire in the stove. I won't be long."

Joy went into Grandpa's bedroom, fluffing the pillows on the bed and straightening the quilt into place. She went behind the screen in the corner of the room and changed her clothes, putting her nightgown on and hanging her dress and petticoat and drawers over the screen till morning. The floor was warmer than the ones downstairs, with this room being right over the kitchen and the heat from the cookstove coming through the vent. She found her place in the bed, pulling the sheet and quilt over herself and turning to face the door.

Gideon was there quicker than she had expected, and he closed the door behind himself. "I looked in on Grandpa and he's sound asleep already," he told her, his words almost a whisper. "I checked Joseph, too, and he's snug as a bug in a rug, all curled up in the middle of the bed. Now it's just you and me, Joy."

She nodded, her heart beating a bit quickly as she watched him approach the bed. He bent to blow out the candle on the nightstand and then he was but a shadow as he took off his boots by the chair before he stripped from his clothing and approached her.

He sat on the side of the bed, then turned and slid beneath the bedding, finding his place beside her. He scooped her up in his arms and held her near, his big body warm as she curled against him.

"I sure do like cuddling with you, Gideon," Joy whispered. "You're warmer than my quilt."

He chuckled, knowing the joy of holding the woman who returned his love in full measure and had given herself into his keeping, declaring her love for him and making him the happiest of men. For he felt he was holding the prize at the end of the rainbow within his arms.

And he couldn't believe his good fortune as he thought of the wedding night he had planned.

Epilogue

Christmas night, 1888

It was snowing again. Joy stood at the window and looked out, remembering a year ago when she'd stood here, watching the same view, not knowing how much her life was about to change. She walked toward the parlor where her family awaited her and stood in the doorway, watching them.

The Christmas tree was ablaze with the twinkling candles that tipped each branch, a sight that seemed to mesmerize Joseph. Grandpa snoozed on the sofa, a quilt tucked up beneath his chin and a pillow supporting his head. Gideon had found a puzzle in the bookcase and he bent over it on the floor, with Joseph helping him fit the pieces together. Joy was content to watch and be silent. She claimed her seat in the rocking chair, keeping an eye on her grandfather, listening to Joseph and Gideon as they worked together on the puzzle they both enjoyed. There was within her a warmth, a joy she'd never known before Gideon came into her life, and the thrill of motherhood as she watched the small boy who called her his mama.

She was happy, not with any great rush of emotion, but with a constant knowledge that she loved and was loved in return.

Now she readied herself to share her secret with Gideon, for it would be his gift from her this year, marking their second Christmas together. With a smile wreathing her face, she slid to the floor to sit beside Gideon and placed her hand on his, gaining his full attention.

He bent to her, dropping a kiss on her cheek and whispering his love in her ear. She turned her head and touched his ear with her mouth, then whispered words she'd been hiding in her heart for several days.

"Would you like to hear about your Christmas gift from me, Gideon?" she asked.

He turned his head to look fully in her face.

"Are you speaking of the new curtains you've been sewing for our bedroom?"

She shook her head. "No, the curtains you can already see, but your gift will take about seven months before you can see or touch it," she said, her smile seeming to be a permanent fixture on her lips these days.

Gideon looked puzzled for only a moment, then his own lips curved into an answering grin, even as he bent to kiss her. "Are you sure? How do you know?" he asked swiftly, hugging her as he tossed his queries at her.

"I'm not absolutely positive, but if feeling queasy in the morning and hating the smell of your coffee and noticing some changes in my usual schedule are anything to go by, then, yes, I'm pretty sure of my facts, sir," she said with an impish grin of her own.

Gideon's face lit up as if an inner glow had possessed him, and indeed it had, for he was filled with delight at the thought that he would be a father for the second time. "I can't begin to tell you how pleased I am," he said softly as he leaned close, placing his cheek next to hers.

"What's going on over there?" Grandpa said from his spot on the sofa.

"Is something wrong, Daddy?" asked Joseph, who had slid closer to his father.

"What's wrong, Mama?" he asked Joy, worry in his tone.

She hastened to reassure the boy. "Nothing is wrong, Joseph. In fact, everything is right. I just told your father that his Christmas gift will be a little late in arriving. It won't be here for seven months, but I wanted him to know about it beforehand, so he can help me make ready for it."

"Well, now, that's about the best present anyone ever had for Christmas, I'll warrant," Grandpa said with a chuckle. "I'm pleased as punch, Joy, for this means I'll be a great-grandfather for the first time."

"You're already a great-grandfather," Joseph said, his puzzled expression bringing a chuckle from Grandpa.

"Your grandpa means he'll have cause for rejoicing, come July," Gideon told the boy. "Your mama will be having a baby right about then, and we'll all have to give her lots of help over the next few months."

Joseph crept closer to Joy and laid his head on her shoulder, leaning close to her ear to whisper words of encouragement. "I'll help you, Mama. I'll tote and carry for you and even help with stuff like churning the butter and carrying in wood for the cookstove and working in the house garden for you. I'll set the table every night for supper, too."

He seemed to have listed all his good intentions and Joy hid her yearning to laugh aloud at his earnest expression, for the boy was certainly sincere in his need to lend a hand wherever he could.

"I'll be ever so grateful for your help, Joseph. I knew I could count on you." Her words seemed to make his chest expand, and his grin spread wide as she spoke.

Gideon patted his son on the back. "You're a good lad, Joseph. Your mama and I will certainly be able to use your help. And yours, too, Grandpa," he said, shooting a glance at Joy's grandfather.

Joseph moved closer to his father and in moments was sitting on his lap. "We'll have a good time with a new baby, won't we, Daddy?"

"We certainly will," his father said, one long arm reaching to pull Joy closer, making a circle of the three of them. "And what better time to begin looking forward to a baby's birth than on Christmas Day, when we're celebrating the birth of another babe, this one in a faraway place. In Bethlehem."

"Our baby won't be born in a barn, though," Joseph said firmly.

"But he'll still need a new cradle to sleep in," Joy said, looking up at Gideon.

"Let's you and me get busy on that, Joseph," Gideon said to his son.

Joseph stood and looked down at Joy, who was still on the floor. "Let me help you up, Mama, before Daddy and I go out to the barn to find wood for the baby's new bed."

Joy took his offered hand and stood with graceful movements. "And I'll get busy fixing a Christmas dinner while you men take care of that," she said. "I have two chickens ready for the oven, so I'd better get busy in the kitchen."

"I'll go with you and have a cup of coffee while I watch you work," Grandpa said.

"Ah, some things never change, do they?" Joy asked, her smile warming her words as she bent to give Grandpa a kiss on his cheek.

"Merry Christmas, Grandpa," she said, and then turned to her husband and son. "And a merry Christmas to both of you, too. I'm so happy you dropped in for a visit last year about this time. It's been a wonderful year, hasn't it?"

"The best ever," Gideon said heartily, and Joseph added his own opinion.

"I've got a new mama since last Christmas, and that makes it the best year of my life." He turned in a circle and included his whole family. "I've got the happiest life in the whole world." He chortled. "I'm the luckiest boy alive."

And the three who watched him could only nod in agreement.

* * * * *

A CHRISTMAS MIRACLE

Carol Arens

Dear Reader

For me, there is nothing like the feeling of love that is the miracle of Christmas. All year long I look forward to finding the perfect tree, listening to beautiful music, and gathering with loved ones to indulge in delicious treats that are forbidden most of the year yet amazingly have no calories in December. But, more than this, I cherish that special feeling in the heart that comes only with the Christmas holiday. Strangers smile and wish each other 'Merry Christmas', even in long shopping lines. People are especially generous—not only with their money but with their time.

Indulge yourself, during this hectic yet happy time, with the story of Rayne and Laira Lynne. May your Christmas be full of joy and warm blessings.

Carol Arens

DEDICATION

To my daughter, Linda Cathleen,
who has been a blessing since the day she was born…
a true gift from God.

Chapter One

"I say we string the fellow up by his ears!" Harvey Molton punctuated his declaration by pounding his hand on the table.

"Tar and feather him! Send him back to his granddaddy good and whooped!" Oliver Post pumped his fist in the air.

Laira Lynne Rowan's fingers skittered across the piano keys with a thunk and a clunk. A dozen and a half children, practicing a Christmas carol, sputtered on a high note.

"Remember where we are, boys," Laira Lynne admonished the men. "Church is no place for such talk."

"Tain't church proper." Harvey heaved his wide body up from his chair and tossed the eviction notice that he had crushed to a sweaty pulp into the fireplace.

"It's only the social room." Oliver tore his own notice in half and let the pieces drift to the floor. He ground them into the polished oak planks with the heel of his boot.

"Sanctuary or not, I'm sure the good Lord can hear your unkind words." Laira Lynne cast the men a frown, but not a severe one. Ordinarily Harvey and Oliver were the souls of kindness, but just now they were under an emotional strain. "Don't you agree that he would rather hear the children singing?"

"There won't be any children to hear singing once Rayne Lantree gets here and forces us all out of our homes," Hilde Molton's voice, high and singsong, trilled from the church kitchen where she was busy warming hot cocoa for everyone. "It's a sad and sorry fact."

The soothing scent of chocolate drifted out of the open door.

"Well, he's not here yet and I, for one, intend to carry on as if he were not coming at all," Laira Lynne replied. "The Christmas pageant will go on and we will deal with the rest later."

A sudden gust of wind rocked the building as though it, too, was cursing Rayne Lantree.

Laira Lynne nodded to the children. They

started from the beginning of the carol, sounding as sweet as angels. Surely if Mr. Lantree arrived and heard them, he would reconsider his plan to evict one and all for the sake of railroad expansion.

Daniel Bolt, postmaster and keeper of the general store, fidgeted in a chair beside the window, gazing out. Judging by the sour look on his face, he expected Mr. Lantree to materialize out of a twist of wind.

"We need a plan," Daniel declared, loud enough to be heard over the voices singing about going a'wassailing. "If we want to save the town from the clutches of that spawn of Satan, we need a plan."

That might be the case, but they did not need a plan this very instant. Laira Lynne stood up, scraping the piano bench across the floor.

"Tonight the children are practicing their Christmas Eve performance. If you want to discuss mayhem, you can do it over at the general store."

The men gazed at her as though she were addled.

"We always discuss town affairs here. Besides, I already banked the fire in the stove."

Oliver Post got up to stand beside Harvey Molton and warm his backside by the fire.

"Let's stuff Rayne with cookies," the elderly Mrs. Blue said, shuffling into the social room with six mugs of cocoa clattering on a tray. "I remember him as a little boy. He did love his sweets. He wasn't the spawn of Satan way back then."

"Nicely done, children," Laira said. "Let's take a break for some chocolate."

While the children gathered about the table, Laira crossed the room to stand with the gloomy-faced people convened about the hearth.

"It's one week until Christmas Eve," she said, turning in a circle and smiling at her neighbors one by one. "For the children's sake, at least, we need to rejoice in the season."

"There won't be much rejoicing on Christmas morning when Santa doesn't come because we are out of our homes," Mrs. Fulton, the mother of four of the members of the children's choir, grumbled.

"I don't believe that will happen," Laira Lynne answered. And she didn't. No one could be so cruel as to put folks out of their homes on the most wonderful day of the year.

"The notice says, as clear as my nose, we

are to vacate no later than December twenty-fourth," Oliver Post snarled. "No Christmas for Snow Apple Woods this year, or any other."

"I am going to call the children back to rehearsal now because I don't believe that." She pivoted in a circle, spreading smiles again. "Christmas miracles happen all the time."

"It would take one. Old Man Lantree loves his money." It looked as if Harvey wanted to spit, but because he was in the social room of the church, he only wagged his finger. "We all know that even two days late on our rents, he charges a fine."

"William, the old goat, has a cold, hard heart," Hilde Molton agreed with her husband.

"I recall that I was in love with him once." Mrs. Blue's eyes crinkled at the corners. "I was quite young then and he was ever so gallant."

"He's not gallant anymore," Daniel huffed. "Not him or his devil spawn."

"Shoo, all of you," Laira Lynne said, flicking her fingers at the disgruntled group. They were casting a pall over the Christmas cheer that should be blessing this time of year. "Go home if you can't feel the joy of the season. Come back for your children in an hour."

"Maybe Laira Lynne doesn't feel the same

about Snow Apple Woods as the rest of us, being a newcomer." Oliver shrugged his slim shoulders and glanced about, probably seeking confirmation.

Luckily, no one seemed to give it to him, since that was simply not true. After living her life in the hustle and bustle of New York City, the peace of this lovely town had healed her soul when she didn't even know it was wounded.

Snow Apple Woods was where she wanted to spend the rest of her life. Raising her cousin's five children would keep her content the rest of her days.

"We can't go home and come back," Hilde said. "Listen to the wind. It's blowing like that time back in '78."

And so it was. She hadn't been here in '78, but she'd heard the tales of that windstorm. Cows, it had been reported, had been blown over and couldn't stand again until the next morning.

"You may stay, then, as long as you sing along with the children."

That ought to take their minds off the arrival of the devil for a while.

It was Laira Lynne's firm belief that a Christmas carol could soothe the heart like nothing else could.

* * *

Rayne Lantree grabbed for his hat, but the cursed wind snatched it off his head and blew it away into the dark.

Curse it! He had planned to arrive in Snow Apple Woods well before nightfall, but frigid wind had fought him and his mount at every turn. If he was shivering under his heavy coat, what must the horse be feeling?

Had it not been for the stubborn folks living in the insignificant town refusing to accept the generous relocation offer that his grandfather had extended, he wouldn't be out in the elements fighting to keep his teeth from chattering.

Snow Apple Woods must be full of foolish people, turning down more money than their homes and businesses were worth.

It was true that his grandfather was not a warm-and-fuzzy man, and that he was dedicated to earning a dollar, but it was just as true that he was fair in his business dealings.

He'd given the folks of Snow Apple Woods six months to move on and they had ignored every offer.

It now fell to Rayne to give them one last chance. With the generous contracts he was bringing, they might mistake him for Santa

Claus. He ought to come riding into town wearing a red suit, a fake bushy beard and grunting, "Ho, ho, ho."

If they didn't take the new offers and move on by December twenty-fourth, the law would evict them as trespassers.

He'd like to feel sorry for them. He'd visited the small town a few times as a child and remembered it as a pleasant place, but the people living there today were acting mule headed. Starting over would be easy with everything his grandfather was giving them. They could buy enough Christmas presents to make their holidays merry this year and next.

All of a sudden the steady plod of his horse's gait changed. It skipped a beat.

"What's the problem, Harvard?" He'd named his mount after the university he had attended, but his affection for the horse surpassed that of his education.

Being away from the ranch where he had grown up had felt like banishment. Grandfather hadn't cared that he'd wanted a future in ranching; he'd shipped him off to Harvard to learn how to earn money.

Hell, he'd learned it, but it still hadn't scrubbed the love of the land out of his blood.

He slipped from Harvard's back, gently

probing the length of his front leg for an injury. It wasn't easy to see in the dark with dust and who knew what blowing in his eyes.

He felt something warm and sticky. Blood leaked from a knot beginning to swell just above the horse's hoof.

"I reckon you'll be fine. We just need to clean your leg and keep it still for a while."

He remembered that the town didn't have a hotel, not even a boardinghouse, but he'd been told there was a woman who let rooms to the few strangers passing through. Her house was the first one that he would come to on the road in.

"We'll take it slow, boy." He patted Harvard's glossy black jaw while he walked beside him. "Sure hope the lady opens the door. With all the debris flying around, she might not hear us knocking."

Chapter Two

Laira Lynne stood in the doorway of the social room, peering outside with her five small nieces gathered about her skirt.

"It's windy," noted three-year-old twins, Abby and Jane. Sometimes when the girls spoke, it was two voices expressing one thought. Since they were very bright and full of thoughts, they were fascinating to be around.

"We's going to…" Jane said.

"…blow away," Abby finished.

"Babies don't know anything," five-year-old Belle declared. "If we jump and flap our arms, we don't have to blow, we can fly."

"Won't you let me walk you home, Miss Laira Lynne?" Oliver Post gazed over her shoulder, watching a bucket tumbling and clanking down the street. "It will only take me a moment to close things up here."

Oliver was a slight-built man, as likely to be blown across town as anyone else.

"That's kind of you." She meant that; his offer was kind. Sand and grit blew so hard a body could barely make out the bend in the street, and Oliver lived on the opposite side of town from her. "We'll make it fine."

The children bid Oliver goodbye with hugs about his legs. He patted each of their heads, then went back inside to close up the church for the night.

"Anyone who will fit, get under my skirt." That would at least keep the dust out of their eyes.

Abby, Jane and Belle ducked underneath, jostling the plaid fabric while they giggled.

At seven years old, Ruthie probably thought she was too old for such an adventure, but by the look on her face, she desperately wanted it.

"Go ahead, sweetie, you'll fit."

Ruthie ducked under and the skirt billowed like ocean waves.

Nine-year-old Lynne grabbed her hand. "I'm much too tall for that."

"And getting taller every day, but here."

Laira Lynne opened her coat. "Snuggle in beside me."

They would appear a sight to anyone who might be peering out their window. They must look like a big plaid ball with a dozen legs rolling past the general store, then the bakery and the barber.

"We've got to have snow for Christmas, Auntie," Lynne, Laira Lynne's namesake, said. Her voice sounded muffled through the wool. "Mama always loved a white Christmas. Since she is going to be here in spirit, we've just got to have snow."

"We will. I'm sure of it."

She wasn't really sure, but she wished it with all her heart. The children had been through so much this last year.

Laira Lynne's cousin and her husband had both been taken by fevers within a week of each other. They'd become ill the day after Christmas and passed before the new year.

When Laira Lynne heard the news, it had taken all of seven seconds to decide to leave her hectic life in New York behind and come to Snow Apple Woods and raise her nieces. In the end, family ties were everything.

"Auntie?" A blast of cold air blew inside her

coat when Lynne parted it to stick her head out. "There's a lantern on in the stable."

"I reckon I left it burning after I fed Old Mule." That had been careless of her. She must have been distracted getting the girls ready for the pageant rehearsal. "Stay close, ladies, we'll just stop for a moment and put it out."

The outside latch was not anchored in place. The barn door rattled in the wind. She must have been more preoccupied than she realized.

She stepped inside the stable and closed the door behind her. The girls scrambled from her clothing like a bunch of chicks popping out from under a hen.

A man knelt, not twenty feet away, rubbing the leg of a huge black horse. Old Mule nipped the collar of the man's shirt and brayed.

Ten little arms suddenly grabbed her about the waist and thighs, hugging tight.

The man seemed as surprised to see them as they were to see him. His clothes were covered in dust, and so was his horse. Clearly, he was a traveler…a very handsome traveler.

His eyes were the same deep green as a Christmas tree, his cheekbones high and manly. His teeth were straight, but his smile was attractively crooked. Black hair, clipped short, fell tousled about his face.

Logically, there was only one person he could be.

"Is that Satan's spawn?" Belle asked, her voice full of accusation.

"Of course not! There's no such thing." Lara Lynne positioned herself in front of the girls in case the man was not who she thought he was…or in case he was.

"Mr. Bolt said he was coming," Ruthie said, peeking about Laira Lynn's skirt.

"To send us all out into the cold where Santa can't find us," Belle declared from where she had once again taken refuge under Laira Lynne's skirt.

The man stood. She had to look up at him; he was that tall. He stepped forward with his hand extended.

"I'm Rayne Lantree, ma'am."

The only polite thing to do was to accept his greeting, so she set her hand in his, palm to palm. His hand was big, callused and blessedly warm. She hadn't noticed how chilled she had gotten on the walk home until his heated flesh wrapped around hers.

Given that she was shaking hands with the devil, she was surprised to find that she didn't really want to let go.

"My horse came up lame," he said. "Yours

was the first place I came to. I hope you don't mind."

Naturally, he would have a voice that sounded like music when he wasn't even singing.

She snatched her hand away because she had let him hold it overlong as it was.

"I'm Laira Lynne Rowan and these are my nieces, Lynne, Ruthie, Belle, Jane and Abby."

"A pleasure, ma'am…girls." He smiled and it was hard, all of a sudden, to hold who he was against him. She couldn't recall ever seeing such a becoming smile. "I've been told you might have a room to let."

"You heard wrong." Ruthie cast him the evil eye.

"You heard right," Laira Lynne corrected. No matter who he was, the money he would pay in board would be a blessing, especially at this time of year.

She had been praying to find a way to provide the girls with a very special Christmas feast. Apparently, the answer had come in the form of the town's archenemy.

Without warning, the wind whipped a slat of wood off the barn door and sent it flying inside.

Rayne Lantree dashed forward and caught

it a second before it would have hit both Jane and Abby.

The lantern tipped over, but the flame went out before it hit the straw. Icy wind filled the stable, racing about and screeching in corners.

Three of the children began to cry.

"Looks like things are getting worse outside." Rayne Lantree's voice was even more seductive in the dark than it had been by lantern light. "I'll help you get the girls inside, then I'll hammer the door back in place."

He scooped up the twins in one arm and Belle in the other. Bent into the wind, he crossed the yard with long strides.

Laira Lynne snatched the other girls' hands and hurried after him. It felt as if she was wearing ice instead of a coat.

Once inside, she lit a lantern.

Mr. Lantree set the children on the floor, then crossed the parlor. He stooped before the hearth and urged the dying coals back to life, then added wood until there was a nice blaze going.

With a nod, he hurried out the front door. A few moments later she heard a hammer pounding wood.

Satan's spawn or not, the man deserved a hot drink when he came back inside.

* * *

As small as it was, the stable was snug. A good thing, too; the temperature was dropping like a stone into a deep well. He was grateful that Harvard was out of the elements.

The hundred-yard dash from the stable to the house had been so cold it stiffened his toes under the boot leather.

God protect anyone caught out in this misery. Coming up the front-porch stairs, he noticed smoke coming from the upstairs chimneys. He watched it blow across the starlit sky, flat and swift in the wind.

He knocked on the front door. It opened in an instant. Miss Rowan must have been watching for him. For some reason that made him feel good.

Since, apparently, even the children of Snow Apple Woods considered him the devil's spawn, she might have locked him out and left him to shiver the night away in the stable.

"You look frozen through, Mr. Lantree. Come and have a seat by the fire."

She indicated a pair of chairs flanking the hearth. On a small table between them, two cups of tea steamed. The scent of peppermint filled the parlor.

He crossed the room and sat down. Damn if

he hadn't landed in a little bit of paradise. The cold leached from his bones and his muscles relaxed. He closed his eyes at the bliss.

"Have you really come to turn us out of our homes?"

Miss Rowan's voice was clear and sweet. The fabric of her skirt whispered as she settled into her chair. Did she sing? he wondered.

"If you have, you are going to meet with a good deal of resistance. Snow Apple Woods has been home to some folks for all their lives."

To call Miss Rowan beautiful did her an injustice. Even if a rock smacked him between the eyes, he wouldn't be able to quit staring at her. He knew her story, just as he knew the stories of everyone in this dot of a town.

She had come from New York, left behind her business of planning social events just when it had begun to flourish, in order to raise her late cousin's children. She had parents, a brother and two sisters in New York. He could only imagine what they thought of her burying herself in Snow Apple Woods.

Yes, he knew the stories of the folks living here. In his opinion, they would be better off taking the bank drafts he had brought with him and starting over somewhere else.

Why they would view him as a messenger of doom rather than hope was beyond him.

There was a long awkward silence, filled only by the fire snapping and the wind battering the walls. Through it, he gazed into blue eyes that were more than a pretty color. The good heart beating in—he couldn't help but notice—her lovely chest, shone out of them.

He judged that she was someone who would care for, what she judged to be, the well-being of the children more than a prosperous future. She'd already given up financial security for them.

This would be a problem for him. If she felt the children would be better off staying in their home, all the good sense in the world would not make her take his grandfather's money.

"The railroad is coming, Miss Rowan. It will bring prosperity to towns all over the county."

"And to your grandfather."

"Especially to my grandfather."

She snatched the pins from her hair and shook it free. Golden-red waves tumbled over her shoulders and down her back. He would rather spend the evening looking at those tresses than discussing unpleasant business.

"Then, naturally, to you when you inherit." She arched a delicately etched brow at him.

That was true. He didn't have great wealth of his own right now, but he would and he wasn't sorry about it. Under his care, the Lantree Ranch would become the finest in the state.

"Look, Miss Rowan, I didn't come here to cause trouble. My grandfather is selling this land to the railroad, but he has offered you folks a fair deal. Take the money and move to one of the towns that will prosper because of it. It's only logical."

"Christmas is in seven days. The Christmas pageant in six. That is the very day you and your grandfather will evict us."

She stood up. Firelight stroked licks of heat on her shapely bosom. It shadowed the nip of her small waist and glowed against the swell of sweetly rounded hips covered by the plaid pleats of her skirt.

"You are welcome to stay in our home, Mr. Lantree. But you should understand that no one in town is going to accept your grandfather's offer."

"It's not an offer so much as an ultimatum." What was wrong with the folks here? There were better, more affluent towns only a day's ride away. "The town lease was up last month. The sheriff will be here on the twenty-fourth whether you all take the money or not."

"It ought to be an interesting day," she said, then spun about and went up the stairs.

She sang softly, going up, her hips swaying gently as she mounted. Her voice was even nicer than he had imagined.

"'God rest ye merry gentleman, let nothing you dismay…'"

The rest of the carol faded as she turned down a hallway.

Chapter Three

So far today, Rayne had had a door slammed in his face, a broom swatted at his backside and a plate of cookies shoved into his hands.

Snow Apple Woods consisted of one main street, five shops on one side and five on the other. A quaint-looking white church flanked the north end of the road with a large, bare-limbed apple tree in front of it.

No doubt, for this pint-sized town, the church was the hub of social activity.

Twenty-five homes dotted a circle around the only street. A hundred and one souls lived in them. Forty adults and sixty-one children.

He knew the facts, who was married to whom and who ran each of the struggling businesses. His grandfather had kept records of his tenants and their stores. It had only seemed good business for Rayne to know who they were before he came.

Rayne bit into one of the cookies Mrs. Blue had shoved at him before she had shut the door in his face. It didn't taste poisoned. If he lasted the walk back to Miss Rowan's house he'd give the rest of the treats to the little girls. Maybe they'd quit looking at him as if he had sprouted horns.

Fortunately, the wind had died down, but the air remained blistering cold.

For all the success he'd had trying to make folks see good sense, he might as well have stayed snug and warm in his room at Miss Rowan's.

For whatever reason, the people of Snow Apple Woods were set against leaving, from the oldest to the youngest.

He'd been certain that when they realized how much money they had been offered to move along peacefully they would have been happy to go.

On his fruitless outing he had made one discovery. Tonight, there was to be a rehearsal for some sort of Christmas celebration. With folks gathered together maybe they'd see things more clearly.

Rayne approached Miss Rowan's stable but didn't go inside because he heard the chatter of young voices.

"We need to give something very special to Auntie for Christmas." If he remembered the voices correctly from breakfast this morning, it was Ruthie speaking.

"What about Mama's brooch?" This was Lynne, the oldest, no doubt about it.

There was a very long silence.

Maybe he shouldn't stand here eavesdropping, but he needed to tend his horse and he didn't want to just barge in on the girls and frighten them.

"Let's make a house that looks like ours out of paste and paper," said Belle, the cute little imp who would have put salt in his morning coffee if Miss Rowan hadn't caught her mid-crime. "We can paint Mama and Papa standing in the window beside the Christmas tree and Auntie playing the piano. That way, when the devil throws us out in the cold, we can remember how Christmas used to be."

"Hush, Belle. Auntie told us not to say unkind things about Mr. Lantree," Lynne scolded her younger sister. "He was raised by his cold-hearted grandfather and they say he never even got a Christmas tree."

"That must be why he's mean," Ruthie said. "Maybe he can't help it."

"I reckon that changes things for tonight," he heard Belle mutter.

"What do you mean?" This from Lynne.

"The pepper in his pillow. I won't be able to do it."

"Santa won't like that, Bellie," one of the twins said.

"We'll get coal," said an identical voice.

"Mr. Lantree must get coal all the time," Ruthie observed. "We ought to do our best to be kind, just like Auntie says."

"Out of the mouths of babes," he murmured.

They had nearly been right about the coal, but the truth was, growing up, he had gotten worse than coal. He'd gotten nothing.

The Christmas that he had been seven years old, the stocking he had hung with his own little hands, full of hope and expectation, had been empty on Christmas morning. All of a sudden he remembered the disappointment so clearly that it hurt.

"There's no such thing as Santa," he had been stiffly informed by his grandfather, then sent to his room to study sums. He'd listened to the children of the ranch hands playing in the snow outside his window while he added boring numbers.

The next year, he had awoken on Christmas morning to find a toy locomotive, carved from wood, outside his bedroom door. It had his initials engraved on the bottom.

He'd proudly showed it to his grandfather as proof that Santa had, indeed, come.

"Don't believe in fairy tales, boy." His grandfather had plucked the train from his hands while he'd tried his hardest to hold on to it. "You'll only be hurt by them. It had to be one of the hands who left it there."

He never saw the train again. Year after year, he watched other children aglow over what Santa had brought, but he knew the truth. Christmas, with all its pretty ribbons and bows, was just another day.

He left the stable without going inside. Setting the cookies on the kitchen table, he walked down the hall to his downstairs room.

The old pain of his grandfather's hard lesson was eased some when he heard Laira Lynne singing "Joy to the World." The clear, sweet tones of her voice filtered through the walls of his room.

He reckoned she was going about some

chore trying to keep "holiday joy" in her heart as she did so.

Maybe there would be joy for him tonight when the people of Snow Apple Woods agreed to vacate on schedule.

It was late. The children had been asleep for an hour when Laira Lynne finally sat down on her cousin's chair beside the fireplace. She took a slow, easy breath and watched steam curl from the cup of tea on the table beside her. Being a mother was infinitely more work than being a social-event organizer and yet vastly more satisfying.

She reached her stocking-covered toes toward the flames, grateful for the warmth.

The dropping temperature had to have everyone worried. A few more degrees and the cold might do damage to the apple trees that surrounded the town.

How fitting that Mr. Lantree, the man who intended to destroy Snow Apple Woods, blew in at the same time as the cold snap that threatened the apple grove…the very apple grove that gave the town its name and its most prosperous product.

Canned apples, candied apples, apple butter, apple cider and fresh, sweet eating apples had brought visitors to Snow Apple Woods for many years.

The front door opened and Rayne Lantree strode inside.

She reached for her knitting basket but grabbed a fistful of air.

Drat! The man was too attractive for her peace of mind. She had to look down so that she didn't embarrass herself by openly staring at the well-shaped curve of his mouth.

"Good evening, Miss Rowan."

She had no choice now but to look at him and return his greeting with a smile.

To attest to the miserable weather, frost glistened in his dark hair. It dusted the shoulders of his coat.

He turned toward the back hallway, walking to his room. The fire in his hearth would be stone-cold. It might be an hour or more before he warmed up.

Since she had been teaching the girls about kindness and tolerance, and he presented the perfect teaching subject, she had no choice but to follow her own lesson.

"Won't you sit awhile?" If she kept her eyes on the hat she was knitting for Belle, she might not be so disconcerted by the fascinating half lift of his smile.

"I'd be obliged, ma'am. It's right cold outside. Hope you don't mind that I left the stove on in the stable for the animals."

She dropped a stitch. One of the knitting needles poked her finger. There wasn't a blessed thing she could do to prevent hearing his voice. It was deep, rich and so smooth it might be mistaken for mulled wine.

What would it sound like singing a Christmas hymn? she wondered. Pure as an angel's voice, maybe? Then again, as alluring as the devil's.

"I'm sorry about what happened at rehearsal tonight," she said, and she meant it.

Mrs. Gilman had spilled hot apple cider on his trousers. The stain still showed in a place she oughtn't be looking at.

"I'm sure it was an accident," he answered.

He settled into the chair beside her with a sigh, stretching his fingers toward the flames.

"I'm sure it wasn't." She set the knitting in her lap, risking a glance into green eyes that made her feel a bit dizzy. "You should know that what you saw of folks tonight is not who they normally are."

"What's that you're working on?" he asked, apparently wanting to change the subject.

"A Christmas gift for Belle." She held up the

half-finished project and turned it to catch the fire's glow. "I've three more to go after this one. I expect I won't get a wink of sleep until after Christmas."

He gazed at her for a long moment, his expression serious. "Can't be easy, raising five little girls on your own."

"I won't lie, it can be a challenge."

"Things would be easier if you accepted my grandfather's money."

She couldn't deny that. The sum the elder Mr. Lantree had offered was tempting.

But… "Those five little girls upstairs have lost too much over the past year. All the money in the world won't ease their pain. This home is where the memories of their parents live. Believe it or not, there are some things that money can't buy."

She picked up her knitting again. She would not—could not—choose financial comfort over her nieces' well-being.

"I'll give you that, but there's no choice to be made. This town is done whether you take the money or not."

"But why Christmas Eve?"

"Why not?" He looked away, clearly avoiding her frown. "It's just another day."

"You saw those children rehearsing tonight.

You heard their voices. Christmas is far from just another day. It's the one time when we all feel joyful…become young again, if only for a little while."

"You do know there's no such thing as Santa Claus?"

He was as wrong as could be about that. Any healthy woman caught up in his teasing smile at this moment would swear that Santa had already left a gift.

"I'll be up until well after midnight—" she clicked her knitting needles at him "—proving that there is."

His laughter washed quietly through the room.

"Carry on, then, Mrs. Saint Nick. I'm off to bed." He stood up, stretched then gazed down at her. "I wouldn't want to stand in the way of the Jolly Old Elf."

"And yet you do."

"What's to say I'm not the Elf? It's all in the way one looks at things." He winked, then turned to stroll down the hallway.

She blessed her stars that she was already sitting down. The man was as tempting as a Christmas present wrapped in a red bow.

"Mr. Lantree," she called softly. "I need some help with the children's choir. They can be a handful. If you'll agree to assist me, I will consider your grandfather's proposal. I'm not saying I'll accept it—I likely won't, but I will mull over what it has to say."

"Call me Rayne, and we have a bargain."

"Good night, Rayne."

"Good night, Laira Lynne."

She listened to his footsteps walking down the hallway, trying to pay close attention to Belle's cap. It was difficult. She had made a bargain with the devil and only hoped it was the first step in winning him over to her side.

Chapter Four

Rayne had hoped that by helping with the children's choir folks might warm up to his grandfather's terms. While no one had dumped hot cider on his pants or called him Satan's spawn, three days had passed and still the only person to accept his grandfather's money was an old man who'd planned to move to another town to live with his daughter anyway.

Rayne turned up his collar against the cold afternoon wind while he walked to the general store where he would send a wire to his grandfather.

The old man wouldn't be pleased, but the people of Snow Apple Woods were waiting for a Christmas miracle. No amount of convincing would make them believe that his money was the miracle.

He sent the wire, purchased a bag of peppermint candies for the girls and then stood by the stove for a moment to gather some heat before he walked back to Laira Lynne's place. While he stood in front of it, the pin fell out of the door hinge, rusted through.

Absently, he picked it up and set it on the counter. He had become preoccupied with a certain pretty young woman.

Laira Lynne…he liked the sound of her name. It was lyrical, just as she was. He was a man to appreciate a beautiful voice and hers was one of the best he'd ever heard.

Last night in the church social room, they had sung a duet, a Christmas carol that Laira Lynne was teaching the children. Everyone down to a fussy baby had become still as stones. He reckoned it was Laira Lynne's voice to steal their breath. He was only a backup to her.

His appreciation of reliving that moment was interrupted when he heard sniffling.

A child was weeping somewhere out of sight. He glanced at Daniel Bolt, who motioned him over to the counter.

"It's little Belle," Daniel whispered. "She

comes here to cry when she feels the need. She doesn't want to bring gloom on her sisters, so she hides behind the ready-made gowns. I let her be, then send her home with a treat."

Rayne lifted the bag of peppermints. "I hope this will help."

He waited beside Daniel until the weeping stopped and Belle stepped out from behind the dresses with her eyes red and her nose damp.

It was unlikely that she would come to him, since of all the girls she distrusted him the most, but he held out his hand.

She looked up at him with wide blue eyes, standing as still as a doll.

All at once she dashed forward and wrapped her small arms around his thigh.

He scooped her up in one arm. She nestled her head against his chest and he had the overwhelming urge to protect her. He'd never felt an urge like that before, but a child so young, so fragile, needed a man to watch over her.

Luckily, the peppermint he placed in her fingers made her smile.

"I reckon your auntie won't mind," he said, carrying her out of the store.

When he glanced back as he closed the door, he noticed that Daniel Bolt was smiling.

"Would you like to talk about why you were crying?"

Belle shook her head.

"My mama and papa died, too. I was just your age."

"They did?" She blinked away the last of her tears. "I was crying about the Christmas tree. My papa always went into the woods and brought us home the biggest one in the whole world. Auntie can't carry one that big."

"I guess she can't," he answered.

A few moments later they stepped inside the house, closing the front door on the steadily increasing wind. Belle dashed off to pass out the rest of the peppermints, laughing as if she hadn't been weeping her heart out a few moments before.

From the shadow of the hallway Rayne watched Laira Lynne shrug into her coat, then put on her hat and gloves. She went outside and quietly closed the door behind her.

It was none of his business where she was going so late at night, but he couldn't help wondering. The town had closed up hours ago and the girls were fast asleep.

He pulled aside the window curtain and watched her go into the barn. A few moments later she came out pulling Old Mule and dragging an ax.

Curiosity won out over none of his business, so he put on his coat and stepped out onto the porch. Cold air filled his lungs. It felt fresh and invigorating. He breathed deeply, savoring the scent of cedar in the nearby woods.

Laira Lynne tugged on the mule's lead while she tipped her face toward the star-speckled sky.

Even in profile she had the face of an angel…purity incarnate, except for one thing. Every once in a while he noticed a glimmer of sass flash in her smile.

Sass in a woman intrigued him. Combine that with Laira Lynne's sweetness and her undeniable beauty… Well, he liked her. Very much.

He'd better have a care to hang on to his heart. Once she took the relocation offer, she would probably move back to New York. In only a few days he would never see her again.

"Come on, you old sky," he heard her say as he came up behind her.

"Are you waiting for a wagon to haul you to the stars?"

She turned around, gracing him with a smile. Her face, framed by the fur lining of her hat, shone with what he could only think was pleasure at seeing him.

All of a sudden he felt warmer by degrees. Laira Lynne had been the only one in the town to give him so much as a howdy-do. That was something he wouldn't forget.

"How did you know? I'm off to the North Pole to ask Santa for snow."

"I wish you luck with that." He turned the collar of his coat up about his neck. The wind had gone down, but so had the temperature. "Where are you really going?"

She tipped her head, considering, he guessed, whether to include him in the mysterious midnight outing. Moonlight caught a twinkle in her eye and shot a shiver clear to his heart.

The sensation was unnerving. His heart had not shivered since that Christmas he had leaped from his bed, eager to see what Santa had left in his stocking.

"It's only two days until Christmas Eve. Naturally, I'm going to the woods to cut down the tree."

"It's late.... It's freezing. I'll help you if you wait until tomorrow."

"That's impossible, Rayne. The girls will expect to see their tree in the parlor when they wake up. It's the family tradition."

"They'll understand."

She pulled on Old Mule's reins.

"Where's the magic in your soul, Rayne?" She hauled the mule behind her, leaving Rayne standing at the barn door.

Where was the magic in his soul? Since when was that a requirement for a responsibly led life? He'd done just fine without it all his life.

"Besides," she said, glancing back at him, "if you and your grandfather get your way, this will be the last Christmas they get to spend in their family home. The girls believe that their parents will be here in spirit, so it's especially important to celebrate the holiday the way they always have."

There was no if about Grandfather getting his way. He always got his way.

Wall Street would cover losses before the old man would go out into the cold to bring home a Christmas tree, even for an eager little boy.

It's not as though his grandfather was a bad man. He wasn't. He was fair, honest in all his dealings. Rayne figured he might be softer if his wife hadn't passed on only a few years into their marriage, and later his only child and his young daughter-in-law. He had replaced his vulnerable feelings with a love of money. Dollars in the bank would never leave a man bereft.

It was his belief that William Lantree was frightened of freely showing affection, even to his own grandson.

He caught up with her.

"Try and keep up," he said, and plucked the ax from her fingers.

The sooner they cut down the blasted tree, the sooner he would be warm in his bed.

"No need to look so glum." She handed him the mule's reins, then tossed him a fetching smile. "Just think of the huge tree the girls will have with your big, strong arms to help."

Truth be told, he wasn't all that glum. Midnight stars…being alone with a beautiful woman… The possibilities blossomed in his mind.

"We'll sing Christmas carols along the way," she said. "You'll feel the spirit in no time at all."

He was feeling something, all right, but it was a bit south of where he figured Christmas cheer resided.

"'Hark! The herald angels sing—'" She began to sing, then stopped when he remained silent. "Surely you know it?"

He knew it…had sung it in secret a few times, even.

"'Glory to the newborn king.'" He added the next line.

"You have an angel's voice, Rayne." He'd heard that said while he'd been away at school, but Grandfather thought the talent a frivolous one, so he didn't sing often.

"'Peace on earth and mercy mild,'" he continued, actually enjoying it.

"'God and sinners reconciled,'" they sang together.

Her voice blended with his as though they were meant to be. The melded tones rang out over the quiet woods.

In the distance he spotted another man and woman walking through the trees. The man carried a small pine over his shoulder. The pair of them stopped for a moment to listen.

Clearly this young couple did not plan to be out of their home before Christmas.

He ought to be worried, even annoyed, but the frigid beauty of the night filled him. He would think about business tomorrow.

Or he might not think about it, after all, because suddenly a picture formed in his mind of five little girls waking to the joy of a Christmas tree in the parlor.

It was a sweet vision, but not quite as spicy as the one he conjured a few moments later when Laira Lynne spotted "the perfect tree."

All of a sudden she stopped, threw her arms open wide and danced rapturously about the eight-foot pine.

"This is it!" Her chest rose and fell with the exertion of her dance. He couldn't see her breasts under her heavy coat, but that sure didn't keep his imagination from conjuring them up.

The woman did make it hard to hold on to his heart as he had determined to do.

He set the ax blade to work at the trunk of the tree. While physical activity did distract him from imagining what was under her clothing, he suddenly took a heated interest in looking at her mouth.

Her lips, smiling and star dusted, reflected pure joy.

He'd like to taste that joy, borrow it from her in a slow, deep kiss. Maybe it would uncover the long-hidden magic missing in his soul.

A quarter of a mile back down the trail, he had spotted a sprig of mistletoe dangling from the bare branch of a tree.

A kiss under it wouldn't change his world.

They could both enjoy the tradition, then keep it as a pleasant memory.

For a moment he wished he was not the devil in the eyes of the folks of Snow Apple Woods. Maybe he wouldn't mind sharing some holiday hoopla with them, just one time.

But an eviction hung over everyone.

Just like years ago, Grandfather, through him, was about to snatch away joy.

Chapter Five

Laira Lynne could not deny that she'd noticed the mistletoe growing on the tree, or that it presented a very interesting image in her mind.

What she didn't expect was to see Rayne climb the tree and pluck it.

"Be careful, Rayne." She looked up, trying to see him through the tangle of branches. "The limbs are frosty."

He lost his footing, then his handhold. With a thump he landed flat on his back.

"Ohhh," he groaned, clutching his prize in his fingers.

"Rayne!"

She rushed forward and knelt beside him, lightly tracing the length of one arm, searching for an injury. She didn't feel anything wrong. Far from it; this was an exceptionally well-formed, muscular arm.

"Are you hurt?"

"Just joshing." He grinned and winked, then poised the mistletoe over her head.

He puckered his lips.

"That, Mr. Rayne Lantree, was not a bit funny." She scrambled away on hands and knees. With a quick jump, she stood as tall as she could, glaring down. "Get off the ground before you freeze."

"I thought this was a Christmas tradition."

He stood up, walked over to Old Mule then lifted the tip of the tree off the ground, taking some of the weight off the animal.

"It is, for folks who are in love."

She arched her brows at him, hoping that he got the message that she would not be dallied with, especially by him.

"Come on, Old Mule." She patted the beast's nose, then took up the reins.

The walk home seemed to take a long time. Whenever she glanced behind her, Rayne was grinning.

She could hardly complain, though. Because of him the girls were going to have a tree that would touch the ceiling.

In spite of everything, Rayne must have a good heart buried under his wallet, because he carried half the weight of the tree all the way to the stable just to spare Old Mule.

"We'll have to be quiet now so we don't ruin the surprise," she whispered.

She stepped lightly up the front steps of the house, then paused to watch Rayne coming up behind her, toting the tree. His arms must be every bit as strong as they had seemed when she'd touched them earlier.

"How can it be a surprise when it's the tradition?" He carried the tree through the front door, then set it on the floor without appearing winded.

"It just is," she said quietly. "It's part of the wonder of Christmas. You know what's coming, but it's magic every time."

"Magic, is it?" He fished the mistletoe from his coat pocket and grinned his crooked smile at her. "You could be right. I wouldn't mind finding out."

She stared at the six-inch sprig as if it was a serpent, and she, caught in its hypnotic spell. To be completely honest, spellbound didn't seem such an awful plight.

When he lifted the greenery over her head, she didn't flee for the stairs. When he slipped his arm about the small of her back and drew her toward him, she didn't resist.

His other hand crept up, his fingers caressing her ribs. He cradled her neck, then tipped her face to his.

The warm breath advancing toward her mouth was irresistible. The aroma of pine clung to him. She caught Rayne's warm, masculine scent even under his coat. She wanted to melt into him, to feel the length of his body pressed on hers and to dissolve into his kiss.

Something was very peculiar…her usual good sense, off kilter. Rayne was simply a man passing though her life and, in fact, leaving havoc in his wake. Besides that, a kiss under the mistletoe ought to mean something.

"This isn't right," she said with the ounce of protest she had left. "We barely know each other."

"Seems a fine way to get acquainted."

"No, Rayne." She stepped backward. Her back felt cold where his hand had been. "This isn't right. You and I…we're at odds. What you want and what I want… I welcome you as a boarder, but…"

Now she did rush toward the stairs because what she was saying was not what she wanted. The fact that they were adversaries did not take away her desire to feel that kiss… and more.

Halfway up, she spun about. “I read what your grandfather offered. It was generous, but I can only decline.”

“Laira Lynne,” he called after her, but in a whisper. “You’re making a mistake.”

Clearly.

Kissing or fleeing, refusing or accepting the money, whichever way she turned seemed to be a mistake.

Rayne had come close to making a big mistake last night.

The play for a kiss, begun as a lark, had suddenly turned into something very different. He suspected that had he indulged his whim to taste Laira Lynne, his life would have been set on its ear.

Nothing would have been the same again. Sure as a dollar, once he’d done it, he wouldn’t be able to turn her out of her home.

Rayne buttoned his shirt and eased into his coat, readying himself for the morning and the task of visiting with the folks of Snow Apple Woods. Maybe this time they would listen to reason.

He stepped lightly, coming out of his room,

figuring that with the house so quiet the little girls must still be sleeping.

The clang of a pot against the stove grate told him that Laira Lynne was in the kitchen. The scents of biscuits baking and bacon frying filled the downstairs.

It struck him, all of a sudden, that he wouldn't have minded growing up in a cozy home like this one where the lady of the house warmed it with good-smelling food and a healthy dose of love. If his parents hadn't passed on, he might have lived this life.

Coming into the parlor, he breathed in a lungful of fresh pine. He glanced toward the window where he had spent an hour last night positioning the Christmas tree so its best side would be presented to the girls when they came down the stairs.

Most of the time, he wasn't such an early riser, but he wanted to watch when they spotted their big tree for the first time.

Cold dawn sunlight trickled through the window, turning the branches bright green… Christmas green.

He was smiling at his work, proud and feeling good about it, when he heard a quiet knock at the kitchen door.

"Daniel," he heard Laira Lynne say. "What brings you by so early?"

Was the older man courting? He didn't care for the way he didn't like the idea.

"I wanted to get here before the girls woke up," said the voice of the owner of the general store. "Here's some hard candy and some ribbons for their stockings."

"Oh, Daniel! Thank you so very much."

"No need for thanks, Laira Lynne. Poor little mites. We do what we can for them. It's going to be a tough Christmas, I'm afraid, what with losing their folks and now their home."

"Can you stay for breakfast?"

"Like to, but no. Got to open early for the last-minute shoppers. I need to earn an income while I still can."

"What will you do, after this?"

"Oh, I'll get by somewhere. It's you all I'll worry about. Will you take the little ones back to New York City, to your family?"

"I'd hate to. Life is so different there and this is the only home they've known. Besides, my family is scattered and none of them are overfond of the city."

"Same for most of us, been here since forever. Say, maybe we can all settle together someplace."

"I'd like that, Daniel…Santa."

He heard Daniel's deep belly laugh, then the door closing.

A door creaked open upstairs along with whispers and giggles.

"We can't cry if there's not a tree this year," he heard Lynne tell her sisters. The shuffle of ten small feet approached the head of the stairs. "It will make Auntie feel sad."

"Maybe she got us a tiny one," Belle said.

"We oughtn't get our hopes up. It was cold last night and she wouldn't be able to go all the way to the woods by herself."

All of a sudden he heard a chorus of high-pitched screeches and a scramble of footsteps pounding down the stairway.

Laira Lynne met the girls at the foot of the steps. He watched them wrap her red plaid skirt in embraces.

"You got us a tree!" Ruthie exclaimed, swiping a tear from her cheek. "It touches the ceiling."

"It's Mr. Lantree you ought to thank. He and Old Mule brought this great big tree home while you were all tucked into your beds."

The girls looked up, noticing him for the first time.

A mass of pink-and-blue flannel dashed at him.

Little-girl arms hugged him the same as they had Laira Lynne. Something shifted in his chest. It left him feeling warm inside.

"You's not Satan's…" Abby said.

"…spoon," Jane completed.

Why, then, did he suddenly feel like it? In two days his grandfather expected him to toss these children out of their home.

For the first time he wondered why it was so all-fired important that the railroad have this particular land.

It was the most direct route and therefore worth more money. He heard his grandfather's voice in his mind saying so as clearly as if the crotchety old Scrooge stood beside him.

When Grandfather had presented the plan, it had seemed so reasonable; easy money in the bank.

But Rayne hadn't always believed that money was so all-fired important.

He glanced over at Laira Lynne. Her lovely smile was luminous while she watched the little girls she had given up everything for gather around the tree and touch its green needles.

Luckily, everyone was absorbed in welcoming the tree, and not paying attention to him. A blow to the gut could not make him quit looking at Laira Lynne.

She hadn't done up her hair yet. It was bound simply in a green ribbon, leaving the soft strawberry-and-cream-colored waves to tumble over her shoulder and across one breast.

He'd be a grateful man if he could find the joy in his soul that shone out of hers every minute of the day…or night.

Wrenching his attention from Laira Lynne, he patted each girl on the head, then went on his way to town.

Leaving the house wasn't easy. He felt like a bear pushed from its den in the dead of winter.

While he walked, he turned about several times in order to watch the girls through the window. They looked happy. He was glad that he had played a part in easing their grief, if only for the moment.

When the house was out of sight, he tried singing a Christmas carol, just to see if a joyful tune would dredge up an echo of the boy he used to be.

Chapter Six

At midnight, sweet silence enveloped the house. The girls, overstimulated from a day of keeping vigil at the window for any hint of a snow cloud, rehearsing their pageant carols and making a secret gift, had finally fallen asleep.

Oh, sweet peace. At long last, Laira Lynne had a moment to sit down and knit another hat. The trouble was, her eyes felt like sand. With her toes stretched toward the fireplace and the warmth wrapping her up, she was certain that she would drift off.

Or maybe not. She hadn't slept well since reading William Lantree's offer.

It was all well and good to refuse it and give the children one more Christmas at home, but on the other hand, she couldn't deny that the money would give them a comfortable start somewhere else. The home was lost to them regardless of whether she took the money or not.

She glanced about the room, seeing memories everywhere. This time last year, she had been sitting beside her cousin, right here, stringing popped corn so the girls could decorate the tree.

Her cousin's husband had placed an old locomotive carved from wood on the mantel, then decorated it with sprigs of greenery.

Laira Lynne had never understood why they put the old toy out every year. It was just something they had found in the attic when they'd moved in. To them, the locomotive was a part of the home's history.

They had loved this house. It was hard to think of it being torn down.

Tomorrow she would search the attic for the train. Her cousin would want to give the toy one more Christmas.

Celebrate Christmas…or take the money? The question plagued her like a toothache. No matter what she did, the choice was on her mind.

She'd weep if it would solve anything.

She would hitch up Old Mule and make the day's ride to William Lantree's home and beg him for another day, but in the end it would do no good and she knew it.

It was well-known that when it came to money, the old man was determined that when his days on this earth were up he would leave as much of it behind as he could.

Oh, great day! Laira Lynne looked down and noticed a missing stitch in the cap. Now she would be forced to unravel four rows of work and set herself back half an hour.

She didn't have the energy, but she would dig it up from somewhere.

No matter what, there were going to be presents under the tree.

Look for the good, she reminded herself, find the Christmas spirit. Oh, but she was tired and her back ached.

She stood up to stretch. The ball of yarn fell off her lap and rolled across the floor. It hit a chair leg, wrapped around it then spun off toward the dining room to catch the table leg.

It bounded here and bounced off there until all that was left of the tidy ball was a tangle of green wool.

Maybe a little cry wouldn't hurt, after all. It might even relieve the emotional pressure gripping her chest. She buried her face in her hands.

Hurrying toward the front door, she opened it and stepped onto the porch where she wouldn't wake anyone.

Only a moment into a good cleansing sob, a big, warm hand gripped her shoulder.

"Laira Lynne, is something wrong?"

Spinning about, she looked up at, really, the most handsome face she had ever seen. This reminded her of one more problem she was weeping over.

All she wanted was a simple kiss, sweet and innocent, under the mistletoe. She might as well want the moon. Just one look at Rayne's mouth and she knew that any kiss between them would be far from innocent.

She pressed her lips together, bit them closed. In a few days Rayne Lantree would leave Snow Apple Woods, taking his railroad wealth with him. He was not going to take her heart, as well.

"What is it, sugar?" With a rough, warm thumb, he wiped the moisture from her cheek.

"My yarn is tangled all over the floor. It's late…there's no snow in sight, I'm tired and your grandfather's money is tempting me like a gift from the devil."

So was the fact that Rayne stood close enough that she smelled the masculine scent of his skin, right where his collar was open and his pulse beat in his neck. The man made her want to toss aside common sense and throw her weary heart against him…literally, her breasts against his chest.

"I can help with the yarn, at least." He rubbed his hand down her arm and up again. "Let's go back inside. My bare feet are about to freeze."

Don't glance down, don't do it…. But she did. How could she not?

His toes were long, perfectly formed and nipped white by the cold.

Her curiosity had certainly paid off, with both a reward and a penalty. His feet were very agreeable to look at, but now that she'd done it, she couldn't keep the vision of them out of her mind. Something about his feet being bare made the wee hours of the night seem cozy… intimate.

To make things even more titillating, beneath her skirt, her feet were also bare.

"Go sit by the fire." Rayne pointed to the pair of chairs in front of the hearth, then he crawled about on the parlor floor gathering and untangling green yarn. "What are you knitting?"

"A cap for Ruthie." She sat down, sighed and then picked up her knitting needles. She stretched her feet toward the flames. Did he notice that her feet were also bare and if he did… Oh, mercy, what was wrong with her? Feet were common, bare or not. It's not as though calves or knees were showing.

"You look done in. Why don't you finish this in the morning?"

"She'll see it and the surprise will be ruined." She closed her eyes, couldn't help it. "Besides, I still have two more to knit."

"Let me help."

The chair creaked when he settled beside her. Knitting needles in the basket between the chairs clinked against each other.

She opened her eyes. Rayne held the needles in one hand and a ball of yarn in the other.

"How about red for this one?" He tossed the ball in the air and caught it.

"Red is perfect. That will be Lynne's hat. I'm making it tomorrow night."

"You work too damn hard, Laira Lynne. Tomorrow night you'll be face-first in your dinner. I'll do this one."

"I don't really have time to teach you."

"No need to." He looped yarn about one needle, crossed points just so and began to knit. "When I was a kid I used to spend time in the kitchen with the cook. She fed me cookies and taught me to knit."

"What? Why would she teach a boy to knit?"

"I was lonely, and she needed someone to coddle. We'd sit by the stove for hours making socks…caps, too, while she told me stories."

"That must have made for a lot of socks and caps." In her mind, she saw him…a little boy hungry for tenderness.

It broke her heart. No child should lack for love.

"We gave them away at Christmas, to the children of the hands and to the orphanage."

"What did your grandfather think of that?" Scrooge that he was.

"He never knew. He'd have made me quit visiting the kitchen if he did. A boy knitting would be worse than a girl riding herd on cattle."

Old man Lantree really must be the tyrant that folks accused him of being.

Outside, the wind kicked up. Blustering gusts howled about the corners of the house.

It was good to be inside with her toes wriggling in warm contentment.

"Maybe the wind will push some snow our way," Rayne observed while he casually propped his foot beside hers.

His ankle turned. His skin brushed hers. She ought to yank back, tuck her toes modestly back under her skirt. The problem was, she was fascinated watching his big, rough foot brush her small, tender one.

"I hope so." Unwisely, she answered his nuzzle by rubbing her arch against the top of his foot. Her response was inappropriate, but somehow she didn't care. "It would mean the world to the girls."

"You really don't plan to be out by Christmas Eve?" His toes stroked the tender flesh of her arch.

"None of us do, Rayne." She closed her eyes because she could not hold them open a second longer. "I'm sorry for how folks are. I believe you mean well…but really, money can only buy so much."

He was quiet for a very long time. She filled her soul with the homey sounds of the crackling fire, the moaning wind and Rayne's knitting needles tapping together.

She drifted to sleep in the chair with his

foot warm against hers and listening while he hummed "Silent Night."

Rayne Lantree, Spoon of Satan and grandson of Scrooge, just might have an ounce of Christmas spirit, after all.

The last thing that Rayne wanted to do this morning was walk to town.

With the house warm and snug, the pile of black clouds skulking on the horizon, ready to slide across the land, seemed all the more frigid.

Given a choice, he'd sit by the fire and watch while Laira Lynne and the girls began what they called the Christmas baking. Already, the six of them were elbow deep in flour, looking sweet in their white aprons.

A man could come to love a life that was anchored by home and family. He could even get used to life in a small town where neighbors were like kin.

Growing up, he'd seen the ranch hands and their families with something similar. Except for the hours he had spent with the cook, he had been on the outside of all that.

He still was, as the next hour was certain to point out.

Well, there was nothing to be done but put

on his heavy coat and give his mission one more try.

Tomorrow was Christmas Eve. Folks needed to begin gathering their belongings.

Upon reaching town, he knew his cause was hopeless. All the talk was about tomorrow night's pageant, Santa Claus and joy to the world.

If anyone was worried about being homeless, they didn't show it.

Clearly, there was no use trying to convince the townsfolk of anything. The Christmas spirit was upon them and all the reasoning in the world would not make them see good sense. The only thing he could do was wire his grandfather and plead for another few days.

He doubted the old man would accept Christmas as a valid reason to postpone his plans, but Rayne trudged up the steps to the general store to give it a try.

"Tomorrow's the big day," Daniel Bolt was saying to a little girl standing beside her mother…Mrs. Hollister and Mary, he recalled. "Santa's probably loading his sled as we speak."

"I've been especially good this year," Mary declared, hopping up and down beside her mother, clearly unable to contain her excitement.

In truth, he hoped that his grandfather would hold off a day. Children should not have their dreams dashed just to pad the old man's already-comfortable pockets.

After Mrs. Hollister and her sparkling-eyed daughter went out of the store, Daniel Bolt turned a frown on him.

Rayne asked to send the wire. He made Mr. Bolt copy the exact words that might make the old man relent a day.

The storekeeper's glare softened; his brows arched in question.

"Those little girls must be getting to you," he said.

Indeed they were, but it was their auntie who had led the way.

"It doesn't matter how I feel, Mr. Bolt. I'm asking for time, but I don't reckon my grandfather will give it."

"Christmas miracles do happen. In fact, I feel the beginnings of one as we speak." He patted his heart and nodded his head.

It would take one to make Grandfather choose this small town over what the railroad was offering.

While Mr. Bolt sent the wire, Rayne glanced about the store. By damn, the girls would have more than hats and ribbons under the tree.

Something in the back of the store glimmered in the light given off by the stove's open door. He walked past and felt the warmth coming off in waves.

"Your stove door is broken, Mr. Bolt." It didn't look safe, hanging askew on it's broken hinge.

"No point in repairing it now." Mr. Bolt shook his head. "Your wire's on its way."

"Appreciate it."

Rayne approached the silver music box that had caught his attention. He opened the lid. A tune tinkled from the delicately etched box. "Hark! The Herald Angels Sing," the carol they had sung together in the woods.

Laira Lynne would appreciate this bit of Christmas in a box.

Still, giving a Christmas gift was as foreign to him as singing in Chinese. His hand was unsteady, picking up the delicate piece.

Why was that? Christmas was just another day. He'd been raised on that belief.

Christmas was not just another day to five little orphan girls, though…certainly not to their beautiful auntie.

Rayne carefully lifted the ornament by its gold ribbon and carried it to the counter.

"Looks like a gift," Mr. Bolt observed. "I

can wrap it up in pretty fabric for you, if that's for Miss Laira Lynne."

"I'd be obliged, and I'll purchase five of those little dolls, too." He pointed to the curly-haired toys dressed in lacy garments of blue and yellow that were on display in a glass cabinet.

"It will be just a moment. I'll wrap them up, too."

Rayne waited, warming his backside by the stove. He swatted away a spark when it caught in his pants. The stove might be a danger, but it was true that it didn't make sense to fix it now.

The bell over the front door jingled and little Belle, her hands white with baking flour, shot across the room to disappear behind the display of gowns.

"Poor little mite." Mr. Bolt shook his head. "Maybe the dolly will brighten the holiday for her."

A home to live in would be better, came a nagging voice in his mind as he took the gifts and left the store.

Chapter Seven

Laira Lynne sat with a twin on each knee, her arms about them, hugging them tight.

"Bellie runned off again," Jane sniffed.

"She going to miss Santa?" Abby clutched a lock of Laira Lynne's hair that had come undone from its bun. She stroked it with her small thumb.

"No, sweetheart, Santa comes tomorrow night." And thanks to Rayne, apparently staying up until the wee hours knitting, the girls would all have caps beneath the tree on Christmas morning.

"Bellie shouldn't be so sad." Ruthie wrung her hands. "Mama and Papa will be here, we just won't see them with our eyes. They'll be here along with the snow."

Laira Lynne sent up a quick prayer for snow. There were clouds, but they were far off and standing still on the horizon.

The front door opened. Rayne, along with a big gust of cold air, blew inside. He carried a sack that he tried to hide behind his back.

"Smells mighty good in here." He stopped to sniff then hurried down the hall toward his room.

He came back a moment later without the bag but with a smile.

Her houseguest might not recognize it, but the Spirit of Christmas twinkled in his eye. Unless she missed her guess, that bag contained Christmas gifts for the girls.

"What's this, little ladies?" He must have noticed the sad faces. "I've heard that Santa's loading his sled right this very minute."

Jane wriggled out of Laira Lynne's lap and dashed toward Rayne. He scooped her up and she hugged his neck.

Poor sweet baby. She missed her daddy very much.

"Bellie runned—"

"Off!" Abby tugged on Rayne's pant leg. "Pick me, too, Satan's Spoon."

"Bellie is at the general store," he told them while he lifted Abby. "She'll be along shortly."

He swayed, rocking the girls. In spite of his reason for being in Snow Apple Woods, Rayne was not a coldhearted man, of that she was certain.

"Bellie cries a lot," Ruthie said, standing by the window and gazing toward town.

"I did, too, when my mama and papa went to heaven. Belle needs to cry sometimes. It helps her."

"Baking Mama's cookies, like we always do, helps me," Lynne said.

"And the Christmas tree," added Ruthie.

"What about mistletoe kisses?" Rayne asked with a waggle of his eyebrows.

All of a sudden, sorrow vanished into giggles.

Rayne set the twins down. The four girls dashed across the room and spoke quietly, heads bent together.

Christmas secrets, no doubt, and Laira Lynne thought she knew which one.

While the girls shuffled toward the fireplace mantel, as discreetly as they knew how, Rayne stood on a chair and tacked his sprig of mistletoe to a rafter in the ceiling.

Stepping down, he shot her a smile…an invitation, rather.

What a gift that would be.

One that she didn't dare accept. The consequences would be life changing. There were casual kisses that could be given and forgotten, but there were others that would live in a woman's heart forever.

The last thing she needed was an itch in her soul for a man who would be out of her life in the blink of an eye.

The only way her lips were going to melt onto his was if it meant something permanent.

"Mr. Lantree," Lynne said, cradling the old locomotive in her arms. "We have a gift for you."

Rayne's smile vanished. He wasn't frowning, but he did appear completely surprised.

"I don't know what to say.... Thank you, ladies."

His smile flashed again when Lynne handed him the worn-out piece of wood.

"This is only the second Christmas gift I've ever received."

"Santa never brought you anything?" Ruthie asked, clearly stricken.

"Poor Satan's Spoon," Jane crooned.

Rayne's ears turned red, having apparently just discovered his mistake about a stingy Santa.

"I'm sure he did, but my grandfather… Well, he thought…"

Clearly flummoxed, Rayne gazed down at the train in his arms.

His face flushed, then blanched. He turned the locomotive engine over in his hands, tracing the initials engraved on the bottom with his thumb.

Laira Lynne looked hard, just to be sure, but certainly there was a sheen of moisture dampening his eyes.

"Do you like it?" Ruthie asked.

He nodded, apparently too overcome by emotion to use his voice. He swallowed hard.

"This is wonderful," he finally croaked out. "Where did it come from?"

"The attic," Laira Lynne explained. "It came with the house."

"Mama and Papa set it out every year and decorated it." Lynne said. "They would want you to have it."

Rayne clutched the old toy to his heart, silent again.

"Rayne, is something wrong? Did something happen?" Laira Lynn asked.

He tucked the train under his arm, hugging it close to his side. With his free hand he touched her cheek, stroked it, really.

"You happened, Laira Lynne. You and the girls."

All of a sudden the church bell rang.

One…two…three…four clangs.

"Fire!" Laira Lynne exclaimed.

Rayne ran for the front door, setting the train on a table on the way out.

"You girls wait here." Laira Lynne dashed out after Rayne. His long legs carried him out of sight before she was beyond the yard's gate.

Without her coat, icy air bit through her dress. She barely noticed, though, watching flames snapping at the sky. Surely they were not coming from the general store.

Smoke whirled up and away. She heard women screaming.

She couldn't see anything yet except the smoke blowing sideways in the wind.

Her stomach squeezed; her heart tripped, then froze. The smoke came from dead center in the town, the east side of the street. It could only be the general store.

"Belle!" she cried.

She ran so hard and fast that her heart and her lungs felt as if they, too, were on fire.

Rounding the corner to Main Street, she spotted the bucket brigade and ran to help pass water along the line.

Where was Rayne?

"Have you seen Belle?" she begged of Mrs. Blue, who hurried to the pump with an empty bucket.

"Mr. Lantree went into that blaze to get her," the old woman gasped, then scurried back to the front of the line to fetch another empty bucket.

Ash filtered down like dirty snow. Laira Lynne locked her knees so that they would not buckle. Belle and Rayne could not be inside that inferno.

It appeared that the whole building was engulfed. Who could survive it?

She glanced frantically about. Where was Daniel?

"Please, oh, please," she murmured over and over as she handed along sloshing buckets. "Please let them survive."

After a few moments, it was clear that the buckets were useless against such hellfire. Hisses of steam spit and sputtered when the water landed, but the flames only grew.

All of a sudden a figure appeared in the doorway, his silhouette blurry with heat. Praise God, it was Rayne, dragging Daniel under one arm and cradling Belle in the other.

Everyone dropped their buckets and rushed

forward to assist Rayne. Someone, she was too frantic to even know who, took Daniel from Rayne.

When it came to handing over Belle to anyone, he would not. He hugged her close while she clasped tight to his neck.

Only when he reached Laira Lynne did he relinquish her.

Belle lunged and she caught her small niece. She did her best to soothe away her fear with coos and gentle caresses.

She glanced at Rayne in his singed coat, covered in ash, his smoke-suffused hair falling over his forehead…and fell madly, completely in love.

While everyone rushed to him, checking for burns, asking questions and giving hugs and pats on the back, Laira Lynne tried to understand what had just happened.

It hadn't even been a week. How could she be this certain of her feelings in such a short time?

At any rate, there it was. She would deal with the consequences of it later. Right now all she could do was rejoice.

Other than the three of them coughing, their hair and clothing reeking of smoke, they were unharmed.

As far as she was concerned, this was an in-the-flesh Christmas miracle delivered by the hands of the town villain.

Chapter Eight

"I told young Lantree that I felt a Christmas miracle coming on," Daniel Bolt declared, sitting at the dining table and munching on a gingerbread man.

Across from him, Rayne, looking fresh and soot cleansed after a good soak in the tub in her bedroom, sipped a cup of hot cocoa spiced with a dash of rum.

She tried not to imagine what he had looked like, bare and sudsy, only a few feet from her bed, but it was no use. Now that she was in love, what was under Rayne Lantree's clothes preoccupied her.

Scrub those pictures from your mind, she admonished herself. A naked, soapy Rayne was a sight she would never behold. Time to put the image away for good.

"Odd miracle when your store burns down," Rayne observed.

"What does it matter? Burned by a spark or torn down by the railroad, it's all the same in the end. Here's the miracle, boy. Tomorrow is Christmas Eve. The three of us are alive and I'll be spending the holiday with you all instead of alone. Santa Claus hasn't visited my house in too many years."

Laira Lynne watched the men from the kitchen where she arranged cookies and baked treats on a platter for tomorrow night's pageant.

Rayne remained quiet for a long time, staring into his drink.

"Daniel." Rayne called him by his first name now because, having saved his life, Daniel thought it was fitting. "I'd like you to accept my grandfather's offer. You'll need the money to begin again."

"That's kind of you, Rayne, seeing that I'm out of my place for good already." Daniel scratched his head. "But you know I can't accept. We all have to stand together…sink or swim."

"I don't want to see you sink. The offer stands if you change your mind."

Daniel stood up. "It's been some day. I'm for bed," he said to Rayne. "If you don't snore… I'll try not to take all the covers."

"You don't talk in your sleep, do you?" Rayne teased.

"Not unless I've got something interesting to say."

With that, Daniel crossed the room to where the girls huddled together, reading a Christmas story. He hugged them good-night one by one, then went down the hall to where he would share the guest room with Rayne.

To Laira Lynne, it was a comfort knowing that Daniel would spend the holiday with them and not by himself in his quarters over the store. Sharing time and joy with others was the very best part of Christmas.

"It's time for bed, girls," she said. "Take the book with you if you like."

The girls, even Belle, smiled great big grins. This was their tradition, to read in bed as late as they could, then wake to greet Christmas Eve.

Lynne skipped across the room to stand before Rayne. She folded her hands in front of her, looking shy.

"Thank you for saving Bellie. It's the best gift we ever got." All of a sudden she threw herself at him in a great hug. Rayne patted her back. "I wish you didn't have to go away."

Lynne ran up the stairs clasping the book to her chest. One by one each of the girls hugged Rayne and said the same thing.

She watched Rayne's face, wondering what he felt, having finally gained the girls' acceptance.

"We thinks you's not Satan's Spoon anymore," Abby said, twirling her way up the steps.

"You's Santa's Spoon!" Jane finished. Giggles, along with running feet, echoed in the hallway. The bedroom door clicked closed.

Laira Lynne was uncomfortable all of a sudden. She and Rayne were alone. It would be harder now to keep her thoughts on a respectable track.

She folded a ribbon, transforming it into a satin bow to put on the tree tomorrow.

She made two more. Unfortunately, keeping busy didn't keep her mind from straying to the forbidden.

What, she wondered, had Rayne meant when he told her that she and the girls had happened to him?

Did they happen good…or bad? Whatever the case, he had seemed emotional about it.

"Show me how to tie up those things, I'll help." He got up from the table and joined her at the kitchen counter.

He stood beside her, so close that she smelled his freshly bathed skin, felt the warmth of his big, manly body. She blinked, trying, all over again, to forget that he had been naked in her bedroom.

"It's like this." She turned the ribbon this way and that until a bow appeared.

Rayne picked up a ribbon but only managed to tangle it in his fingers.

"You'll have to illustrate how, in the flesh." He held the dangling ribbon in his hand. His fingers waggled and his smile was, no doubt about it, flirtatious.

"Do it this way." She lifted the ribbon from his palm and his fingers closed about her hand. They felt strong and warm. She wanted to wriggle free…she wanted to keep her hand in his forever.

"Why did you say I happened to you?" She had to know. If she didn't ask she would spend the rest of her life wondering. "Did it have something to do with the train?"

"That toy belonged to me, for a few minutes one Christmas morning, until my grandfather took it away. Those initials carved in the bottom are mine. How on earth did you come by it?"

"It was in the house when my cousin moved in. Her husband was fond of it so they set it on the mantel every year." He hadn't let go of her hand yet. She couldn't help it, she squeezed his fingers. "I'm glad it found its way back to you, especially since there won't be a mantel to set it on next year."

He glanced down. Drat, he dropped her hand. The ribbon floated to the floor like a long crimson snowflake.

"My grandfather is coming.... If you all take his money or not, he'll show up to see that the town is destroyed. You might as well have something for it."

Of course, she'd known that all along. They all had. It didn't mean that her heart wasn't breaking over it.

It didn't mean that they wouldn't all continue to hope for a miracle.

She snatched up the ribbon from the floor and tied it while she walked toward the tree, just to have something to do other than weep.

Big masculine footsteps thumped behind her, then stopped halfway across the room.

After placing the ribbon on the tree, she went back for another one.

Rayne stood in her way. She walked around him, pretending not to notice that he stood smack under the mistletoe.

He caught her hand. She glanced back at him over her shoulder.

"I plan to stand with you," he said. "With you and the town."

"How can you? Against the railroad…and your grandfather? Rayne, you have so much to lose if you do."

"I have more to lose if I don't." His thumb caressed her wrist, then the palm of her hand. "Like kissing you under the mistletoe."

"Not unless it means something." Her mouth went suddenly dry while her eyes flooded. "I won't take—"

"It means everything."

Rayne drew Laira Lynne toward him. It seemed a bold move to appearances, but his insides pitched about. If she snatched her hand out of his, it would be the worst moment of his life, but if she didn't…

"Everything? It has to mean that you want more than this kiss." She leaned toward him, her eyes bright and misted. "It's you and me for good and all. And the girls…we all come as one."

This day had shown him that there was nothing he wanted more. His feelings for Laira Lynne and the girls had hit him fast and hard. They would not change with time and reflection.

This morning he had experienced the first Christmas joy of his life. Holding that old train after so many years, to have it given to him by the girls only days before it would have been destroyed was more than coincidence. It was magic. Holiday magic.

Grandfather had tried to teach him that December twenty-fifth was just another day, but Laira Lynne had showed him different.

Right now, feeling her come to him, press against him then lift her face to be kissed was more than holiday magic…it was a Christmas miracle.

He was a believer.

"I'm asking for your hand, Laira Lynne, and the hands of all who come with you. Will you marry me?"

"Yes." She touched his cheek, then cupped his ear and feathered the hair at his temple.

"You don't feel that I'm rushing you?"

"I love you, Rayne. All the time in the world, waiting to make sure, won't change it."

"Marry me tomorrow, then, after the pageant. We'll already be in church with everyone gathered together. We'll wake up on Christmas morning, man and wife. What do you say?"

"You can kiss me now."

"There's no going back…this being a mistletoe kiss."

"Where would I go, now that there's you?"

Desire for her made him want to chomp down on her lips and feast, but he'd never given a permanent kiss before. This one needed time and savoring.

He nibbled softly, tasting the plump swell of her lower lip, smelling the sweet warmth of her breath.

"You are my heart, Laira Lynne."

All of a sudden, his intended climbed on top of his boots, wrapped her arms around his neck and showed him just what a feast his future would be.

Chapter Nine

Laira Lynne rose from her bed before dawn, not that she had slept a wink in it.

Today was December twenty-fourth. A day of days all by itself, but this Christmas Eve was going to be like no other.

This would be the first Christmas the girls would spend without their parents, her first without her cousin. Her prayer for this morning would be for the grace to give the children the comfort they needed and the strength to find joy in this day.

Everyone in Snow Apple Woods would need strength today. She suspected that the good Lord was hearing a bucketful of prayers at this moment regarding the evictions.

And the most amazing, most unexpected

thing was that this was her wedding day. She had to stomp her feet and give her head a vigorous shake to make sure this was not just a dream that she hadn't yet awoken from.

The floor was cold; the windows rattled in the predawn wind.

She picked up her robe from the foot of her bed, put it on then hurried downstairs. She needed to get a fire going to greet the girls when they got up.

Halfway down the steps she heard the snap of burning wood.

"Rayne?" she called softly.

Footsteps padded across the parlor; his head peeked around the doorway. When he saw her he grinned, then approached the foot of the stairs.

From the third step, she launched herself into his arms. She buried her face in the crook of his neck and he spun her about.

"Merry Christmas, love," he said, setting her on the floor with a long, wonderful kiss.

"In spite of everything, it is a merry Christmas." She squeezed him about the middle and gazed up at his face. "Are we really getting married tonight?"

"No matter what else happens today, we're standing in front of the preacher. Even if we say our I dos on the road to…somewhere, we'll be man and wife."

She took his hand and pulled him along to the kitchen. She needed to light the stove and put the cinnamon bread in the oven. Christmas Eve morning had never begun without it.

Five little girls were bound to feel the presence of their mother when they came downstairs.

Early today, before she had even got out of bed, she had sensed her cousin. There had been a feeling…something just out of sight that was a joyful presence.

With the baking begun and the scents of nutmeg and cinnamon in the air, Rayne lifted her to the countertop and nuzzled his hips between her thighs.

"I have something for you…a Christmas present." He drew a small wrapped package from his pocket.

He looked so happy about the gift, not a bit like the man who had only days ago believed that Christmas was just a day among many.

He tugged on the ribbon and the wrapping fell away to reveal a beautiful silver music box. It glittered in the lamp's glow. She lifted the lid and listened to the pretty carol.

"It's exquisite," she said. "But I don't have anything for you."

He took her face between his wide palms and kissed her. She was out of breath when he let her go, her limbs as pliable as taffy.

"Nothing but a family."

"I love you, Rayne. I suppose we should give some thought as to where we display this music box next year."

She ran her fingers over the etching of a Christmas tree on the silver lid.

"I don't think the girls would thrive in New York," she added.

"We'll thrive anywhere, as long as we're all together, but this is where the children need to be."

"It doesn't seem possible with the railroad.... Your grandfather?"

She hugged Rayne tight about the middle. Her wool robe was pressed to his flannel shirt. Without undergarments to get in the way, her breasts absorbed the warmth of his chest. She felt the solid beat of his heart.

Without a doubt, this is where she wanted to be for the rest of her life.

"What about expecting a Christmas miracle? You can't back out now that you've got me believing."

"Oh, I believe." How could she not? This time last week she didn't know the man of her dreams existed; today she was marrying him.

"Look, my grandfather is a hard-nosed moneyman, and that's the truth…but I can be hard-nosed, myself. Let's just see if we don't end up staying here."

"Would you be happy here? It's a different life than what you are used to. The ranch is your inheritance. Someday it will be your duty to take it over."

"My duty…my promise is to you and the girls…our girls now. The details will come together as they're meant to."

"Their daddy would have liked you."

"If the girls are right, there's no 'would have' about it. I'll need to prove myself worthy in the here and now since he will be here for Christmas."

"Here come the girls now." Footsteps and giggles bounded down the stairs. "I hope our news makes them happy."

He kissed the tip of her nose, then set her back on the kitchen floor.

"Oh, my!" Lynne gasped.

"Santa's Spoon kissed Auntie's nose," Abby and Jane declared in unison.

"That's because we're getting married tonight."

"You gonna be my new daddy?" Belle asked, the frown on her face dark and severe.

Rayne knelt down, took her chin in his fingers and looked her in the eye. "You'll always have your daddy. I won't pretend to be him. What I will do is love you and take care of you like he would ask me to."

"All right, then." Belle hugged his neck.

"Could be that you are our Christmas gift from Daddy," Ruthie observed with a hitch in her voice.

In truth, Laira Lynne could not say that he was not.

At six o'clock the church bells chimed, calling the residents of Snow Apple Woods to the Christmas pageant.

Rayne carried the platter of fancy cookies, watching his bride-to-be walk beside him toward town.

He could scarcely blink or breathe for fear that she would vanish, that none of this had really happened.

He'd come to Snow Apple Woods a man nearly as callous as his grandfather. That man was as gone as last summer.

While the town folk waited on their own miracle, he had already received his. She walked beside him looking like an angel in her fur-trimmed cloak, her smile and eyes sparkling.

"There might be snow," she observed, scanning the cloudy sky.

"Of course there will be, Auntie." Ruthie, walking ahead with her sisters, turned her head to grin. "It's Mama and Papa's gift… besides Uncle Rayne, that is."

Rayne watched the girls strolling ahead. They tipped their heads skyward as they scanned the clouds. Each one of them held his heart and had his devotion.

Coming into the church, Rayne was greeted with friendly handshakes, smiles and apologies for treating him as they had.

He couldn't blame them for being resentful. He'd come to turn them out into the cold…and on Christmas Eve, no less.

He reckoned there really had been a bit of Satan's spawn in him last week.

Tonight he listened to the children's choir singing, some of them at perfect pitch and some off-key. It was the most beautiful sound he had ever heard. Their shining faces, full of the joy of the holiday, filled in the ache that had crippled his joy for most of his life.

If only Laira Lynne could teach his grandfather what she had taught him. There was no need for him to be such a bitter old man. Especially now that he had five little girls to call him great-granddad.

The singing ended, but the children remained standing where they were.

Preacher Jones read the story of the nativity, then closed his bible.

Rayne took Laira Lynne's hand. He squeezed it.

"You ready, love?"

She nodded, squeezing his hand back. He led her to where the preacher stood at the front of the church before a tall stained-glass window.

The children sang something pretty, something holy sounding, as he and his bride walked hand in hand down the aisle.

The preacher called the group dearly beloved, he told of faithfulness and love. All the while Rayne couldn't take his gaze off his Laira Lynne's face.

When at last he said "I do" and she vowed it back to him, the preacher said he could kiss his bride.

This was a direction he followed with great dedication. Everyone cheered, and some eyes welled up.

With a hand under her knees, he scooped his bride up into his arms and kissed her again.

“Look out the window behind you, Mrs. Lantree,” he whispered in her ear. “It’s snowing.”

“Ruthie!” Laira Lynne called to her niece, who, standing with the choir, had her back toward the window. “Look outside!”

Ruthie covered her face with her hands. She hopped up and down, weeping and laughing at the same time.

“They came,” she hiccuped. “Just like I knew they would.”

The doors to the church blew open. Cold air sucked the warmth from the sanctuary.

Grandfather and the sheriff stood side by side with swirls of white at their backs.

Chapter Ten

"What, Rayne Lantree, are you doing clutching a woman in your arms?" William Lantree's voice boomed off the walls of the sanctuary.

"Marrying her." Rayne grinned in that crooked way that made Laira Lynne's heart swell. "You showed up just in time to wish us well."

The silence that crushed the room was as loud in its way as the elder Lantree's bellow had been.

"William?" Mrs. Blue's voice, high and birdlike, broke the stillness. "Is it really you?"

"Who did you expect, Santa Cl—" William Lantree squinted at the woman advancing upon him between the church pews. "Beatrice Blue?"

"I'm disappointed in you, Willie. You've grown thin and mean."

"Bettie, you're the same as I remember."

"I only wish you were. My Willie would never sell my house out from under me."

"That's an unreasonable way to look at it. My grandson, on my behalf, has offered you more money than the place is worth."

"Tell me, what is a memory worth? I can't fathom that you want to tear down the very room where we first…" Mrs. Blue stood on her toes and whispered in his ear.

Rayne also whispered, "I've never seen my grandfather blush before."

As much as she wanted to remain in the security of her new husband's arms while she met his notorious grandfather, she wriggled out from his embrace.

"As long as you're here," Mrs. Blue said, "I suppose you might as well stay. Partake in the Yule tidings, but don't you dare eat one of my special sweetie buns. You, Sheriff, may eat as many as you like, since the old fool probably dragged you from your family…and on Christmas Eve."

Mrs. Blue shot William Lantree a long, scorching glare.

"Come along, children." The petite woman fluttered her hand at the choir, who stared, round eyed, at the men in the doorway. "It's time to celebrate while we all wait for Santa."

The man charging up the aisle behind her looked like an older version of Rayne, except that he had hard scowl lines creasing the corners of his mouth. They scratched the edges of his eyes, as well.

Even so, it was easy to see that fifty years ago William Lantree would have been a man that Mrs. Blue would have been mad over.

Instead of following Mrs. Blue into the social room, Mr. Lantree halted in front of her and Rayne.

"Explain yourself, boy."

"Merry Christmas, Grandfather."

Rayne slipped his arm around her waist, apparently undisturbed by his grandfather's ill humor.

"Merry nonsense.... I raised you better than that. Kindly explain what these people are still doing here."

"Celebrating the most joyful day of the year...and our wedding. Wouldn't you like to meet your new granddaughter?"

The old fellow did look shamefaced for an instant.

"I beg your pardon, Mrs...." Faintly, but she saw it, pain darkened the old man's eyes. He swallowed hard. "Mrs. Lantree. I was taken by surprise. I've never known Rayne to be impulsive."

"As I heard the story, you married my grandmother after three days," Rayne said.

"That was different. We were young and in love...foolish."

"I used to agree with you." Rayne looked at her, his eyes flashing a message of *just wait until I get you home.* "Not anymore."

"Clearly," William Lantree grunted.

"I've learned something since coming here, Granddad. You won't like it, but I've discovered the truth. Christmas is not just another day. It's special. Look around. All these people refused your money because they wanted to spend it together, one more time. This isn't just another day to them...or to me."

"They're fools. They'll be out of their homes tonight and broke to go with it. I've brought the law to see it done."

Laira Lynne glanced toward "the law." The sheriff stood at the dessert table with a sweetie bun in one hand and a cup of steaming cocoa in the other. Mrs. Blue was evidently telling him something very interesting, because he glanced back and forth between her and William Lantree with his eyebrows raised.

"You, my dear—" he nodded at Laira Lynne "—do not need to worry. You will have a home at my ranch."

"That's kind, but I don't want a home at your ranch."

"Of course you do. It's a sprawling house with a cook and housekeepers. It could use a mistress."

"What about five little girls?" Rayne asked.

"The orphans? Are you the aunt who came from New York?" His eyebrows shot up in his forehead. "I offered you extra because of them."

"They don't want your money," she said. "They want the home they grew up in…where the memories of their parents live. And very possibly, they might want a great-grandfather."

"I couldn't possibly be a—" He glanced about. "Which ones are they?"

"Those five little ones huddled in the corner, looking like they've spotted the devil."

"That's good…children can't be too careful. Wouldn't be wise of them to take to a stranger."

"Let's get down to business, Grandfather." Suddenly Rayne looked like a man she hadn't seen before. A man of business who was used to getting his way. "You want us out and we are not leaving. Not tonight or tomorrow. In fact, we aren't leaving at all."

"I've brought the sheriff to make sure you do."

"The sheriff is busy with my sweetie buns," Mrs. Blue declared, coming back into the sanctuary.

It was impossible to miss the effect she had on Rayne's grandfather. The hard lines of his face softened. Laira Lynne couldn't be sure, but she thought he nearly smiled.

"He'll be too stuffed with holiday cheer to get out of his chair. He's a family man, did you know, Willie? Says he'll quit his job before he forces us out. Oh, listen, the fiddler is beginning to play. Remember how we were, Willie, way back when?"

Mrs. Blue caught William's hand to her chest and tugged him along into the social room where the doors were flung wide and the dancing beginning.

"Did you know that your grandfather and Mrs. Blue used to be in love?"

He shook his head and caught her around the waist. "Let's go see what becomes of it."

Bettie and Willie danced.

Laira Lynne and her groom did, too, along with everyone else, even the sheriff, who toe-tapped about the room with a sugary treat in each hand.

When the music stopped, the girls timidly approached William.

"You don't look like Satan," Belle announced, staring up with her small hands fisted on her hips.

"That, my dear, is because I am not."

"He don't have…" Jane said.

"…horns," Abby finished.

"As it appears, I am your new great-grandfather."

"If that were true," Lynne said, peering at him with squinted eyes, "you wouldn't take Mama and Papa away."

"I didn't…I wouldn't. I lost someone, too."

"If you wreck our house, they won't know where to find us," Belle said. "The store burned down."

William sputtered something, but Laira Lynne couldn't hear what it was.

"Merry Christmas, Great-grandfather." Ruthie stepped forward and formally shook his hand, and then she ran off with her sisters following.

"Out of the mouths of babes, Willie, out of the mouths of babes." Mrs. Blue shook her gray head solemnly. "While you may not be the devil, you are Scrooge, in love with your money instead of people."

"Their parents are dead. They'll need to face that. Besides, I wasn't trying to cheat anyone."

"Oh, but you have been, all these years. You've cheated us of your charming self. I believe you need a sweetie bun."

Mrs. Blue snagged William's hand and tugged him toward the dessert table.

"What do you make of that?" Rayne asked. They had been close enough to hear every word that had passed between the couple.

"I'm not sure, but apparently Mrs. Blue has some influence over your grandfather."

"Look at that! She's making the old man smile!" Rayne blinked his eyes as though he could scarcely believe what he was seeing.

"Ordinarily, that expression is reserved for looking at his bank balance."

"Well, Rayne, it is Christmas, after all."

The fiddler came back and everyone danced again, except for Mrs. Blue and William Lantree. They sat shoulder to shoulder eating sweetie buns.

If folks were agitated about William Lantree's presence and what it meant, they didn't show it. Laughter and good wishes filled the room.

Greetings of "Merry Christmas!" passed from person to person.

Rayne whirled her toward the mistletoe hanging between the sanctuary and the social room. He kissed her long and sweetly.

"I've got a different sort of kiss in store for you later, Mrs. Lantree."

"I love you, Rayne." This time she kissed him.

Somehow it didn't matter that she had loved him for only a short while. Love, she was learning, didn't recognize time.

From the corner of her eye she spotted William approaching with a very odd look on his face.

He seemed younger.... So did Mrs. Blue,

walking beside him as if years had been wiped from her posture.

The old woman's eyes, normally twinkling, now had stars in them.

Beyond the stained glass, the snow fell harder.

Sitting in front of the big window with the children gathered about her skirt, the preacher's wife read "'Twas the Night Before Christmas."

William Lantree cleared his throat, glanced at a nodding Mrs. Blue then back at Rayne.

"Mrs. Blue has made it clear that I will never taste another one of her pastries unless—" Rayne's grandfather took a long breath and held it.

"Go on, Willie..." Mrs. Blue winked and the old man smiled, genuine and wide.

"Very well.... Bettie believes that I don't need to die with so much money. I'm giving the railroad the longer, cheaper route. You can keep your town."

Someone must have overheard then passed the news along. Cheers and hallelujahs rolled through the room in a wave.

"Looks like we got our miracle," Rayne whispered in her ear.

"Move over, boy." William elbowed his grandson aside.

Laira Lynne pulled Rayne a few steps closer to the preacher's wife, who picked up her story where she had paused.

William Lantree gathered Beatrice Blue to him under the mistletoe and gave her a long, lusty kiss.

"'Happy Christmas to all, and to all a good night,'" the preacher's wife declared.

* * * * *

CHRISTMAS WITH HER COWBOY

Lauri Robinson

Dear Reader

When I was asked to write a story for the *Christmas Cowboy Kisses* anthology I knew I had to give my heroine a red cape with a white fur trim. Yes, because my favourite colour is red, but also because, to me, Christmas isn't Christmas without red—be it a coat, blouse, sweater or dress. Why? Well…

My father's favourite colour was red. He was also a 'Christmas Eve shopper'. I tried to get him to shop earlier, but finally had to concede it wasn't going to happen. So, no matter how many people I was expecting for dinner that night, I knew Christmas Eve morning would be spent shopping with my dad for one particular present. A red dress for my mother. We deviated a bit over the years—a red skirt and jacket, or one year it was a red coat—but for the most part it was a red somewhat fitted dress. My parents were married for almost sixty years, and my mother always acted as if it was the first red dress she'd ever received upon opening his package.

When my father died in 2007 I told my sister I was going to buy a red dress for the funeral, and that tumbled throughout the family. At Dad's funeral all the girls, right down to my granddaughter, not yet six months old, were dressed in red and the men of the family wore red shirts or ties. That year, though I didn't buy it on Christmas Eve morning (I now dedicate that morning to remembering my dad by *not* shopping), I bought my mom a red blouse, not wanting to try to replace Dad's gifts but to keep the tradition going. And I did so every year until 2011, when Mom passed away. Since then I've bought myself something red to wear at Christmas, just to keep the memories flowing.

I hope you enjoy picturing Anna in her red cape, and I hope you enjoy her and Tanner's story!

May you all have a blessed and merry Christmas!

Lauri Robinson

DEDICATION

To my oldest granddaughter, Isabelle.

Born on December 23rd, she continues to be
a Christmas miracle we enjoy year-round.

Chapter One

Wyoming
1881

Tanner Maxwell tugged his hat down and flipped the collar of his coat up to protect his ears from the biting wind whipping around the corner of the depot. Planting the sole of one boot against the wooden building behind him, he crossed his arms and leaned back.

The judge must have drawn straws. No one would have volunteered for this job. Tanner sure hadn't, and assuming he was the short straw didn't help his temperament. Neither did the gray sky or the bits of snow swirling about. Hauling Anna Hagen back to the ranch was going to be unpleasant enough; he sure didn't need a storm to fight along the way.

Never seeing the judge's granddaughter again would suit him just fine. Guilt had nothing to do with it either. He hadn't done anything to be guilty about. She, on the other hand—

Nope, he wouldn't go there either. He'd just go on counting his lucky stars he'd stopped before venturing down that lane. He respected Walter too much to put something like that between them.

Then and now.

Huddled in fur and wool coats and holding on to hats the wind attempted to steal, a queue of passengers stepped off the train. No hat could hide Anna Hagen's mess of brown curls, and Tanner's mind tried to take another detour, which he stopped short. Instead, he recalled how she'd disappointed the judge time and time again.

And that he was the short straw.

The noise of people shouting above the wind, the clanging of doors and the pounding of heels scurrying across the platform died down a bit. Tanner peered closer at the women who had departed, wondering if Anna had changed so much in the five years since she'd gone to live with her father in Kansas City that he'd overlooked her.

Not one of them looked familiar, but being a man, one who appreciated beauty when he saw it, Tanner couldn't pull his eyes off a slender woman wearing a long red cape. The hood was up, protecting her head from the elements, and the white fur surrounding her face made a stunning picture. For the briefest of moments, Tanner wished he was the man holding that woman's elbow, escorting her toward the depot. He wanted that—someday—a wife, a family that was truly his.

As if she sensed his stare, the woman in the red cloak turned. A friendly smile formed as her eyes met his. A flutter happened inside his chest. Tanner lifted a hand to touch the brim of his hat, giving her a subtle acknowledgment. Maybe being a short straw wasn't all bad.

She reached over and patted the hand holding her elbow. The man, taller than her by several inches, bowed slightly to give her his full attention while she graciously nodded toward the building.

Tanner pushed off the wall and scanned the train cars. That woman was taken, and he wasn't a thief—no matter what others believed. Where was the judge's granddaughter?

It would be like her to not be on the train. To have gotten Walter's hopes up, just to destroy them by not showing up. If she had done that again, Tanner might just buy himself a ticket, travel all the way to Kansas City and tell Anna Hagen what a spoiled brat she was. Just like her father.

That's how Tanner saw it. When you grew up without a family, you tended to notice how poorly others mistreat the ones they have.

The man, dressed in a tailor-fitted black coat and top hat, and the woman in her red cape, weaved around a few lagging passengers, making their way toward him. Tanner was just about to give them a parting nod when the woman spoke.

"Tanner?"

A cold, invisible fist gripped his spine as he examined her more closely. Thickly lashed eyes, a friendly smile that enhanced her cheekbones and a simple, somewhat button nose that when put together were undoubtedly stunning. Maybe it was the white rabbit fur that trimmed the red hood, but she looked almost angelic, like an image on one of the Christmas cards the judge received this time of year.

"Tanner Maxwell?"

"Yes," he said cautiously.

"It's me," she said, flipping the hood off her head. "Anna Hagen."

Air rattled in his lungs. To say he was surprised would have put it too mildly, but he wasn't about to let her know that. With a nod, he replied, "I see that." Without the white fur distracting his vision, he could see she was the one the entire ranch referred to as *the granddaughter*. He'd thought he was prepared for this—seeing her again—but a sinking feeling said there were no lucky stars left for him to thank. Anna Hagen had grown up.

She laughed again and without any warning leaped forward and wrapped her arms around his neck. "I can't tell you how good it is to be home."

Tanner wished he wasn't backed up against the wall so he could escape her hold. As it was, he took her upper arms and set her aside, all the while trying not to notice how sweet she smelled, the softness of her velvet cape or how his mind flung one specific memory—that of how sweet her lips had once tasted—around faster than the wind spit out snowflakes.

The clearing of a throat had her giggling. "Oh, John, darling, forgive me," she said to the man, taking his arm with both her hands.

"This is Tanner Maxwell, my grandfather's right-hand man."

Tanner was more than a bit amazed to hear her call him that. Considering what her father called him.

She turned those sparkling blue eyes back to him. "Tanner, this is John Hampton, my fiancé."

It wasn't that Tanner was tongue-tied, he just didn't have a response to that.

The other man extended a hand. "Mr. Maxwell."

Tanner's insides had turned as cold as the wind, yet he took the man's hand, shook it. "Mr. Hampton." He nodded toward the edge of the platform, where a wagon with the Double Bar brand burned in the side of the wood sat amongst several others. "I'll get your baggage."

"I'll help," John Hampton said as he put an arm around Anna. "Go inside, dear, out of the weather while Mr. Maxwell and I load the wagon."

"That's not necessary," she responded. "I'm too excited to be cold." She hugged the man with both arms. "Oh, John, darling, you're going to love it here as much as I do. I just know it."

Tanner's mouth had filled with a bitter taste. Probably due to the *darling* and *dear*. Seeing the porter, Wes Marley, waving at him from the baggage car, Tanner skirted around them as John *darling* started to say something else about the weather. The Double Bar had shipments come in on a regular basis, so he knew most every railroad man, including Marley, who was now shaking his head.

Tanner saw why when he arrived at the open doorway. Trunks were stacked five high. "All that?"

"No, the bottom one is someone else's," Wes replied. "Old Judge Hagen has to be grinning from ear to ear at having his granddaughter home for Christmas."

"Yes, he is." Tanner reached in to grab a trunk handle.

Wes caught hold of the opposite handle and as they started walking toward the wagon, he asked, "Does the judge know about the fiancé?"

"Not much gets past Walter," Tanner answered, yet he harbored the same question. In all his talk about Anna coming home for Christmas, the judge hadn't mentioned anyone accompanying her. Tanner had asked if Will, her father and the prodigal son, was coming.

Walter had said no, which had every man at the ranch letting out a sigh of relief. The judge had never said Anna was alone either. Leave it to Walter to surprise everyone. Including him.

A fiancé?

Anna and John *darling* helped with the luggage, and other than a parting comment assuring Wes he'd see him at the Christmas party the ranch was hosting later that month, Tanner kept his thoughts to himself. He had plenty of them—thoughts—and they kept growing as the three of them climbed onto the wagon seat and set out for home.

It would be a long ride, fifteen miles, and the wind was picking up; so were the flakes of snow. His temperament grew more sour with each revolution of the wagon wheels, too, but that had a lot to do with the *darlings* and *dears* that kept spewing from the couple's mouths.

He'd never begrudge anyone for falling in love and getting married, but these two had him sick to his stomach. It was worse than sitting in a hard chair watching actors on the stage at the playhouse in town. He'd gone there once, when Rosalie had begged him to take her, and swore he'd never sit through that torture again.

The real-life version was worse.

* * *

Anna was so filled with joy nothing could wipe the smile from her face. Not the wind or snow or even Tanner's grumpiness. He'd barely said three words to her. Less to John. But that was Tanner. He'd never been overly talkative, and she was glad he hadn't changed over the years.

Five years.

She'd asked her grandfather if she could visit too many times to count. He'd always said yes, but each time, at the last moment, something had happened to prevent her from going. Usually it had to do with her father's schedule.

She loved him, her father, she truly did, and assisting him had been her top priority, so she never let on how disappointing not going home had been. To do so would have been wrong. He'd needed her and she'd been there for him, but now, although she felt selfish admitting it, she was so very glad that part of her life was over. Seeing Tanner—grumpy or not—confirmed it. She was home.

Turning to the stone-faced Tanner beside her, she asked, "Did you hear my father remarried?"

"No, I can't say I did."

He never took his eyes off the road ahead of them, and his aloofness could have tainted her contentment, but she wouldn't allow that. "Well, he did. Two months ago. Her name is Virginia and they're very happy."

Tanner nodded, which was about all she could expect. Grandpa must not have mentioned the marriage. She'd written him all about the wedding, even though her father had told her not to bother. It wasn't a bother to her, but a milestone. The end of her having to choose between the two men she loved unconditionally.

Noting the blanket covering her and John wasn't spread across Tanner's legs, she found the corner and flipped it across his thighs, then, as the impulse appeared, she went with it and gave his midsection a big hug. "I'm just so happy to be home," she declared. "I could hug everything in sight."

"Well, I'm right here, darling, and you can hug me all you want," John said, tugging her back toward him.

She hugged him in return. Without John she wouldn't be here, and she was appreciative of that.

His hold tightened. "With this wind, I'd appreciate all the hugs you can give."

Unable not to, she giggled. John was attentive by nature but had grown more so during their travels, using endearments, which, considering some of the characters on the train, she'd grown to appreciate and had found herself using them in return. It did seem wrong to carry on so now, though, and she'd have to tell John that when the opportunity arose. Remind him the engagement, no matter how contrite, had been her only choice. "You're going to love the ranch," she told him now instead. "There's no place like it on earth."

Immediately full of ranch thoughts, she turned to Tanner. "Fill me in on what's happened since I left. Is Slim still cooking for the boys in the bunkhouse?"

"Yes, he's still cooking," Tanner answered, shifting the reins in his gloved hands.

"And Merilee? Is she still cooking for Grandpa?"

Tanner answered affirmatively and she turned to John. "Wait until you try her spice bars. She only makes them at Christmastime and they are so delicious. Truly wonderful."

"About like you," John said.

"Oh, you," she answered, playfully slapping his shoulder. She grinned, too, for John's agreement to accompany her had ended her father's protests; therefore, here she was. Home.

She twisted and wrapped both hands around Tanner's arm. It was solid, full of muscles from working every day, and she held on tighter. She'd always admired Tanner's strength and endurance. Even that once, when he'd used it against her. That was in the past, though, and she'd learned not to dwell on it. "Tell me Thunder is still at the ranch. She is, isn't she?"

His gaze was on her hold, and it was a moment before he lifted his eyes. They were as brown as his hair, and how he kept them so expressionless was beyond her. No one ever knew what Tanner Maxwell was thinking unless he wanted them to. Which was never.

"Yes," he finally said. "She's still at the ranch. Had another foal this spring."

Her excitement doubled. "Is it a buckskin, too?"

He nodded, but then with his low, slow drawl, he said, "Thunder hasn't been ridden much the past few years, so you'd best be careful if you take her out."

At one time the horse had been her best friend, her only friend, and Anna was as excited to see the animal as she was her grandfather. "I will," she assured him.

"You haven't asked about Walter," he said then, snapping the reins.

An inkling of fear appeared through her joy. "He's doing all right, isn't he?"

"Yes, he's doing all right."

Tanner was staring at the road again, and the stillness of his profile had the fear inside her growing a bit more. "You're scaring me, Tanner," she admitted, close to a whisper.

"Walter's missed you," he said rather coarsely. "And he's been disappointed when you kept promising to come but never did."

She couldn't fault his infinite loyalty to her grandfather—it had always been there, and knowing Tanner was with Walter while she couldn't be had helped each time her plans to return home had fallen through. But watching his profile, noting the twitch in his cheek, Anna had to wonder exactly why Tanner was so mad she'd finally come home. Her father claimed if anyone inherited the Double Bar, it would be Tanner. She'd thought that was just talk—her father's way of holding on to the bitterness he felt toward the Double Bar. Surely he was wrong.

Chapter Two

The ride home had proved long and cold, yet the chill in Tanner's bones had little to do with the weather. He stayed clear of the homecoming, other than to watch Anna fly into Walter's open arms after John *darling* had lifted her out of the wagon.

As soon as a couple of cowhands had unloaded the trunks and carpetbags, Tanner drove the wagon away from the house, unhitched the horses and led them into the barn.

He'd just finished giving the second horse a good rubdown when the barn door opened. Along with a solid blast of frigid air, Walter Hagen walked in, brushing snowflakes off the arms and shoulders of his buffalo-hide coat.

"Good thing you got home when you did. It's really coming down out there."

Tanner nodded. "Saw it coming." He gave the horse a pat on its rump, sending it into its stall. "The horses did, too. Had a heck of a time keeping them from running most of the way home."

Age hadn't altered the judge much. He was still big and burly, and though some thought he was past his prime because he no longer oversaw the wild courts of most of Wyoming, Tanner knew differently.

"Smart critters," Walter said, leaning against the top rail of a stall. "Smarter than some men."

Tanner fought not to grin. It had been this way between him and Walter practically since the day the judge had hauled his fourteen-year-old butt home rather than send him to jail as he had the rest of the Taylor gang. "I'm assuming you mean me."

"Who else?"

"Why?"

"I told you to fetch my granddaughter."

"That's what I did."

"Well, what's that other thing you dragged home?"

Tanner did grin when he caught the one on

Walter's face. "That," he said pointedly, "is her fiancé."

"You don't say." With an exaggerated shudder Walter added, *"Darling."*

The rapport between the two of them had always been dry, and Tanner enjoyed it. Besides giving him a chance, the judge—outside his mother and a few youngsters way back when—had been the first person not to hate him on sight, and Tanner had appreciated that since day one. He crossed his arms and set both elbows on the stall. "What did you want me to do, *dear*, leave him at the station?"

Walter guffawed before he pulled up a disgruntled frown. "That would have suited me fine."

"Yeah, well, it wouldn't have suited Anna fine," Tanner answered.

The judge took a few steps in order to pat the nose of a very coveted horse. Thunder was not only an excellent broodmare, she'd been Anna's favorite, therefore Walter's favorite, too. "She told me she was bringing a friend with her," the man said. "I assumed it would be a girl. You know, a companion of sorts."

"Considering they're engaged, I guess you could call him a companion," Tanner said.

"Soon to be a lifelong one." That galled him in ways it shouldn't.

Walter spun around and the squint of his eyes flared something else inside Tanner.

In the ten years he'd known the judge, Tanner had learned how to read him well. The man had waited five years for his granddaughter to return home and the thought of sharing her—with anyone—irked him. That wasn't new, though. Years ago Tanner figured out any man who tried to come between Walter and his granddaughter had a good chance of finding himself at the end of a gun barrel. "The way I see it..." Tanner began, having no qualms about pointing out the truth. The judge expected that of him. "There's not a lot you can do about it. She's a grown woman."

"Maybe, but she's still my granddaughter."

Tanner pointed out something else. "You couldn't tell her what to do when she was a child, so do you think you can now?"

Walter tipped back his Stetson before he folded his arms across his barrel chest. "I'm not going to tell her what to do."

"That's good," Tanner said, already imagining a showdown between two of the most stubborn people on earth. Anna may have grown up, but the way she'd cajoled her soon-to-be husband on the trip home, Tanner was set to bet half the time she called John *darling* she was acting, using the man to get her way.

"You are," the judge said.

Caught only half listening, Tanner stuttered, "Wh-what?"

The judge nodded.

An entirely different kind of chill rippled his spine. "Oh, no, I'm not." Pushing off the stall, Tanner took a step closer, just to make his point clear. "She's your granddaughter. I didn't have anything to do with her when she lived here five years ago and I won't have anything to do with her now." That was the line he'd almost stumbled across years ago, and he had vowed it would never happen again. Without Walter, he'd most likely be dead by now, and he'd never forget that.

Walter didn't move. He didn't square his shoulders or stretch on his toes, yet all of a sudden he seemed taller. The man had the ability to do that. With little more than a certain look, a gleam that appeared in his eyes, Walter could exude authority like no other. Tanner had seen it numerous times, but it was rarely directed toward him, which is how he wanted to keep it.

"No way, Walter," he said, shaking his head.

"You'd still be rotting in jail if it weren't for me," the man said. That wasn't anything Tanner hadn't heard before, but the judge was usually joking when he said it.

Not this time.

That was something Tanner couldn't quite believe, or accept, which had him wondering if Anna had told Walter about their *encounter* in the barn years before. That possibility didn't take hold, so he said, "No judge would have sentenced a kid to prison for life just for holding horses." Walter had told him that on more than one occasion.

"You were holding the get-away horses while the Taylor gang robbed the bank."

"But they didn't get away," Tanner argued.

"That's beside the point."

"No, it's not," Tanner insisted. Walter knew the Taylor gang had more or less held him captive and for years, when it came up, this conversation had been flipped around, with Tanner accepting his guilt and the judge defending he'd been too young to know better. He'd been young, and he'd known better, which is why he'd knotted the reins together, made sure the getaway hadn't happened.

Walter turned to Thunder and stroked the

horse's elongated face. "You ever hope for a Christmas miracle, Tanner?"

Understanding none of this conversation was really about him, the seriousness of Walter's tone had Tanner's nerves biting his skin. "Yeah, but I've got a feeling what you're envisioning as a miracle others might call murder."

Hearing Walter laugh allowed Tanner once again to breathe freely.

Walter stepped away from the stall and slapped him on the shoulder while walking to the door. "I don't want you to kill John *darling*, just get him the hell off my property."

In all his twenty-four years of living, Tanner couldn't recall being left speechless, yet it had happened twice today. Once by Anna with her fiancé proclamation, and now by Walter.

Frustrated, Tanner set into the evening chores, but in what appeared to be a snail's breath of time, cold air once again swirled around him. Frozen for a moment, he watched the wind whip the red velvet cape around her as Anna tried to pull the door shut.

He'd planned on being long gone by the time she came out here. Blowing stale air from his lungs, Tanner moved forward and closed the heavy door for her.

"Thank you," she said, smiling brightly.

"Grandpa said you were out here, that you'd show me which one was Thunder's latest foal."

He'd known it wouldn't take long before she'd visit the horse, and watched as she opened Thunder's stall to walk in and hug the horse's thick neck. The fur-lined hood had fallen from her head, and though her hair was still brown, there were no waist-long curls like before. Instead, it was neatly pinned into a smooth bun on the back of her head. He had an urge to pluck out those pins, see if the curls still fell over her shoulders and down her back, and he wondered—

Stopping himself, he asked, "Where's Joh—Mr. Hampton?"

She flashed him a bright smile. "Don't be getting all formal, now, Tanner. The only person you've ever called mister was Grandpa, years ago." After planting a kiss on Thunder's cheek, she rested the side of her face against the horse. "John is with Grandpa. He's showing him his gun collection."

"Walter is showing John his gun collection," Tanner repeated for himself. The judge was too smart to flat out shoot the fiancé, but he knew his guns, and an accidental shooting, *that* he could arrange.

"Why are you frowning so?" Anna asked.

"Oh, just thinking about Christmas miracles," Tanner lied.

Skepticism shimmered in her eyes as she shook her head. "You believe in Christmas miracles?"

"I'm starting to," he mumbled, while his mind flashed images of the judge's gun-lined office.

"Why do I have a feeling we aren't talking about the same thing?"

Tanner shook his head. "Everyone's miracles are different." With a wave of one hand, he gestured toward the other end of the barn. "Thunder's latest foal is in the last stall."

Anna waited until he walked past her, and then matched his footsteps. "What's her name?"

Irony settled in as he answered, "Your grandfather named her Little Darling."

"Oh, that's sweet," Anna cooed.

"Isn't it," Tanner answered drily.

Chapter Three

The foal was a buckskin. With a coal-black mane and tail, and a hide as golden brown as freshly baked bread, Little Darling was as beautiful as her mother. Yet Anna had a hard time concentrating on the animal. "You don't like me any more now than you did when I left, do you, Tanner?"

"I don't dislike you," he said. "Never did."

By default—Tanner not liking her had won out when she'd moved to Kansas City. Before then, he'd been her friend, let her get away with things others hadn't.

On more than one occasion her grandfather had insisted she didn't rule the roost, so to speak—usually when he'd sat her down for a lecture on something she'd done. An only child with thousands of acres at her disposal, she'd chapped more than one cowhand's hide by getting in the way. Those were also her grandfather's words.

But things had changed. Her father had returned. Tanner hadn't lived in the house then, not as he did now, and once again her father's suggestion echoed in the back of her mind. John thought the same thing—he'd voiced how annoyed Tanner appeared to be about their arrival a short time ago when she'd showed him to his room. She'd ignored John's statement, but ignoring Tanner had never been possible.

Anna gave the horse a final pat, and then turned to face him. Her adversary. If that's how it had to be, though she did hope differently. "I almost can't believe I'm home."

With a look that said he didn't believe her, Tanner huffed out a little breath before he walked back up the row of stalls.

She took a deep breath. Inhaled the aroma of horseflesh, hay and the lingering other scents that filled the barn. Some found it offensive. Not her. She thrived on it and had missed it with all her heart. "You have no idea how hard it was for me to leave this place."

"Seems to me you did it easy enough." He was filling a can with oats when she arrived at his side, and then shouldered his way around her. "Never even bothered to visit."

Frustration wormed its way in, overshadowing some of her joy. "I wanted to visit, but it just didn't work out. Not with Father's schedule."

He was dumping the oats in a bucket for one of the horses and didn't look her way. "What about Walter?"

"He had you," she answered honestly.

"I'm not his family," Tanner said, coming back for a second canful.

"In his eyes you are." She followed him this time, remained inches behind him as he dumped the oats. "In his eyes you're the son he never had." The years of letter writing, where her grandfather wrote of little else besides Tanner, had been bittersweet. As much as she was glad her grandfather wasn't alone, she'd wanted to be here, be a part of the progress assuring the Double Bar thrived for future generations.

"Walter Hagen has a son," Tanner said as he walked past her again. His tone and attitude spoke volumes. "His name is Will, and he's your father."

"Does reminding yourself help?" The sting her words created inside her was ugly, but maybe her father was right—that she'd been remembering things differently from how they'd really been. "My father never wanted to be a rancher. It wasn't in his blood. Not like it is in Walter's. Not like it is in yours. He wanted to be a doctor, was destined to be a doctor, and watching my mother die, not being able to save her, was more than he could take."

Her explanation, though it made her throat raw, didn't seem to affect Tanner. His glare was as frosty as the single window next to the barn door.

"That's what he is now," she said. "A doctor. And he's happy. I know he and Virginia are going to have a wonderful life together." His silence said her words still hadn't got through, so she continued, "He wanted more for me, too. He wanted me to see the world outside this ranch." She didn't add that that world had mainly consisted of taking care of her father, cooking, cleaning and helping him study. It was over now and didn't matter.

"Really?" Tanner paused long enough to eye her squarely. "The daughter he'd abandoned two years before."

Why was she the only one who understood and forgave her father for his behavior while mourning her mother? "We all make mistakes,

Tanner." In order to contain other memories from sneaking forward, she concentrated her efforts on defending her father. "I was the only person my father had who would support him. Walter—"

"Walter," Tanner interrupted, "left the bench because of you. Retired from being the best judge the courts ever had to take care of you when your father deserted you, and he never went back after you left, hoping you'd come home."

"Walter had you, Tanner," she said, fighting hard to stay focused. "He didn't need me."

Tanner shook his head.

"It's true, ask anyone. From the time you moved in here, you became his favorite." She'd been nine, and with both parents alive and happy, her life had been too full to notice the young cowhand. Three years later, though, when her mother died, her world had turned inside out. Tanner might not remember it, but she remembered how he'd comforted her, told her how sorry he was. He'd held her hand, too, while they placed her mother in the ground on the hill north of the house. And later, when her father disappeared, Tanner had become her friend, or perhaps idol. Until two years later when out of the blue her father had returned and told her they were moving to Kansas City, where he was enrolled in school to become a doctor. She'd protested, but—

"Anyone?" The repulsion on Tanner's face was as strong as any she'd ever seen. "Don't you mean ask you or your father?" he continued. "That's what it comes down to. He hated me from the minute I stepped foot on Walter's land."

"No, he didn't," she replied, frustrated by his accusation.

"I recall it differently."

There had been a terrible row, and her father had lashed out at Tanner, calling him an outlaw and other nasty names, but he'd been despondent, full of grief and taking it out on anyone nearby. "My fath—"

Tanner stepped forward, glaring at her with more aversion. "Your father never let anyone forget moving here wasn't my choice. That it was court ordered. In place of going to prison, I had to serve seven years on Walter's ranch."

Anna's insides trembled with anger. Somehow he'd turned this all around. She'd hoped that now that her father was happy, living his life as a doctor, she could start living hers. But she couldn't put the past behind, where it belonged, if Tanner refused to. Right now, he was acting so mean and hateful she didn't want to share the air she breathed with him.

"Your seven years were up three years ago," she snapped. "Why are you still here?"

His laugh was bitter and cold. "So the truth comes out. The real reason you finally came home."

She gave her head a single shake, trying to catch his exact meaning. "Which is?"

"To get rid of me."

He stepped forward, which caused her to step back. His proximity, for he was a tall and muscular man, was somewhat suffocating and had her heart beating frantically. The first stall was right behind her, and her back bumped into it, preventing her from moving any farther away. He kept coming, though, and trapped her by placing both hands on the rail behind her. His brown eyes held no compassion, no concern for how cornered she was. He was not the Tanner she remembered.

"Let me assure you," he all but growled inches from her face, "I'm not going anywhere."

"Why? Because you think you deserve this place?"

"No." He grasped her chin with one hand,

held it firmly. "Because that old man's going to need someone when you leave again."

She wanted the laugh to come out sounding as if she knew exactly what she was doing. Instead, it sounded as if she was being strangled. All the same, she answered, "I'm not going anywhere. This is my home and I'm staying."

"We'll see about that."

The challenge in his eyes ignited determination in her. This was her home, and this time she was old enough that nothing and no one would stand in her way. "Yes, we will." Fueled by the fight inside her, she added, "We'll also see how long you last once I'm in charge."

He threw back his head and let out a harsh laugh before he brought his nose inches from hers again. "This place would fall apart with you in charge of it."

Anna wasn't exactly sure what snapped inside her. For five years she'd catered to her father, and though she loved him dearly, and was happy for him, she'd never again put her desires and dreams in second place. Her dreams—more like the one memory all her dreams were based upon—blasted forward, propelled by all the emotions she'd buried with it so many years ago. The day Tanner had found her here in the barn, crying.

She'd felt torn in two that day. Her father insisting she leave with him and her grandfather worrying if she went, her father might abandon her again. She'd wanted to please them both.

Tanner had hugged her and asked her what *she* wanted—something no else had done—and then, not so different from right now, a deep-centered desire had burst forth inside her.

She'd acted upon it. Kissed Tanner. Not a simple peck on the cheek. Oh, no, back then she'd never done anything halfhearted. With all the ferocity of a snake sinking its fangs into an innocent bystander, she'd planted her lips on Tanner's.

The heat that had exploded between their lips had shocked her. Even now, the sheer memory instilled other sensations. Those of wanting more. Of wanting Tanner to kiss her the way he had all those years ago.

He'd responded to her kiss that day, returned it as hotly and fiercely as she'd begun the action. His fingers had dug into her hair and kept her from pulling away. Not that she'd wanted to, even when his tongue had slid along the line between her lips before entering her mouth to create a firestorm she'd never known before, or since.

The intimacy of it, or maybe the wildness, had thrilled her.

She may have only been fourteen, him eighteen, but Tanner Maxwell had ruined her that day, with that kiss, for all other men.

He about broke her again right now, by letting out a low growl that shattered her treasured memory into a million little crystallized pieces that flashed behind her closed lids like a constellation of stars being cast away by some mighty beast.

She opened her eyes and knew Tanner had been remembering the incident, as well. He was breathing as hard as she was, and they were staring at each other as if on a battlefield, defending their very lives. Perhaps they were. She was, anyway. The life she now wanted. Had earned, and wouldn't give up for anyone. This time she was prepared to fight. Whether Tanner knew it or not, she'd heard him that night, all those years ago, when her grandfather asked for his advice and Tanner had said letting her go to Kansas City with her father was the best thing for everyone.

He'd told her something that day, too. That she'd better never act so foolish again. She was too young to be kissing men, he'd said, before he'd stormed out of the barn. That kiss—Tanner's anger afterward—had fueled something inside her. She'd gone to Kansas City then because her father had needed her, with the goal of returning, grown up and old enough that no one would tell her what to do again.

She had grown up. Had returned. And now had to wonder if Tanner had tried to scare her into leaving with that kiss so he could lay claim to the Double Bar.

He took a step back, and removed his hat to comb back his somewhat long and unruly brown hair with one hand before he returned the Stetson to his head. "Isn't it time for you to see what John darling's doing?"

Locked precariously between the past and present, Anna asked, "Who?"

"John Hampton. Your fiancé. The man Walter is showing his gun collection to."

"What about him?"

"Shouldn't you be in the house with him?"

Her father's insistence that she couldn't travel alone, then that she couldn't travel with John unless they were engaged hadn't stopped her from coming, and it wouldn't stop her from staying, either. But it might give her the protection she needed. The desire to kiss Tanner again, just to prove she had grown up, was building much too strongly inside her.

Anna stepped away from the stall and flipped her hood up, as if that might conceal the deception of her engagement. "John comes from a family of lawyers and has taken on women's rights as his specialty. Especially those when it comes to inheritance, and he understands how important the Double Bar is to me."

Tanner didn't so much as blink. He may be acting as if nothing mattered, that the past hadn't been dredged up, but it had been, and her original plan of working the Double Bar alongside him was growing more impossible by the minute.

Lifting her chin, she said, "The Double Bar is my home, Tanner, and it'll take more than a Christmas miracle for you to remain here."

His gaze roamed from her toes to her nose. "I never said I wanted a Christmas miracle." The glare in his eyes was deadly serious when it met hers. "But you might want to start praying for one."

Chapter Four

Anna Hagen had returned home, all right, and it galled Tanner she was the reason he hadn't been able to sleep. Thoughts of that one, stupid, youthful hormone-driven kiss hadn't kept him up at night for years. He'd known the exact moment the memory had entered her mind. It had hit him at the same time. Like a shotgun blast. So had the desperation he'd seen in her eyes. She wanted something—badly—and he couldn't quite figure out what. The ranch was already hers. It was her birthright, and she certainly didn't need a lawyer fiancé to get it for her, so what exactly was she after? Why had she come home? It couldn't be money. Walter sent a goodly sum to her and Will monthly.

Following the smell of coffee brewing, Tanner made his way down the back stairs. It was early; the sun had yet to rise, but the judge and Merilee, the other person who lived in the ranch house, would be up. Merilee had moved in more than thirty years ago, shortly after her husband and Walter's wife had died during an Indian attack, to take care of Will. Walter had become a judge then. He'd claimed the law was the only thing that could tame the territory and had taken it upon himself to see it happened.

Tanner thought it a bit ironic how the women in Walter's family had been pivotal in putting him on the bench and pulling him off it. To say Tanner liked that was wrong, but to say it taught him just how much influence women held over men was dead right. Before stepping into the kitchen, Tanner reminded himself that he and his wife—when he found her—would be equal partners.

When the image of Anna flashed before his eyes, he shook his head. No way; his wife wouldn't have an overbearing father, either. Or be the light of her grandfather's eye.

"I expected you at the dinner table last night," Walter grumbled as Tanner entered the room.

The judge was never cheerful in the morning, no matter what the season, and his gruffness rarely bothered Tanner. He shared a grin with Merilee, who was rising from her chair at the table. Only three people knew exactly whose bed the older woman slept in most nights, and they were all in this room. It was little things like that that Tanner liked. They made him feel as if he belonged here, yet the thoughts that had kept him up last night were still banging away inside his head, telling him he really didn't.

Belong, that is. Will Hagen had told him that on numerous occasions, and Tanner was more than a bit put out he'd let that bother him again yesterday while talking—arguing—with Anna. She'd got to him, though, defending her father as she had. The man had treated her like a slave instead of a daughter, and Tanner, having been treated like that at one time, didn't like it.

"Well?" the judge said expectantly.

Tanner grasped the cup Merilee handed him, took a sip and sat down at the table before answering. "I figured you'd like some time alone with your family."

Walter snorted like a bull, but it was the sound of Merilee slamming a pan against the stove top Tanner reacted to. Guilt that he'd eaten in the bunkhouse last night had him glancing her way, silently apologizing.

Her gray hair was tucked into a bun at the back of her head as usual, and she wore a familiar blue dress covered with a long white apron, but there was something different about her this morning. It was in her eyes. They were still green, but they weren't twinkling like normal. Instead, they sent a plea, telling Tanner he couldn't let the judge down now.

An eerie sensation crept up his spine.

"John darling's a lawyer," Walter said.

The nickname they'd shared yesterday was no longer humorous. "I heard that."

"I want him gone, Tanner."

Tanner didn't. John Hampton was the barrier he needed, which he wasn't going to speculate upon. Five years ago, he'd stuck his nose in where it didn't belong, told the judge to send Anna to Kansas City with her father, and had regretted it every day since. Not that he was stupid enough to think he'd influenced the judge's thinking—or Anna's decision. No one had that ability. They were both too bullheaded. Tanner set down his cup. "Walter—"

"Before Christmas," the judge interrupted.

Another thing that had kept Tanner up last night was one poignant statement Anna had made. His seven years were up. Had been for three years.

He hadn't labored until his hands bled putting up barbed-wire fences, or caught pneumonia driving cattle through a blizzard three years ago, or taken a bullet in the shoulder while defending the ranch's borders from cattle rustlers just for himself.

All that had been for Walter. He owed the man for his freedom, for the very life he knew. Admitting he respected Walter, loved him like the father he'd never known, or that he loved Merilee in much the same way didn't change the fact they weren't his family. That the Double Bar wasn't his home. He had no God-given right to claim it was. He hadn't forgotten that, knew it without Anna's reminder yesterday, yet it held more weight this morning.

Tanner spun his coffee cup in a circle. Walter still needed him, but the man needed his family more, and the ranch wasn't big enough for him to hide from Anna. "Maybe," Tanner finally said, "you just need to get to know him."

"Who?" Walter demanded. "John darling?" Snorting again, he continued, "I had supper with him last night."

"That's not enough time to get to know someone," Tanner insisted.

"How do you know?" Walter asked dryly. "You weren't at the table." Waggling a finger, he continued, "It takes me less than thirty seconds to know what's inside a man."

The judge was excellent at pinpointing a person's character, but this time his emotions were involved. Not to mention his age. Tanner, of course, couldn't and wouldn't point either of those things out. Instead, he said, "Anna must like him."

"What does she know?"

Not answering was his best choice, so Tanner took a long swig of coffee.

"I'll tell you what else she doesn't know," Walter continued. "Ranching. What my granddaughter knows about this ranch could fit in this coffee cup."

Anna froze in her approach to the kitchen, both her feet and her heart. The harshness of her grandfather's words, floating on the quiet morning air, shocked her. Easing her way to the wall to hear more without being discovered, she held her breath.

"If she loved this place like she claims to,

she'd have stayed here five years ago, or at the very least come home now and again."

That statement stung, too, and told her Walter didn't understand why she hadn't returned even though she'd explained time and time again in her letters.

"You don't mean that, Walter."

Anna snapped her head up, astonished to hear Tanner's reply.

"Yes, I do. My wife died defending this land, and I'll die defending it, too."

"Well, you're not going to die anytime soon. Now eat your breakfast."

That was Merilee's voice, and Anna wasn't sure she was glad the conversation had been interrupted. Who was her grandfather defending the ranch from?

When the only sound became forks clinking on plates, she pushed off the wall.

Convincing her grandfather she did love this place, and that what she didn't know she was willing to learn, might not be easy. He might never understand how badly her father had needed her, for he was stubborn and set in his ways, but he was happy she was here. That had been evident on his face last night. She just had to convince him she'd never leave again, and that she, too, would defend the Double Bar to the death.

Planting a smile on her lips, she marched the rest of the way down the hall and around the corner. "I haven't slept that well in years."

Anna didn't miss the scowl on Tanner's face or that the tension in the air was thicker than gravy, yet head up, she crossed the room and kissed Walter's cheek. "Good morning, Grandpa." Glancing to Merilee, she produced another bright smile. "Breakfast smells wonderful."

Tanner had the good grace to stand and pull out a chair for her, which, rightfully, caused her to pause briefly. She hadn't expected such gallantry from him. Then again, he was probably putting on as much of a show as she was. With a single nod, she acknowledged his courtesy and sat.

"Where's the lawyer?" her grandfather asked gruffly.

John hadn't made a very good first impression on Grandpa. Anna wasn't exactly sure why, for his manners were impeccable and he could carry on a conversation with anyone. Unless Walter saw through her ruse. He wasn't one to have the wool pulled over his eyes, and the thought of telling him John wasn't really her fiancé made her stomach hiccup. "I'm sure he'll be along shortly," she said, making a mental note to explain to John that rising before the sun was a must in her grandfather's home. Once their old rapport—that between her and her grandfather—returned, she'd tell him everything.

The butter was still melting on her flapjacks when Tanner pushed away from the table.

"Where are you going?" her grandfather asked.

"Got work to do," Tanner said.

"I wasn't done with our conversation," Grandpa said.

"It'll have to wait," Tanner replied. "There are cows to feed, fence lines to check, ice to break."

"You've got a bunkhouse full of men to do those things."

Anna hid the grin her grandfather's response evoked.

"I know," Tanner agreed. "And they won't get started on any of it until I tell them to."

A trigger flipped inside Anna's mind and she quickly swallowed the food in her mouth. "Wait, I'll go with you."

"No, you won't," Tanner declared.

"Yes, I will," she insisted. Her grandfather expected honesty at all times, and in this case, she could provide it. Turning to him, she said, "Five years ago I was a child. Now I'm a woman, and I'd like the opportunity to learn everything I can about the Double Bar. It's where my heart is, and it's where I want to be."

She saw the smile that tugged at her grandfather's lips, even though he tried to hide it behind his coffee cup. Tanner, though, she noted out of the corner of her eye, was scowling again.

Anna had never been in a courtroom he presided over, but her father often said Walter Hagen could hush an entire building without making a single move. It was a presence he conjured up, and he did that now.

It seemed an hour passed before he finally said, "Go get the men started, Tanner."

Anna's hand balled around her fork at the deflation inside her.

"Then come back," her grandfather added. "Anna will be properly dressed then."

"For what?"

The growl of Tanner's low voice added to the elation springing forth inside her.

"To give my granddaughter a tour of the ranch, of what the hands are doing, of what needs to be done on a daily basis."

In an effort not to display just how much this win meant to her, Anna slid a forkful of food into her mouth. She wasn't a fool. Though she may have just won this battle, there were more to come. Wars were like that. Dozens of minor battles to be won before victory could be claimed.

Tanner left the room without another word and Anna cut another section off her flapjack.

"Don't be getting too smug there, little girl."

The wind once again left her sails as Anna glanced up and saw the seriousness in her grandfather's eyes. She laid down her fork and knife. "I'm sorry, Grandpa, but I don't know what more you want me to say. How else you want me to say it. I tried to come home, but Father's schedule just didn't permit it." Frustration at reliving this all over again hit hard and fast. "You know the condition he was in when we left. What my mother's death did to him."

"I watched my wife die, too," he said, "but I didn't abandon my family afterward."

"I never felt abandoned," she replied. "I had you." The one thing she'd never quite understood was her grandfather's reaction to what had happened. "You're his father," she said. "Where's your compassion?"

"Compassion?" He reached over and

wrapped his fingers around her hand. "I love my son, Anna, and I love you. That's never changed, but I can't say I abide his behavior."

"You were a judge for years, you believe in reform, you know people can change. That's why you gave Tanner a chance. Why can't—"

"Tanner didn't need reforming, he just needed a home, and I'm proud to say I gave him one." He nodded for Merilee to refill his coffee cup. "Just like I gave you and Will one. Where do you think the money came from for the two of you to live the past five years?" He shook his head then, and for the first time she noticed how much he'd aged in the past few years. "But this isn't about Will. It isn't about Tanner, either."

"Then what is it about?" Anna asked.

"You," he said, taking a drink of his coffee. "Now that your father got married again, he sent you here, expecting me to hand over the ranch. Even sent a citified lawyer with you to help make it happen."

A chill entered her veins, turning her blood icy. The way he said it made it sound wrong, wicked even. "It is my legacy," she said out of justification.

"Legacy," he huffed. "You sound just like your father, and that's where you're wrong, little girl. It's not your legacy, nor Will's. It's mine, and I can give it to anyone I want. No lawyer on earth will change that."

It was as if the pancakes she'd swallowed had never gone down, were just sitting in the back of her throat. Her father had let her come this time, even though he still claimed to hate the ranch—for killing her mother. He also claimed Walter had wanted a son who was as ornery and stubborn as himself, which is why he'd hauled Tanner home—something else her father hated.

But she didn't hate the ranch. Or Tanner. Attempting to corral her thoughts, she asked, "So what you're saying is you don't want me here."

His fingers tightened around hers. "No, honey, that's not what I'm saying. I've dreamed of you coming home. Of living here."

"But I'll never inherit the Double Bar."

His stare must have been one he'd used in the courtroom, hard and clear. "The Double Bar might become yours someday, but not because some fancy-pants lawyer says so. If you want it, you'll have to earn it."

"Earn it? How?"

"That's up to you, little girl."

Chapter Five

Not even riding astride Thunder quelled her melancholy, nor did it calm the guilt churning inside Anna. Coming home was all she'd wanted, but the way she'd gone about it was wrong. Rather than assure her she'd get what she wanted, it now threatened to make her lose everything.

If only she hadn't left five years ago. But she'd had no choice, and that hurt, made her angry. How everyone held it against her—that she'd taken care of her father when he'd needed her to—seemed blatantly unfair.

"There's a line shack a few miles ahead," Tanner said, riding his big black stallion beside her and breaking the thick silence that had hung between them since they'd left the ranch some time ago. "Fred's spending this month up there. The hills in this area give the cattle plenty of natural shelter when snow falls, and it's important someone's up here at all times to break the ice off the creek once it freezes, make sure the cattle have water when there isn't any snow."

There was snow now, what had fallen yesterday and last night, covering the earth with a pristine white blanket. Ahead of them it had not been touched, and behind them there was nothing more than the even tracks of the horses' hooves. The vastness, the open space that went on for miles with no buildings to obstruct her view or constant city sounds to interrupt her thoughts was what she'd longed for and exactly as she remembered.

She remembered Fred, too, just as she did most of the other hands. So far since they'd left the barn, what Tanner had told her were things she already knew. Such as how someone had to live in the line shacks this time of year to keep the animals safe and fed.

There were many things she recalled about ranching; she had lived here for fourteen years. Yet it seemed she was the only one who remembered that.

Maybe she did need that Christmas miracle

Tanner had told her to start praying for. It had crossed her mind last night, after she'd entered her old room, complete with the knotty pine walls she missed and loved so much.

Lying in the comfort of her bed, covered with the quilt her mother had made years before, along with the matching curtains, she'd thought about his parting words—not necessarily a miracle, but a wish. There, in bed, she'd wished things had gone differently. That she and Tanner hadn't argued. Seeing him at the train depot, knowing he was waiting for her, had filled her with a unique kind of wonderful.

Which was now shattered.

"Something's not right."

Tanner's statement was more a self-mutter, and Anna followed the direction of his gaze. The line shack was a short distance ahead, nothing more than a small gray-weathered building surrounded by fresh-fallen snow and butted up against one of the majestic hills of the long range that ran through central Wyoming.

The entire area boasted tranquillity, and nothing seemed out of the ordinary. Other than the furrowed frown on Tanner's face. When he kneed the stallion into a faster gait, she followed suit, all the while searching to see what he saw that she didn't.

"What is it?" she asked, growling beneath her breath at him for not pinpointing whatever had signaled his alarm.

"There's no smoke coming out of the chimney," he pointed out.

"Maybe Fred's not here," she suggested, even while the coil of hope that had sprung forth unraveled inside her. A pony stood in the fenced-in lean-to on the far side of the tiny cabin and there were no footprints in the glistening snow.

They were still several yards away from the door when Tanner stopped his horse. "You wait here." He scanned the area while swinging out of the saddle. "And don't dismount."

Her first instinct was to disagree, but the glare he shot her way quelled it. With a slight nod she took the reins he handed her.

"If I tell you to ride, do it, fast. But stay in the trail we just made."

Anna nodded again. She hadn't forgotten lessons learned years ago. The ranch was heaven, but dangers lurked even in familiar places. Which was why Tanner had stopped where he did, out of pistol range from any hiding spots.

He didn't cower, zigzag or display any caution as he strode toward the cabin. Anna knew why. To do so wouldn't have been Tanner. The wide-brimmed Stetson on his head suited him as well as the long black duster that hung past his knees, drifting slightly in his wake. His long strides moved him forward, shoulders squared with confidence and just a hint of animosity. The determined swagger epitomized him. A man who knew the country he lived in, one who thrived in it and wasn't afraid to challenge anyone or anything head-on that might attempt to thwart him.

A shiver, not from the weather—for the wind was barely blowing and the sun graced the earth with warming rays—rippled over Anna, and a flash of fear made her chin quiver. She wouldn't want to be the person on the other side of the cabin door. Opposing Tanner Maxwell would never be a good idea. Not for anyone.

Unable to pull her eyes away, she watched him push open the door and disappear into the darkness. Ears peaked, she waited, yet heard nothing more than the horses snorting and stomping now and again.

In reality, it was probably minutes, or less,

but it felt like hours or years, and she couldn't stand the wait.

After dismounting, Anna led the horses forward and tied them to the hitching post before she squared her own shoulders. Wishing she could carry herself with half the amount of self-confidence Tanner exuded, she marched toward the open doorway. Attempted to march anyway, as the slick bottoms of her new boots—the ones she'd purchased just for this trip—were not good in snow. Her feet wanted to slide right out from beneath her, in several directions. The boots she should be wearing were sitting back in her bedroom. She'd thought about putting them on but they were scuffed from use and the leather was cracked from sitting so many years; ultimately, they wouldn't have looked as nice as the new ones did with her brown wool riding suit.

Foolish. John may have scolded her for wearing old boots but Tanner never would have.

She reached the threshold as a match flared, and the anguish on Tanner's face erased the boots from her mind as fast as it squeezed the air from her chest. "What is it?" she asked.

A small wood-burning stove, two chairs, a table and a set of bunks, where one bed was nailed to the wall above another one, filled the dimly lit cabin.

"It's Fred."

Tanner replaced the chimney, and Anna, catching a moan coming from the bottom bunk, instantly went that way. "What's happened?" she asked, removing her gloves. "Bring the lamp closer."

"Miss Anna?"

Though weak, Fred's voice warmed her chest. The man had to be close to her grandfather's age, and had been a part of her life for just as long.

"Yes, Fred." She knelt beside the bed. "It's me."

"I told the judge you'd come this time."

It could have been the frailness of his voice, or his words, that caused her eyes to smart.

"It's been so long," the man croaked before he started to cough.

"Yes, it has," she answered, pressing a hand to his forehead. Heat stung her palm as if she'd just touched a baking oven. Looking over her shoulder, she whispered, "He's burning up."

Tanner nodded. "He said the ax broke while he was chopping wood. The blade lodged itself in his leg."

"Where?" she asked, attempting to push Tanner out of the way.

As stubborn as ever, he didn't move. "I need you to ride to the ranch, have someone bring a wagon out here and send someone else to Homer to get the doc."

"Move," she insisted, shoving harder with one hand while grabbing the blanket covering Fred with the other.

"Anna, don't." Tanner grasped the blanket.

Perturbed, she wrenched the blanket from his hold and squeezed between him and the bed. "I've spent the last five years helping my father through medical school, and then assisting him as he started his practice. I'm sure I've seen worse."

When she uncovered Fred's leg, she swallowed, realizing she may not have seen worse. At the same time, knowing this was Fred, Anna forced herself to look beyond the swollen and blood-crusted skin. This was the man who had taught her to ride and shoot, much to her mother's chagrin, and he needed her. "When did this happen, Fred?" Keeping her voice from shuddering was impossible. "How many days has it been?"

"Don't know," the man groaned. "Thought

it was yesterday, but I can't say for sure anymore."

"Hand me the lamp," she told Tanner.

"Anna—"

"Don't argue," she snapped. "Give me the lamp."

He held it for her as she attempted to examine the wound. Fred's pant leg, once blood soaked, was dried tight to his skin. The gash could be much smaller than it appeared, or much larger. There was no way to tell until she cleaned it. Without glancing around, for she remembered well what the line shack held and what it didn't, she turned to Tanner. "You need to ride to the ranch, bring a wagon back. I can't clean him up here. And I can't stitch him up until I can wash that leg."

"I already told you to—"

"Now's not the time to figure out who's the boss," she said. "While you're gone I'm going to pack some snow around that leg, try to get the swelling to go down, and I'm going to get some fluids in him. He's dehydrated along with injured." Meeting Tanner's gaze with one just as determined, just as confident, she continued, "I want a wagon big enough to fit this entire mattress in the back, and I want it here now."

A tick formed in his cheek as his jaw firmed up, but then, without a word to her, Tanner knelt beside the bed. "I'm going for help, Fred. You hang in there."

"I will, son," Fred rasped. "But hurry. I swear I can hear an angel."

"That's not an angel," Tanner whispered. "It's Anna."

Though he never looked her way as he rose and strode out the door, Tanner's words filled Anna with something rather profound.

"I'm not dreaming, am I?"

She turned back to the bed, knelt down next to the lamp Tanner had set on the floor. "No, Fred. You're not dreaming. I'm going to have you fixed up in no time. I have to. Who else will dance with me at the Christmas party?"

The man grinned, but his heavy sigh said he was fading. Fast.

Anna went to work. She started by building a fire in the stove and then did all the things she'd told Tanner she was going to do. She wasn't a doctor, had never taken a test, but she had read every book in order to quiz her father before each of his exams and had known the answers as well as he had. More than once she'd cared for a patient while her father prepared for surgery or saw to another patient, and she could do this. Would do this. Fred would not die on her watch.

Even with all the self-encouragement she continued to muster, a great relief washed over her shoulders when she heard horses approaching. Fred had swallowed a few spoonfuls of the snow she'd melted atop the stove, but he was still burning with fever. The snow surrounding his leg had melted into the mattress, and she worried about hauling him through the cold like that, but she had to get him to the house where she had an abundance of hot water and light. Not to mention the other things she needed. Scissors, a needle and thread, alcohol, bandages. She'd made a complete mental list.

"Anna, darling, what on earth were you thinking, staying out here by yourself? You know better than that."

John's voice had never made her flinch before, but it did now. So did the pacifying grimace on his face as he climbed off the wagon seat.

"How bad is he, girl?" her grandfather asked, hoisting himself out of the driver's seat.

"It's not good, Grandpa," she answered, ignoring John's question and not looking toward Tanner. Sensing his exasperation was enough. Other men climbed off horses, and she started giving orders, explaining how carefully they had to carry Fred and his mattress at the same time, not moving his leg any more than necessary, which she insisted was not at all.

The fact they'd brought a wagon equipped with sleigh rails, which would make the ride to the ranch smoother than wooden wheels added to her relief.

Once Fred was loaded and Anna was satisfied the covers were tucked tightly around him, she climbed out of the wagon and walked toward Thunder. "Take it slow, Grandpa, but not too slow. We have to get him home."

"Anna, darling, you ride here in the wagon with us," John said, gesturing toward the seat.

Tanner was already handing over the reins to her mount, and she couldn't help but glance up, meet his gaze. Anna couldn't say it was pride glistening in his eyes, but there was enough understanding that her confidence remained intact. She swung into the saddle and steered Thunder about. "Get in the wagon, John. We don't have time to spare."

The ride home was long, and everyone, sensing the urgency, remained quiet. By the time the house came into view, Anna's stomach was churning. Fred was part of it, but the patronizing glares John kept delivering were the main reason. She kneed Thunder to trot around the wagon and made a beeline for the front porch, where Merilee stood wringing her hands in her long white apron.

Anna had barely arrived at the other woman's side when Tanner stepped up beside them.

"Where do you want him?" he asked.

"I have the backroom ready," Merilee answered.

Anna froze. She hadn't been in that room—the small bedroom off the side of the kitchen—since the death of her mother. Feeling eyes on her, she lifted her gaze to see Tanner watching her, waiting for her reaction—or maybe her answer. There was more in his gaze—understanding—and it penetrated, had her confidence flaring to life again.

"The backroom is perfect," she said.

"What else do you need?" Tanner asked.

Perhaps it wasn't her confidence she felt but his, his confidence in her. Anna spun about and started spewing out the list she'd mentally created to Merilee, ending with, "Water, lots of boiled water."

"Already have some cooling and more boiling," the woman answered.

"Go get the supplies," Tanner said. "We'll carry Fred in."

Everyone had a job to do and set to it, except John, who followed her as she gathered items and carried them into the room. "What do you think you're doing?" he asked several times. "You're not a doctor."

Anna was doing her best to ignore him but it was hard. He'd never irritated her the way he was now and she wasn't sure what to do about it. Her silence must have worked, because eventually he quit asking questions and disappeared.

Fred had been settled on the bed and Anna was laying everything she'd need on a table that had been set up nearby, when her grandfather entered the room. "What do you think you're doing, girl?"

Tanner couldn't say what snapped inside him, but he'd had enough. Moments ago he'd heard John grumbling to Walter about Anna and her abilities, or lack thereof. The way she'd taken over back at the cabin and rattled off what needed to be done had been enough to convince him she knew what she was talking about.

"She's about to save Fred's life," Tanner said.

"I sent Willy to town for Doc," Walter said. "He'll be here soon."

"He can assist Anna once he arrives," Tanner said, blocking Walter from moving closer to the bed. "Until then, she has a lot to do, and you need to leave her to do it."

"Who do you think you are?" Walter bellowed.

"The man who's going to make sure Fred's injury is seen to." He and Walter had gone head-to-head before and Tanner had no qualms about doing so again, especially when the life of one of his men was at stake. He waved a hand toward John. "Take him with you and shut the door behind you."

Walter's face was red and his eyes narrowed, but in the end he spun around and gestured for John to leave the room ahead of him.

The air took on a stilled silence as the door clicked shut, and Tanner had to wonder about the outcome of what he'd just done. A decision, one he'd stood by despite Walter's opinion, had never included the man's granddaughter before. He'd always made sure of that.

"Thank you."

Tanner turned, and the apprehension glistening in Anna's eyes led him to believe whatever happened tomorrow had no bearing on today. "What do you need me to do?"

She held out a pair of scissors. "You can cut

off his clothes. Start with the shirt. I have to soak his pant leg, get it to let loose of his leg before we can remove it."

Removing the old man's layers, right down to his skivvies, didn't take long, but the task of removing his left pant leg was a tedious one. Every time Anna swapped out the warm, wet towels, the water in the basin turned red, showing just how much dried blood crusted the leg.

Merilee kept switching basins, keeping the water clean as Anna instructed, and Tanner, somewhat awed by all she seemed to know, listened carefully when she gave him a task to complete. Her hands were steady, her attention fixed as she worked, and he sensed his admiration rising, as well as his hope for Fred.

"Tanner, help me roll him on his side," Anna said. "The cut goes all the way down the back of his leg."

He did so, rolled Fred and then helped Merilee prop pillows to keep the man from moving. The inside of his left leg appeared to be ripped open from knee to ankle.

As soon as the pants were cut completely away, Anna examined the large gash meticulously. "It's deep, but he didn't nick the bone. That's a good thing."

Tanner had seen a lot in his days, but he found it hard to look at the damaged, swollen and oozing flesh. “What do we do now?”

“I’m going to sterilize the wound with some whiskey, and then stitch it up.” The way her smile wobbled belied the confidence in her voice.

Words couldn’t seem to form in his mind. Instead, Tanner was thinking about kissing her again. Not with youthful lust like years ago; just a comforting one, for encouragement. He couldn’t do that, though, so he reached over and squeezed her hand. “I’m glad you’re here, Anna, and I know Fred is, too.”

Chapter Six

Tanner stayed close as Anna worked. It made sense that he hadn't recognized her at the station. He'd been expecting the Anna he used to know. The girl who wore britches more often than dresses and had forever been riding off in one direction or another. He remembered, too, how Fred had often been at her side. That had been before her mother died. Snake bite. Walking along the stream where she'd stumbled upon a den of rattlers.

He hadn't been at the homestead when it had happened, couldn't recall all the details, but clearly remembered the day he'd returned from branding cows on the north end of the ranch and heard the news. He'd come across Anna sitting in the barn, tears trickling down her face. It was a poignant memory, in part because it had evoked others. Made him recall the day his mother had passed away in the back of a saloon down in a Colorado mining town. He'd been eight, and pretty much on his own until the judge brought him home six years later.

Those years had been lonely and cold. His father, a man he'd never met, had died a hero before Tanner was born. That's the story his mother had told him. They'd been in love, she'd said, but her father had refused to allow them to marry. Said she was needed at home, until he learned she was pregnant. Then he'd turned her out. She'd cried, too, on her death, at how hate had distorted her life. Even then, as young as he'd been, Tanner hadn't considered finding his grandfather. He'd lived with one of the other dance-hall women, her kids anyway, in a shack on the edge of town for a couple years, until she'd married a miner. Invited to tag along, he'd spent the winter in a cave with eight others. He'd learned a lot about life that year, at the ripe old age of eleven, whether he'd wanted to or not.

Fred groaned, and Tanner, glad to leave the past behind him, stepped forward to rest a hand on the man's shoulder.

"Wipe his brow with a cool cloth," Anna said. "I'm sure he's feeling each stitch I make."

Merilee reached the basin first and wrung out a rag. As she went to Fred, Tanner squeezed the water out of another cloth and walked up beside Anna. Then, careful not to obstruct her view, he wiped at the sweat beaded on her temples. He could only imagine the stamina it took for her to sew up Fred's leg like patching a quilt.

"Thanks," she said, never turning from her duty.

She had to restring the needle several times with the thread she'd put in a pan of steaming water, and he noted how her hands shook each time, but it wasn't until she set the needle down that he saw the tears in her eyes.

He couldn't say why, other than he knew her strength was waning. He didn't know how to help her, but he stepped forward and folded his arms around her shoulders.

Anna wrapped her arms around Tanner's waist and held on. It was exactly what she needed, just as it had been when he'd held her hand at her mother's funeral. No chastising or belittling, just a comforting outside source of strength to replenish what she'd used up.

Without a word, Tanner held her until her knees stopped wobbling. Then he simply stepped back and asked, "What do you need me to do now?"

It was amazing how a man this sturdy and powerful kept looking to her for directions. Yet, much like his hug, it fueled her. "I have to bandage it," she answered. "And then we can roll him onto his back, but we'll have to prop up the leg. I want to keep it moist, too," she added, thinking aloud. "I don't want the thread to dry out and tear the skin."

"All right," Tanner said. "Just tell me when and what to do."

"You've been a great help." She glanced up, having almost forgotten the other person in the room. "You, too, Merilee. Thank you, both of you."

"You've done all the work," Merilee said. "I'm amazed."

"Me, too," Tanner said, addressing Merilee. "Although I don't know why. She's always accomplished anything she set her mind to."

"Ain't that the truth," Merilee replied.

Unfolding a long length of bandage, Anna bit her lips together, both at a smile and the heat streaming into her cheeks. "That's enough flattery from you two, we still have work to do."

"Flattery?" Tanner asked. "I was referring to your stubbornness."

Merilee was the first to laugh, and when Tanner joined in, Anna gave herself permission to giggle slightly. It felt good, and she let go of a bit more tension by laughing harder. The room took on a different ambience then, one of hopefulness. Anna let it fill her as she bandaged Fred's leg, and with Tanner and Merilee's help, repositioned the man more comfortably on the bed.

"We need to get some fluids into him," she said, gently covering Fred with a blanket. "Could you make him some chicken broth, Merilee?"

"Of course," the woman replied. "As soon as I clean this up, I'll see to it."

"I'll clean up," Anna assured her.

"I'll help," Tanner offered. "You go get the soup started, Merilee."

It didn't take long for the room to be set in order, and as Tanner carried the last load of things out the door, Anna couldn't help but stare at it, wondering where her grandfather was. Surely he'd want to know how Fred was doing. Expectation continued to rise. He'd have to appreciate her abilities, too.

Tanner was the only one who returned. "I'll sit with him if you want to go change your clothes or something."

"No," she said, glancing toward the open doorway. "I'm fine." She'd long ago removed her heavy coat, as well as the wool jacket that matched her riding skirt. After inspecting the front of her blouse, which was as white as when she'd put it on this morning, she rolled down her sleeves to button the lacy cuffs. "I want to make sure his fever doesn't spike again."

Tanner carried the rocking chair from the corner to the side of the bed, and although she sat and thanked him, Anna couldn't help but glance toward the door again.

"Do you want some coffee or tea or something?" he asked, resting a hand on her shoulder.

"No, I'm fine." She was about as far from fine as ever, and doctoring Fred had little to do with it. Glancing up, she met Tanner's tender gaze. There was no one else like him. Never had been and never would be, and understanding that had her rethinking several things.

He leaned down and his lips, warm and

firm, pressed against the top of her forehead. "You did a great job. I'm proud of you."

Her eyes started to burn and she blinked forcibly to make them stop. Changing the subject was the only way to explain the tears, so she said, "Fred's not out of the water, yet. Gangrene or blood poisoning could set in."

"I doubt it," Tanner said as he straightened. "Not on your watch." He squeezed her shoulder. "I'm going to go find the judge."

She nodded and watched as he pulled the door closed behind him. He was proud of her. No one had ever said that to her.

Little more than minutes later, the door opened and John, scowling, asked, "What are you doing now?"

It seemed impossible to think yesterday she'd been hugging him and calling him darling. Turning her gaze to the bed, she answered, "Watching my patient."

"You're not a doctor, Anna, and this is becoming ridiculous." He'd arrived at her side and folded one hand around her upper arm. "Now come. You've done enough."

She twisted, but he didn't release her arm. "I'm not going anywhere. Fred could wake up at any time."

"And what will you do if he does?"

There was no way for her to know that until it happened. "Give him fluids, ask how he feels," she suggested.

"Someone else can do that." He tugged on her arm. "You should go change your clothes. You probably have blood on your dress."

"No, I don't. And even if I did, I wouldn't leave right now."

"Darling," he said, his voice now condescendingly soft. "I know Fred is a friend of yours, but you mustn't wear yourself out."

A shiver shot along her jaw and down her neck with such intensity her shoulders shuddered. One thing made sense. Why her father had approved so heartily of John. The two were very much alike. Whenever she didn't immediately mind them, they cajoled her into following orders.

"Come along now." John tugged on her arm yet again. "You need to eat something. It's been a long time since breakfast."

She peered into his face. His eyes were a faded blue, his features well-defined and the blond curls covering his head were cropped short, yet wayward enough they'd always made her smile. Yes, John was handsome, and kind, but why hadn't he so much as blinked an eye when her father had insisted they become engaged before traveling out here? He couldn't love her. They'd never discussed that. Actually, in the six months she'd known him, they'd never discussed much of anything. They'd never argued, either. When he was miffed at her, he'd just clam up and look at her with disappointment in his eyes.

Like he had during the ride home.

Like he was now.

Like her father.

The door opened and Merilee bustled in. "Tanner asked me to fix you some tea. I added a touch of honey to it." The woman skirted around John to pass over the cup and saucer. "Excuse me, Mr. Hampton, I didn't know you were in here. Would you like some tea, too?"

"No," John answered. "Thank you."

There was nothing not to like about John. His reply to Merilee had been gracious, not clipped, and her father raved about his accomplishments. Yet Anna's stomach churned. Why had he agreed to accompany her? Even after she'd explained she wanted the Double Bar, not marriage.

"Well, I have a fresh pot of coffee done," Merilee said. "If you'd like some."

John cast a long look her way before he answered, "Yes, I would."

As he left the room, Anna wondered if it was him churning her insides. Perhaps not. It could be her. Explaining her false fiancé to her grandfather was not going to be easy. Maybe she should never have come to the ranch. Maybe this was no longer home.

Twisting about, she set the cup and saucer on the table behind her and then stretched forward to place a hand on Fred's forehead. He was cooler to the touch than earlier, and she ran a hand down his whiskered cheek. If she hadn't been here, he may have died.

Leaning back, she pushed off the floor with one foot to set the rocking chair into motion. If she hadn't come home, she'd never have known how it felt to receive a hug, support, at the very moment she needed it, or heard Tanner say he was proud of her. Or, most important, remember the one wish she used to have.

Chapter Seven

The judge was in his office. Tanner had known that's where the man would be. He took a few minutes to visit the bunkhouse, where he sent Slim out to the line shack to fill in for Fred before visiting the judge. He lived with the man, worked beside him day after day, and this was the first time he'd been apprehensive about talking to him. Because of Anna. It goaded him Walter wasn't beaming with pride over what she'd done.

"Doc wasn't in Homer," Walter said as Tanner entered the room. "He's gone down to Rawlings to pick up some medicine for Lamont Key's son."

"Rex told me that," Tanner said, closing the door. "He also said he'd sent a telegram for

Doc to stop here on his way home." Homer was only eight miles north of the ranch, while Rawlings, where he'd picked up Anna, was fifteen miles south. The doc's route home would bring him within a mile of the homestead, but Tanner no longer saw an imminent need for the doctor to stop in. Taking a seat in one of the wingback leather chairs, he added, "Fred's all stitched up. Your granddaughter did a mighty fine job."

The judge leaned back in his chair and rubbed the back of his neck with one hand. His hair, gray for years, had turned whiter lately, and the curves of his fingers, plagued with arthritis, had grown more prominent. "Merilee told me. Said Anna saved Fred's life," Walter replied roughly.

"I suspect so," Tanner agreed. "I hadn't planned on checking the line shacks for a couple more days." The somewhat disgusted sigh Walter let out had Tanner saying, "I don't get it. You've wanted Anna to come home for years, yet you act like you don't want her here."

"Maybe I don't want her here."

Tanner was taken aback, and more than a bit concerned by the coldness in the judge's tone. "Why not?"

Walter rested both elbows on his desk

and took on an almost deflated appearance. "Maybe Will was right. The ranch is no place for her." He let out another long sigh. "The Anna who arrived isn't a girl—she's a woman."

Tanner had already deduced that and was still struggling with how it affected him. "Yes, she is."

Walter stood and walked to the window, where he stared out into the fading daylight. "At one time, her grandmother and I lived in a cabin no bigger than that line shack, and when I saw Anna standing in that doorway today, I was taken back. Years." Shaking his head, he almost whispered, "Her grandmother died on this land, and her mother. That could happen to Anna, too."

Tanner held his opinion on just how hardy he thought the Anna who'd just patched up Fred was, yet knew that wasn't what Walter needed to hear. "Accidents happen everywhere, Walter. People die in Kansas City just like they do here."

Walter turned from the window. "That lawyer wants to get married on Christmas Day," he said, as if he hadn't heard Tanner's statement.

"You still want me to get rid of him?" The idea had taken on more appeal.

"No," Walter said, leaning against the window frame. "Marrying him is what Anna needs. He'll take her back to Kansas City where she belongs."

"Walter," Tanner started, prepared to argue his point.

The judge shook his head sadly and walked across the room, toward the door. "I have to go see Fred."

This morning, Tanner might have agreed that Anna marrying the lawyer and going back to Kansas City was the best thing all the way around, but what had happened today had changed his mind. The strange part was, and he questioned it as the door shut, the steadfast alliance he'd always held toward Walter had shifted. Whether the judge saw it or not, Anna belonged here.

What scared him was there was no guarantee she'd stay. Her father might request her to return to Kansas City and she'd go. Where would that leave the judge? Or him?

Tanner exited the office more torn than when he'd entered it, and he was still questioning his motives hours later when he entered the room off the kitchen to check on Fred.

He wasn't surprised to see Anna sitting in the rocking chair. She hadn't joined the family for supper, nor had she left the room after Doc Andrews had stopped by.

The doc had told everyone, especially Walter, that he couldn't have done a better job of stitching up Fred himself, and assured everyone the man would be up and walking in no time. Neither Walter nor John Hampton seemed impressed by the doctor's declaration, and that irked Tanner more.

"How's he doing?" he asked, walking up to the bed.

Her smile was brighter than the lamp flickering on the table beside her. "Good. He ate an entire bowl of chicken soup, not just the broth, and drank a full cup of coffee. I'd say that's a good sign."

"Me, too," Tanner agreed, watching the steady rise and fall of Fred's chest. "No temperature?"

"No, and Dr. Andrews left some medicine for the pain. I gave it to him after he ate. That's why he's sleeping so soundly." Anna couldn't keep the joy out of her voice or the grin off her face when Tanner smiled as he sat in other chair the doc had pulled close while questioning what she'd done before stitching up Fred's wound.

"So he's going to be all right?" Tanner asked.

She had no reservations sharing her one niggling doubt with him. "Fever could still set in. I'll know by morning if he's clearly on the mend or not."

"I take it that means you don't plan on leaving this room all night."

That was Tanner. Not telling her she shouldn't, just accepting her behavior at face value. A frown tugged at her brows. If John was handsome, what did that make Tanner? Then again, it wasn't just his looks that made Tanner so, well, memorable. His dark hair, long enough it wedged beneath his shirt collar, only added to his overall charisma—an attractiveness that caught her off guard every time she looked at him. He caused her heart to flutter, too, and her stomach. Even her blood pulsed harder in her veins.

Yesterday at the train station, she'd assumed it was simply because she recognized him, and in the barn, because he irritated her, but if so, why would it continue to get stronger every time they encountered each other? It might be because he was the only one not upset with her. Grandpa and John certainly were. Which was partly why she wasn't leaving this room. Either one of them might corner her, and she wasn't prepared to take them on. She wasn't afraid, just exhausted, and she wanted a bit more time to consider all her options. Her ability to assist Fred had turned both men into tyrants. Only Tanner, and Doc Andrews, seemed pleased by her actions.

Something else the doctor had said filtered through her thoughts. "So," she said, setting the rocking chair into motion, "you're courting Rosalie Andrews?"

Tanner lifted a single brow as he gave her a penetrating stare. "No, we aren't courting."

"Hmm," she mumbled through a fake smile. "Doc said she's excited about the Christmas party this weekend because she hasn't seen you in some time. That you've been too busy to visit."

"Walter says you and John are getting married on Christmas Day."

Fire shot up her spine and both her heels scraped the floor, bringing the chair to an abrupt stop. "John and I may be engaged," she had to admit, "but a wedding date has not been set."

"Oh," he said, scratching at the back of his

neck. "Sorry. Maybe I just let the cat out of the bag."

"I assure you, Tanner, there is no cat to be let out of the bag. John knows I'm not ready to set a date."

"So you're engaged, but you aren't ready to marry him?"

She nodded.

"I don't get it."

"What?"

"I don't get it," Tanner repeated. "Why did you say yes if you weren't ready to marry him?"

Anna didn't have an answer, not one she could tell him. "Because he's handsome and kind and generous." Those things were all true.

"But you don't love him?"

Annoyed at how quick he pointed that out, she replied, "I didn't say that."

"You didn't say you did, either," he insisted rather snidely.

"What about you?" she asked with arrogance. "Do you love Rosalie?"

"No," he replied in a snap. "And I've never given her any reason to believe I do."

Anna couldn't challenge that. Tanner would never pretend to feel something he didn't. That had been obvious years ago. Wishing she had more of the ability to see things as black and white instead of several shades of gray, she asked, "How do you know you don't love her?"

His expression softened, as if he understood the battle going on inside her. With a shrug, he answered, "I just do."

The air that moments ago had seemed charged toned down, almost as if night had just fallen, filling the room with its peaceful quiet. Something else she'd missed. "It's never quiet like this in Kansas City. There are always train whistles, and wagons traveling about, and people. Hordes of people everywhere. Even in the middle of the night you can hear them."

Tanner's only response was a simple nod.

"Have you ever been there?" she asked.

"No."

"You wouldn't like it," she said, and then proceeded to tell him why. While chuckling, he agreed she was right. They continued talking, and laughing now and again at memories or something she'd tell him about, until late into the night. So late that Anna didn't remember when they stopped. When he left the room. It had to have been after she'd fallen asleep because when she awoke, still sitting in the rocking chair, and there was a quilt covering her and a pillow resting beneath her head.

She stretched her arms over her head while inhaling the familiar aroma filling the room.

"I sure could use a cup of that coffee," Fred said, apparently smelling the same thing.

"How are you feeling?" She pushed aside the quilt to stand and press a hand to his forehead.

"Leg feels like it should belong to someone else, but the rest of me is good."

"I'll take a look at your leg and then get you some coffee."

A good amount of the swelling had gone down, so she did as promised, delivered a cup of coffee to Fred. After he'd eaten a hearty breakfast, all the while insisting he didn't need her sitting beside his bed, Anna left his room to visit her own. There she changed her clothes and took a moment to gaze out the window at the new day dawning.

She recognized Tanner as he stepped out of the barn, not from his swagger or clothing but by the reaction inside her. That, as well as the inspiration she'd gained while watching the sun rise, made her spin around. There were five days until the ranch's Christmas party, and then three more until Christmas Day, and she was going to need every minute.

Some miracles needed help.

Chapter Eight

If a man didn't know when he was being taken, that was his own problem. Therefore Tanner kept his mouth shut. Watching John darling being run roughshod over didn't bother him a bit, but Walter was a different story. However, the man was so grumpy—probably because he knew what was happening and couldn't stop it—that Tanner let it slide. After all, Anna had learned from the best. She was Walter's granddaughter, and the man hadn't presided over the territory for so many years without knowing how to manipulate a few things when needed.

Even with all her party preparations, Anna hadn't let her care of Fred slip. The man was well on the mend and glowing like a freshly shined apple at the attention he was receiving. The house glowed, too, inside and out, with all the cleaning and decorations she had the hands hauling in and putting up. Every breath Tanner took was full of pine and spice, and there was a sort of festive fever rampaging through the place.

He'd caught it, too, and didn't mind helping Anna out when he'd find her searching for some type of decoration or tool. Seeing her eyes twinkle and hearing her laughter was all the reward he needed. There was a downside, though. The desires she evoked inside him were wreaking havoc.

"There you are."

Tanner dropped the can into the feed bucket at the sound of her voice, and when he straightened after picking it up, she was standing next to him.

"What do you need now?" he asked, trying to sound grumpy. "There can't be another pine tree on the property."

Enjoyment filled her eyes. "No, I have plenty of pine boughs."

She smelled as good as the house, except instead of pine needles and spice it was sugar and vanilla. "Then what is it?"

"I want you to ride to the line shacks with

me," she said, moving aside so he could walk to the next stall.

"What for?"

"Because I have cookies and apple cider for the men out there," she said. "In case they can't make it to the party tomorrow."

"They can ride in for the party if they want to. Walter won't deny them that." He continued going about his morning feedings. Filling buckets of grain for the stalled horses.

"I know. But if they're as dedicated as you, they might not. Therefore, I want to take them each a bit of Christmas joy."

He tried not to smile at that. Her and her Christmas joy had become contagious the last couple of days. "It'll take most of the day to visit all three shacks."

"I know. That's why I'm all set to ride." She gestured to the clothes beneath her red velvet cape.

Britches and well-worn boots, as well as… "Is that one of my shirts?"

"Yes, I hope you don't mind. It's warmer than anything I own, and I want to wear my cape." Flipping up the white fur-lined hood, she asked, "It looks Christmassy, don't you think?"

He thought, all right, but he wasn't about

to admit to what. "Why don't you ask John to ride with you?"

"He doesn't know where the line shacks are. Besides, Grandpa said the only way I could go is if you'd take me. I have everything ready for the party—the things I can do before tomorrow—so will you? Please?"

Tanner was about to give in and didn't like it. "Why do you want to go so badly?"

She took the can from his hand and filled it from the large bucket he was carrying from stall to stall. "Because it's Christmas, and I want everyone on the ranch to know I'm thinking about them."

"Why?"

"Because that's what a good ranch owner should do. If not for the men who work here, we wouldn't have a ranch."

He couldn't fault her on that. The past two years there hadn't been a Christmas party, and drooping morale had shown the men missed it.

"While we're visiting," she continued as she dumped a can full of oats into Thunder's bucket. "We can personally invite the men to attend the party, just as long as they return to their posts as soon as possible."

"Why is this so important to you?" He was

stalling. Being alone with her could be dangerous.

Seriousness overtook her features, had the smile on her lips strained. "Because I want all the men here to like me. That way, if Grandpa tries to send me away, they'll stick up for me."

"It'll take more than cider and cookies to make men go against Walter's orders," he warned.

"I know." She dropped the can into his bucket. "He doesn't want me here, Tanner, and that hurts."

The sadness on her face had him wanting to pull her into his arms. "Fine," he said, irked by how strongly the change in her demeanor affected him. "Go get your goody bags."

She pointed to several flour sacks decorated with red bows lying near the barn door. With eyes once again sparkling, she said, "I'll saddle Thunder." Then she stretched onto her toes and kissed his cheek. "Thank you, Tanner."

Half an hour later, as they rode out of the ranch yard, Tanner's left cheek was still tingling. He was no better than her fiancé and grandfather, falling into her trap like this, but he could handle it. He wasn't in love with her the way the other two men were.

The snow that had fallen previously was mostly gone, and the ride was easy. The men, Padre, Weston and Slim, were all happy to see her, and touched—he could tell that by the pink hue of their cheeks—that she'd ridden out to personally invite them to the party.

She'd packed lunch for the two of them, too, which they shared between visits beneath an outcropping of rocks that sheltered them from the wind, and gave the horses a chance to rest after drinking their fill from the still-flowing stream. Conversation flowed easily between them, as it had the other night, but this time it didn't include memories. The future was what she talked about, and it pulled him in. She spoke of how meatpacking plants in Kansas City were doubling, and having one nearby would increase their profitability. Shipping meat in refrigerated cars eastward, where the demand for it continued to grow, would secure the ranch for years to come, she insisted.

Tanner was amazed by all she knew, and told her so.

"All the while I was gone, the ranch was never far from my mind," she said.

She jumped to her feet then, claimed it was time to continue, and they did.

Tanner wasn't about to admit how much

he'd enjoyed the day, nor how disappointed he was when the homestead appeared before them, signaling it was over. Anna grew quiet then, too, as they rode the last half mile home. Outside the barn, once they dismounted, he took Thunder's reins from her hands. "I'll put the horses up, you can go in the house."

"No," she said, moving to the barn door. "I'll brush down Thunder first."

He didn't argue; there wasn't any use.

Anna held the barn door as Tanner led both horses inside, and then pulled it shut behind her, letting out a sigh both at the strength it took to close the heavy door and at the perfection of the day.

In a sense, this had been her plan all along—a way for her and Tanner to share the ranch. Being with him as she had today had her imagining just what the future could be like if her plan worked.

Pushing off the door, she strode toward Tanner and the horses he was now unsaddling. "Where'd you live before coming here?" she asked while putting up Thunder. He never talked about his past, and she had a desire to know everything about him.

"Nowhere really," he answered.

"It had to have been somewhere."

"I met up with the Taylor gang down in Colorado, if that's what you're wondering."

The brush she was running along Thunder's back paused. She'd forgotten that—his gang association; then again, it had never mattered to her. "How long did you ride with them?"

"I didn't ride with them," he said.

She peered over Thunder to catch a glimpse of him several stalls down. He was looking back, so she asked, "You didn't?"

He was quiet for a moment and then started brushing his horse again, and doing the same, she was a bit surprised when he said, "I came across their hideout when I was hunting one day. I was about twelve or so, and an extra mouth to feed for the miner's family I'd lived with since my mother had died, so I stayed there. Two years later, they took me on a raid with them."

"You just stayed at their hideout all that time?"

"I didn't have anywhere else to go, and I had more than I'd had in a long time. A roof over my head, a bed, food. I knew they planned on robbing a bank, and knew it was wrong, but I agreed to go."

She set the brush on the shelf and when she

exited the stall, Tanner was there to close the gate for her. There was more to his story, she sensed that, yet also knew he said so little for her protection, not his. "Is that when you were arrested? That first ride?"

He nodded. "That was the last job the Taylor gang pulled off."

"So you never were an outlaw."

"Does that surprise you?"

"No," she answered honestly. "It confirms what I always thought."

His grin was a bit bashful as he shook his head, and the intensity that now constantly resided inside her doubled. It seemed natural, and easy, so she did it, slid her arms inside the opening of his long coat, all the way around his waist.

"Thank you, Tanner," she whispered, pressing a cheek to his chest. "For riding with me today."

He'd turned stiff, and the way he patted her back made her smile increase. Many times the past few days she'd sensed he wanted to kiss her. She hadn't encouraged it. To do so wouldn't be right. Not while she was still pretending to be engaged to John. After the party—once her grandfather recognized how invaluable she was to the ranch—she would tell him everything. Tanner, too.

Increasing her hold around his waist, she sighed. "It was a wonderful day, wasn't it?"

"What are you doing?"

"Doing?"

He took her shoulders in a firm grasp, separating them slightly. His frown was heavy, and a tiny warning that she was wrong, that he hadn't wanted to kiss her, ticked inside her brain.

"It won't work, Anna."

"What won't work?" The alarm rising inside her made her voice squeak. She couldn't have been wrong. Not again.

He shook his head.

Full-fledged panic that he was about to push her away erupted and without a second thought, she hiked onto her tiptoes and covered his mouth with hers.

Time stood still. Every beat of her heart echoed in her ears, but she refused to budge, just kept her lips pressed against his.

He didn't move for several more moments, but then his arms wrapped around her like steel bands and he kissed her. Heaven above, did he kiss her. Like years ago, with his lips parted and his tongue exploring the inner regions of her mouth.

It was as if they were battling, their tongues swords, to see who could kiss harder, faster, more intensely. Her determination renewed, Anna hooked her arms beneath his and went in with all she had. It was exhilarating and lit a flame inside her that went clear to her toes and shot right back up again, fueling her with steam and stamina.

When the kiss ended, they were both gasping for air and staring at one another, waiting to see who would make the first move. Unlike last time, Tanner didn't step away. Didn't tell her she was too young. Instead, he took her face with both hands and gently pulled her toward him. His lips met hers with all the tenderness of a butterfly's touch. Completely in awe, Anna barely had time to react before he pulled away, making her arch forward, toward him. He did that several times, just touched his lips to hers, softly, affectionately, and then, when he did deepen the kiss, it was so gentle and tender that a whimper rumbled in the back of her throat.

His hands left her face; one arm circled around her shoulders and the other her lower back. Tanner leaned her backward then, over his arm, and continued kissing her. She felt almost suspended in air. One of her feet had left the ground. If not for his hold she would have fallen to the floor. She was holding on to him. Tightly. Digging her fingertips into his arms. The fire inside her grew to a smoldering heat that included every ounce of her being.

It was a bit frightening. He was in complete control and she had none. Not over the reaction inside her or the way he kept her off balance. Her feet and her senses. It was exciting, too, knowing his strength, and trusting that he wouldn't drop her. Not Tanner.

Gradually he brought her upright, still holding her attention with his lips. It was several more kisses before his mouth left hers and his lips brushed her cheek, then temple, while pulling her close.

Anna was beyond breathless, and the buzzing in her ears made hearing impossible. Tanner must have whispered her name two or three times before she finally managed to reply with, "Yes?"

"It still won't work."

Still questioning her hearing, she leaned back. "What?"

He tickled the underside of her chin with

the knuckle of one finger. "I won't go against Walter. I can't. Not even for you."

Anna didn't have the ability to respond. It took all she had just to grasp the stall gate with both hands in order to stay upright. What had she done now?

Tanner strolled to the barn door and, pushing it open as if it weighed no more than a feather, he said, "I'll tell John darling you'll be in shortly."

Chapter Nine

The party was in full swing by the time Tanner made an appearance. He'd considered not going, but that would disappoint Walter. Truth was, it would disappoint Anna more. Staying away from her had proved more difficult than he'd anticipated. After leaving her in the barn, he'd gone to the bunkhouse, where he'd spent the night, and this morning he'd ridden into Homer before the town had awakened. There were always things to see to in town. Feed, supplies, cattle deals to make—things he tried to use to fill his mind.

He spent the entire morning there, even bought himself a bath, a close shave and a hair trim. However, with everyone talking about the party, not thinking about Anna was impossible.

It just so happened he'd met up with Doc Andrews on the trail. The man, his wife and their daughter, Rosalie, as well as the occupants of the dozen other wagons taking up the road, were all on their way to the party. Doc had gestured for him to ride beside his buggy, wanting to know how Fred was doing. Rosalie had been in the back and asked how he'd been, adding it had been several months since she'd seen him. Fall was a busy time at the ranch, he'd told her in reply.

Now, as he walked down the stairway after changing into the suit he wore to funerals when need be, he caught sight of Rosalie again. Couldn't miss her; she was standing next to Anna. He'd never call Rosalie homely, for she wasn't. Her blond hair was curled and pinned up stylishly, and her pink dress was covered with lace and bows, but standing next to Anna, Rosalie might as well have been a wallflower.

Anna, with her mass of brown curls hanging loose, wearing a dark green dress that had white fur at the cuffs and hem, was most certainly the belle of the ball. Not just because she was the hostess, either. One would have to look far and wide to find a more beautiful woman.

Tanner gave them a nod, since they were both staring at him.

"Oh, no, you don't," Rosalie said, catching his arm as he stepped off the stairway to make his way toward the judge's office. "You promised me a dance."

He hadn't, but saying so would have been rude.

The furniture had been hauled out of the front parlor. Nothing but the Christmas tree and four chairs for the musicians occupied the room, except for the people dancing. The back parlor was where the drinks and treats were set out, the main food—half a beef that had been roasted—was in the kitchen and the men, a good number of them, had probably taken cover in the judge's office. Which was where Tanner wanted to be.

Instead, he was on the dance floor, nodding as Rosalie went on about how lovely the house looked. At least that's what she had been talking about before his attention was drawn across the room, to where John sashayed Anna across the floor.

Whatever medicine the doc had brought home for Lamont Key's son must have worked, because the kid was at the party, too. He and a couple other boys his age, fifteen or so, were running around with sprigs of green, claiming it was mistletoe and holding it over people's heads. Kent Key held it over Anna's head right now, and she was laughing.

She and John stopped dancing, and after nodding to the crowd, Anna puckered her lips for John to kiss.

Tanner's jaw twitched as he watched the man take Anna's shoulders and kiss her, longer than necessary. The crowd whooped and clapped as the couple broke apart, and Tanner considered turning away, when Anna's eyes found his. Instead, he held her gaze for a moment, wishing he could read her mind. Guilt at kissing her the way he had yesterday was playing havoc inside him and, mixed with the desire now closer to the surface, he was about as twisted up as he'd ever been.

A commotion surrounding him pulled his eyes away and he found Kent holding the sprig over Rosalie's head. She'd already closed her eyes and pursed her lips much the way Anna had done for John.

As much as he didn't want to, Tanner couldn't not kiss her, so he leaned forward and placed a tiny peck on her lips.

The crowd groaned with disappointment, and John, still beaming and receiving pats on the back for the way he'd kissed Anna, yelled, "You call that a kiss?"

That didn't get to him as much as how Anna slapped John on the front of his shoulder. Tanner gestured for Kent to hold the sprig over Rosalie's head again, and this time he took her in both arms. Bending her over backward, he kissed her until the crowd cheered.

"Oh, my," Rosalie muttered when he stood her on her feet again.

The crowd cheered again. The kiss had done nothing for Tanner, not like the one in the barn last night. When he lifted his head, already regretting what he'd just done, he expected a glare from Anna, but all he saw was the back of her green dress as she left the room.

As soon as the dance was over, Tanner apologized to Rosalie and her parents for the spectacle he'd made of them. After receiving good-hearted assurances no harm had been done, he left the room. He considered looking for Anna, but there wasn't anything he needed to say to her, so he went to the office, where a good number of men were gathered, including Fred, proudly showing off the fine sewing job Anna—his Christmas Angel—had completed.

Tanner spent most of the afternoon in the judge's office, talking cows, weather, grain prices and railroads, while wishing he didn't have to make the choice he had to make.

It was hours later, after everyone had eaten their fill of beef and pastries, when an announcement proclaimed the judge wanted everyone in the front parlor. Tanner hung back, letting others crowd into the room. Walter would just wish everyone a merry Christmas and thank them for coming.

That was exactly what the man did, standing next to the tree with Anna beside him, and John behind her, resting both hands on her shoulders. "I'm sure you all know how happy I am that Anna made it home for Christmas this year," Walter continued. "I hope she makes it home for a few more Christmases, too, considering she really knows how to throw a party."

The crowd cheered, but Tanner flinched, noticing the way Anna's smile faded.

"For those of you who don't know, Anna and her fiancé, John Hampton, are getting married Christmas Day. They'll head back to Kansas City soon afterward, where they'll live. John's law practice is there."

Silence was growing heavier with each word Walter spoke, and Anna turned paler.

However, inside Tanner, steam was forming. The judge had to know what he was doing to her. Why couldn't anyone see she had a mind of her own, and that it was a good one?

"There's one more thing I want to share before we get back to dancing," Walter said. "As of January first, I'll no longer be the owner of the Double Bar."

Gasps filled the room, and Tanner, steam and all, froze.

"I've sold it." Gasps turned into mumbles, and before they grew too loud, Walter added, "Don't worry, you all know the new owner."

Tanner's attention, a large portion of it anyway, was still locked on Anna, catching the panic she was trying to hide.

"Nothing much will change around here," Walter declared. "Other than I might be traveling a bit, down to Kansas City to see my granddaughter." He wrapped an arm around Anna, who looked as stiff as a board. "But, back here, business will go on as usual at the Double Bar. The new owner, Tanner Maxwell, will see to that."

Tanner would have left the house if not for the look of defiance in Walter's eyes. The man was challenging him, but beneath that, the judge was begging him not to let him down.

It was the last thing he'd ever expected from Walter—to back him into a corner that included a lie.

Anna called upon every ounce of strength she had. Hearing Tanner had purchased the Double Bar was one thing, but having everyone, especially him, thinking she was marrying John on Christmas Day was a completely different issue.

She accepted congratulations, hugs and cheek kisses, while ignoring her grandfather and John, and even Tanner, who had a receiving line of his own. Eventually she found her way into the kitchen, where she made her escape by claiming the need to use the facilities out back.

Escaping John wasn't so easy. He was waiting when she stepped out of the outhouse.

"I'm sorry, darling. I wanted it to be a surprise." He kissed her temple. "I had it all planned. How the preacher would show up Christmas morning and—"

"What are you doing?" she protested. "Our engagement isn't real."

He settled a rather dull stare on her.

Anna glanced around. Her choices were few. The house was full of people, and they couldn't stand out here talking, but she had to put an end to this ruse.

"Let's go to the barn for a moment."

John didn't respond, which wasn't unusual, until they'd entered the barn. There, while he closed the door, she glanced around, made sure the space was unoccupied by guests seeking a private place.

"I'll wire my father," he said. "See how we can stop the sale of the ranch."

This isn't about the ranch, she wanted to shout, but knowing how John felt about arguing, she softly said, "That's not what we need to discuss."

"What else is there?" he asked. "We can leave tomorrow, and once we get home, back to the city, I can—"

"I'm not going back," she interrupted, glad he at least suggested leaving before the supposed wedding day. Sighing heavily, she said, "Thank you for all you've done, but—"

"But what? If Walter sells the Double Bar to Tanner, you'll be penniless." He cupped her cheek. "We can still change that. In the beginning, we might have to travel back and forth, but eventually we'll be able to oversee this place from Kansas City."

"What?"

He tilted her head. “We can’t live here. My practice is in Kansas City.” Grinning slightly, he said, “That’s the reason you agreed to marry me, isn’t it? So I’d come out here, use my legal skills to assure you’d inherit the Double Bar?”

“No, I agreed to an engagement because my father said I couldn’t travel with you unless we were engaged. You knew that.”

John let go of her face. “Yes, I did, but I thought—”

“Thought what?”

“Well, that we all wanted the same thing.”

“We all?”

“Yes,” he snapped. “We all.”

His tone gave her anger the opening it need. “Who is *we all*?”

John grasped her shoulders. “Anna, you know arguing will get you nowhere, and it’s useless. Now, let’s just—”

She twisted out of his hold. “Maybe it’s useless to you, but once in a while, I like it. It’s the only time I get to voice my opinion.” Pointing a finger, irritated he could remain so calm all the time, she asked again, “Who is *we all*?”

“Your father,” he said condescendingly.

Her shoulders sank. “My father?”

John stepped back and straightened the lapels of his suit coat. “The Double Bar is a worthy piece of property. You don't think he'd allow that outlaw to inherit it, do you?"

Fury ignited inside her. "Tanner is not an outlaw!"

"Shush! Do you want everyone to hear?"

"I don't care who hears," she seethed. "You disgust me."

"Well, that's the pot calling the kettle black if you ask me," he retorted. "You, *darling*, played the role of a fiancée very convincingly." He stepped forward and ran a hand down her arm. "We still could get married. We make a good pair, and Maxwell wouldn't stand a chance in court."

Anna wrenched her arm out of his reach. "I suggest you leave."

He pivoted on one heel, but then spun back around. "I may, but let me point out something. If I do leave, you'll be without a ranch and a fiancé. What will your plan be then?"

"What it should have been in the beginning," she stated, head up. "I'll be honest about what I want."

"And that is?"

"None of your business, but I'll tell you this much. The Double Bar is Walter's and he can do whatever he wants with it. No matter who thinks otherwise." To know her father had gone to such lengths after all she'd done hurt, but it also made sense. She'd hoped his new wife would lessen it, but now questioned if she'd ever truly be able to break the hold her father insisted on keeping on her.

John marched out of the barn and Anna followed, but just to close the door before all the heat escaped. Then she leaned her head against the hard wood, wishing every last guest was long gone. She needed to talk to her grandpa.

That was exactly what Tanner was wishing: that the house was empty, except for him and Walter. Most folks wouldn't be ready to leave for hours, so Tanner left, but only went as far as the bunkhouse. There he built a fire in the stove and sat down. His mind was like a spiderweb, catching everything that flew by. Christmas Day. Sitting there, he tried to convince himself it was the best thing—Anna marrying John.

"I thought I'd find you here."

Tanner waited until the man closed the door. "That was a terrible thing you did, Walter," he said. "She might never forgive you."

"Who? Anna?" Walter pulled out a chair and sat at the long table.

"Yes, Anna. This place is all she's ever wanted."

"Then you give it to her," Walter said. "It's yours now, or soon will be."

"No, it's not. I didn't buy anything." The once-tasty beef had turned to lard in Tanner's stomach. "I won't lie and pretend I did."

"The paperwork in my office says differently. All you have to do is sign it."

"Where am I supposed to come up with the money to buy the Double Bar?"

Walter patted the table with one hand. "The first seven years you worked here, I never gave you a wage."

"I've always been paid a wage."

"Pocket money. Not nearly what you were worth." The judge stood then and hitched up his britches by the waistband. "I put that money in the bank, in an account under your name. Just so happens to be the exact amount I'm selling the ranch for."

"Walter, I could put my wage in the bank for fifty years and not have enough money to buy the Double Bar."

"Haven't I taught you anything?" Walter asked, heading for the door. "It's the seller who sets the price, not the buyer."

"It's not the price, Walter."

The man stopped with one hand on the doorknob.

"I don't want the Double Bar," Tanner said.

Chapter Ten

Anna waited until the last guest departed, and then sought out her grandfather, whom she found in his office, precisely as she'd expected.

"Hello, girl," he said as she poked her head around the door. "That was one heck of a party." Gesturing toward the chairs near the fireplace on the far side of the room, he invited, "Come sit down."

After drawing a deep breath, she closed the door behind her and, shoulders squared, led the way across the room. Once seated, she blurted, "I'm not marrying John on Christmas Day."

"You don't say."

The ease of his tone, the lightness of his

mood, had her peering at him. "You already knew that, didn't you?"

"I suspected."

There was definitely something different about him. Actually, for the first time since she'd arrived he reminded her of the man she used to know. The grandfather she'd missed so much. "Then why did you tell everyone I was?"

"It was time for me to call him out." He reached over and patted her hand. "You, too. Oh, he's a nice enough young man, but if you two really loved each other, you'd have got married in Kansas City and never cared a whit about me and this old ranch." His fingers then folded around hers and squeezed tightly. "Wouldn't you have?"

She couldn't deny that.

"When's he leaving?"

"Tomorrow, I presume," she answered.

"Good. I couldn't take much more of him telling you what to do." He tugged on her hand. "Sounded too much like your father to please me."

Her stomach gurgled.

"He's the one who hired John, isn't he?"

She nodded.

"You know what he was trying to do, don't you?"

"I do now."

He twisted in his chair so they faced each other more directly. "I can't say I blame him for wanting to keep you in Kansas City. Life isn't full of roses anywhere, but this country is hard. People out here have to be tough, strong, resilient and even a bit rough around the edges."

Hurt took over now, and it had nothing to do with John or her father. "I know you don't want me here, but I'm not leaving."

He shook his head. "I do want you here, honey. As much as I shouldn't, I do."

Even through the sting of her eyes, she smiled. "Well, get used to it. I'm not marrying John and I'm not going back to Kansas City. Not even selling the ranch to Tanner will change that."

"Well, that's not a problem."

"What do you mean?"

"Tanner doesn't want the Double Bar."

A knot twisted inside her chest. "That's not true."

Her grandfather shrugged. "He refused to buy it. You may inherit it after all."

Chilled to the bone, she only shook her

head. "I don't want to inherit it," she finally whispered. Then she sat up, unsure when she'd slumped in her chair. "Where is Tanner?"

"I don't know," her grandfather said. "Willy said he rode out a while ago."

Three days later Christmas Eve arrived, but Tanner still hadn't. Slim had, though, and therefore Anna knew where she was going. The line shack.

"Where you off to, girl?" her grandfather shouted as she hurried down the stairs, fully dressed for the weather that included tiny flakes of snow.

"Where do you think I'm going?" she asked in reply.

He let out the belly laugh she remembered from years ago. "The longer you're here, the more you remind me of, well, me."

She stopped long enough to kiss his cheek. "Then I know you won't worry if I'm not back before dark."

"It's not going to be easy—convincing Tanner, that is."

"You just leave that to me," she said, pulling on her gloves. "You've got other things to see to. Merilee has my list."

Anna left the house with laughter floating

behind her and held that sound in her heart as she and Thunder traveled the miles to the line shack. There had been time to talk the past few days for her and her grandfather, and they had. About many things, including her father, her mother, her grandmother and Tanner. Especially Tanner.

Anna said a prayer while she rode for the Christmas miracle she now wanted with all her heart, and believing it had a chance of coming true filled her with determination.

When the line shack came into view, the first thing she noticed was smoke spiraling out of the chimney.

Hope hitched up another notch.

Tanner was at the side of the shed, chopping wood, and he set down the ax as she walked Thunder the last few yards to the cabin. "What are you doing out here?"

"Looking for you."

"Why?" he asked.

She swung out of the saddle and then led Thunder into the corral housing Tanner's stallion. The two horses snorted at one another and Anna couldn't help but smile. A stallion and a broodmare only got along at specific times, when nature intended, and that reminded her of her and Tanner.

"Don't you have enough to do back at the ranch?" Tanner asked. "Seeing how you're getting married tomorrow."

"Merilee has my list, and she's seeing to the wedding preparations in my absence."

Tanner was at her side now, and her insides were dancing like sparks of a freshly lit fire. He was so very handsome, and even now, eyeing her with caution, he was steadfast, powerful and indomitable. In truth, she liked what she saw more than ever.

"What are you doing?" he asked as she started to loosen the leather saddle cinch.

"Taking off the saddle so she doesn't sweat."

He laid a hand over hers. "No."

She took a moment to weigh her options before she shrugged. "Fine. You take it off. I'll go make some fresh coffee."

It was a moment before Tanner realized what had happened, and by then Anna was already heading toward the cabin, her red cape floating behind her as if her feet weren't even touching the ground. He cursed under his breath and unsaddled the horse, all the while wishing he'd ridden down to Colorado instead of only as far as the line shacks. He couldn't leave, though, not until he knew what was going to happen. To Walter. To the Double Bar.

"Tanner," she shouted from the doorway. "Bring in my saddlebag, will you?"

He grabbed the bag, only because he hoped Merilee had sent food—he was already tired of beans and hardtack—and marched to the cabin. "Don't get too comfortable," he said, throwing open the door. "You have to head out soon or you'll be riding in the dark."

"Then hopefully this won't take long," she said, laying her red velvet cape on the upper bunk. Turning to face him, she declared, "I'm not leaving without you."

He'd only been gone a couple days. How could she have grown more beautiful? His good sense said it was impossible, but missing her as he had, it seemed it was true. Dreams didn't compare to the real thing. "I can't leave." He set her saddlebag on the table. "Someone has to keep the creek flowing."

"It hasn't frozen that hard yet," she said, crossing the tiny space. "It won't be until January that someone has to chop ice every four hours. Once a day is fine for now." She was pulling things out of her bag. "I'm sure you've opened it up today. The cattle won't die of thirst before Willie arrives tomorrow."

He couldn't deny the truth of that, so he

asked, "If Willy's coming out tomorrow, why are you here today?"

"We always open our gifts on Christmas Eve." She handed him a package wrapped with red paper and a big green bow. "I brought you your present."

His cheeks hadn't burned like this for years, and he set the package down on the table, hoping that would help. "I, uh, I don't have anything for you," he stuttered while his mind shouted, *"Liar."* In his saddlebag, lying on the top bunk beneath her cape, was her present. An oval keepsake box made of glass with a buckskin painted on the lid. He'd seen it while in town the day of the party and couldn't help but buy it for her.

"I didn't expect you to," she said, handing his present over again. "Open it. Please? I bought it for you in Kansas City."

Her smile touched something inside his very core. He could say no to men by the dozen, even Walter. Saying no to any other woman never bothered him much either, but telling Anna no was impossible. No matter what she asked.

"Go on, open it."

He did so carefully, handing her the bow before he undid the paper. Inside the cardboard box was a black string tie. The slide clasp was made of porcelain and had a black stallion painted on it. Tanner couldn't help but chuckle.

"Do you like it?"

"Yes, I like it."

She sighed. "Good. I bought it some time ago. I saw it one day and it reminded me of you. Of the day you brought your stallion home and Walter said you'd never be able to train it. Never be able to ride it."

"That was a long time ago," he said.

"Seven years," she said. "Right after my father left."

Some of the shine left her eyes. He walked over to the beds and dug beneath her cape for his saddlebag. When he returned to the table he handed her the present wrapped in brown paper, with no bow—he'd planned on rewrapping it.

She frowned. "I thought you said—"

"I lied," he interrupted. There was nothing else he could say, and he might never have another chance to give it to her.

Although she eyed him curiously, the stars had returned to her eyes, and when she opened the box, she gasped. "Oh, Tanner, it's beautiful. It looks just like Thunder."

The way she was gazing at the keepsake box had him wanting to go to her, tell her all the things he'd thought of the past couple days, including how it hadn't been just the judge who'd been disappointed when her trips home had been canceled. He wanted to tell her that he'd lied the other day, too. That he could go against Walter. For her. Therefore he was glad the coffeepot started to spit and sputter, giving him something else to do.

As he skirted around the table, and her, to the stove, she said, "I love it, Tanner, thank you."

"You're welcome," he answered, moving the pot to the handmade bracket built on the side of the stove for just for that purpose.

"I had yours engraved. Turn it over."

The string tie was still in his hand, and turning it over, he could see the porcelain was set in gold, but the dim light didn't allow him to read the engraving. He moved closer to the table where the lamp sat.

To Tanner Maxwell. Love, Anna Hagen.

He tried to stop his heart from skipping every other beat, but it was useless, even though he knew people used the word *love* without meaning it. "That's nice, thank you."

She reached over and took the tie from

his hand. "When the jeweler asked me what I wanted engraved, I rattled this off without thinking." She set the tie down and took hold of his hand. "Do you want to know why?"

The warmth of her fingers was sending a charge up his arm, into his chest. "Why?" he asked, unable not to.

She stepped closer, holding his hand tighter. "Because loving you wasn't something I ever needed to think about. It was a constant."

Although Tanner liked what he was hearing, he didn't want to take it out of context. "Anna—"

Two fingers from her other hand pressed against his lips. "I love you, Tanner. I have since I was a little girl and you found me crying in the barn." Her hand moved to cup his cheek. "Over the years, when I thought of coming home, it was to you, not the Double Bar."

His heart stopped. "I'm not buying the Double Bar from Walter."

"That's fine. We don't have to live here." She grinned up at him. "It's not the ranch I love."

"What about John?"

She shrugged. "He should be back in Kansas City by now. I can't say for sure, though."

He didn't know if delight had ever raced through his body as fast as it was right now. "You're not marrying him tomorrow?"

"No. I was never really engaged to him." She shrugged. "My father said I couldn't travel out here alone, and when John agreed to travel with me, my father said only if we were engaged, so we pretended to be."

"Your engagement was false?"

"Yes," she said. "I wasn't going to let anything stand in my way this time."

Tanner was glad she hadn't, but felt inclined to remind her, "Your father hates me. Always has. I'm an outlaw."

"You are not an outlaw, and I don't really care what my father thinks."

"You don't?"

"No. He's had women looking after him from the minute he was born. I'm glad it's no longer me, and he'd better keep Virginia, because I'm not going back."

Tanner had to chuckle. Anna did have a mind of her own. One he loved.

Chapter Eleven

Anna had been fully prepared to argue until the sun set and rose again. As it was, she'd never been so peaceful in a conversation. So content with what she had to say. Then again, Tanner had a way of calming her.

His smile faded, though. "What list is Merilee seeing to for you?"

"My wedding list," she answered. "I'm still getting married tomorrow."

"To who?"

"You."

Another smile played at the corners of his lips. "I never asked you to marry me."

"I know. That's why I'm here. To ask you to marry me." She let go of his hand and placed both hands on his shoulders. "I have to warn you, though, the Double Bar is Grandpa's to do with as he pleases. Being born his granddaughter doesn't give me any rights other than the right to love him. Be thankful he's my grandfather. But, honestly, Tanner, it never was the ranch." A single tear slipped from her eye and she let it trickle down her cheek. "The moment I saw you at the train station I felt as if I'd come home, and ever since then, the only time I felt that way was when I was with you."

When Tanner didn't immediately respond, she continued, "We might *have* to live here, though. My grandfather adores you. Almost as much as I do, and he's very happy with my choice. Someday, once he learns I'm my own person, my father will come to love you like Grandpa and I do, but the truth is, Tanner, I don't really care what anyone else thinks. It's my life, and I know what I want."

His hands slid around her waist. "You do, don't you?"

"Yes, I do." She wanted to arch into him, stretch upward to kiss him, but there was one more thing she had to say. "All I ever wanted was someone who would walk beside me. Not in front, telling me where to step, or behind, telling me what I was doing wrong, just beside me, holding my hand as we go forward together. You've always done that." She stretched on her toes then, to whisper next to his ear, "But if I ever see you kiss another woman like you did the other night, I'll hunt you down like a rabid coyote."

Tanner's arms tightened, brought her up against him in a strong, unbreakable hold. "The feeling's mutual," he said.

She closed her eyes as happiness swam through her veins.

"The only reason I kissed Rosalie was because I was raw inside from watching you and John. I apologized to her afterward, and to her parents."

That was so like the Tanner she knew so well and loved so much. She leaned back then, just her head, to ask him, "Will you marry me, Tanner Maxwell?"

He didn't say yes or no; instead, he answered with, "I have to warn you, besides a small savings account, I'm pretty much penniless."

"I don't care," she said honestly.

He lifted a brow. "I'm not so certain I even have a job anymore."

"I am. Walter knew you wouldn't desert him. Matter of fact, we had a disagreement over who you'd have a stronger allegiance to."

"Who won?"

The way he was looking at her lips had them trembling, and she had to lick them before answering, "Me."

"Only because Walter can't say no to you."

His gaze was still alternating between her eyes and lips, and she couldn't wait much longer. "What about you? Can you say no to me?"

"You know I can't."

"So you'll marry me?"

"Yes."

She barely had time to relish his answer when his lips touched hers and shattered her ability to think. He didn't stop kissing her until she was so breathless and limp she may have entered a different universe for all she knew. Then as reality returned and she found herself truly home, she asked, "Tomorrow? You'll marry me tomorrow?"

"I wouldn't have said yes if I wasn't prepared to marry you tomorrow."

"I love you," she whispered.

"I love you, too," he said. "I think I have since the day I found you in the barn, but having never felt it before, I didn't know what it was. Not until Walter announced he'd sold the ranch to me. I knew then if I ever had to make a choice between the Double Bar and you, I'd choose you. Even if that meant walking away so you and another man could live here."

"I don't want to live anywhere without you," she insisted. "Not ever again."

Tanner kissed her again, and this time there was no coming up for air. The passion between them grew steamy and fiery, and nature stepped in, took its course. Tanner unbuttoned her shirt, teasing her with warm kisses and asking when he'd given her permission to wear his shirts.

Anna assured him he'd never given permission, but he'd never said she couldn't either, and laughed while disagreeing that his shirts looked better on her than him. The shirt, along with the rest of her clothing and his, were soon forgotten.

Tanner lowered her onto the bed as if she was as fragile and breakable as her new keepsake box, and Anna liked that. It made her feel cherished and loved. Tanner's words though, softly whispered and followed by kisses that had her body humming, were even more wonderful.

He took his time, caressing and teasing specific points on her body until she was wrought with desire so strong she could barely breathe. The promises he kept whispering of what was to come had her heart thumping and, when his mouth, warm and moist, found one of her nipples, she buried her hands in his hair while becoming so caught up in the sensation she sank deep into the mattress, relishing the intensity of it all.

There was more, though. His body was hard, taut with muscles and contours, and he tasted so wonderful, she couldn't stop herself from suckling on his neck, his shoulders, or from running her hands along the length of his back when he shifted, positioning himself on the bed beside her.

Warmth spread through her loins as his hand slid over her stomach, across her hip and along her inner thigh. The smoldering heat there was like red coals, ready to burst into flame, and with the pressure of his touch, a gentle, firm weight was all it took.

"Tanner," she gasped, "I can't take much more."

"I want you to be ready, so it doesn't hurt."

She grabbed his face, tugged his lips to meet her frantic ones. After a thorough kiss, she explained, "Trust me, the pain can't be as bad as the waiting. It's killing me."

"You always were impatient," he said.

"I've waited my entire life," she insisted.

His kiss was more potent than any drug she'd read about, and the commotion he created between her thighs by entering her with his finger had her body aching and burning, begging for more. She grasped his sides and tugged for him to roll on top of her, knowing what she wanted, what she needed.

Finally he shifted, and Anna, unable to wait, tugged harder, wanting him to hurry. Just as she thought she might lose her mind from wanting, he entered her—barely. That's when she knew a form of bliss mixed with torture. It wasn't enough and she strained upward, opening for him to fully take her.

The strength and power of his body was magnificent, the feel of his muscles working beneath the skin as he tried to move slowly, captivating, yet Anna's desire could no longer be held in check. She wrapped her legs around his thighs and arched her hips.

Not even the quick slice of pain made her flinch. She'd been on the brink, the very edge of existence, and that one swift movement brought her home.

She moaned aloud at the pleasure it instilled, and again when Tanner started moving. Each gliding thrust took her forward, toward some destination only the two of them knew about, and it became her one desire to arrive. Tremors overtook her body, and her hands, wrapped around Tanner's upper arms, felt the way his arms shook.

Still, they traveled onward to that unknown destination, until she once again felt suspended, as when he'd kissed her in the barn. Momentarily hanging there, on some unexplainable plane, their gazes met, smiling as they arrived at the same time.

The calamity was divine, a perfect and just riot of sensations that burst between them. Offshoots spread through her system, wave after wave, and she held on to Tanner the entire time, as if they were on a boat together, riding the wild swells as one.

When everything slowed, Anna was so spent she didn't have the energy to lift a finger, yet had never felt so wonderful. So complete.

Tanner rolled off her, kissing her shoulder as he snuggled up to her side, and leaned over her to gently ask, "Are you all right?"

Her vision was blurred; at least it should have been. However, there was no fog. His handsome face was crystal clear. Her brain took a moment to process everything, then with a nod, she replied, "Better than all right. I'm home."

He lifted her hand then, kissed the fingertips before wrapping his fingers around hers.

"I guess Walter was right."

"How's that?" she asked.

"There are Christmas miracles. Angels, too." He kissed the end of her nose. "All wrapped up in one little package. My bride-to-be."

She laughed and ran a fingertip along the side of his face. "And here I thought you were my Christmas miracle."

"We'll share."

"Oh, yes," she answered. "We'll share."

They shared another miracle a year later. Tanner Maxwell Jr., who many, many, years later inherited the Double Bar Ranch from his father.

* * * * *